The Star Chamber Vol-II

by

William Harrison Ainsworth

The Star Chamber Vol-II
by William Harrison Ainsworth

Copyright © 2024

ISBN: 978-93-57273-63-3

Published by

DOUBLE 9 BOOKS

2/13-B, Ansari Road
Daryaganj, New Delhi – 110002
info@double9books.com
www.double9books.com
Tel. 011-40042856

ABOUT THE AUTHOR

A 19th-century English historian and author, William Harrison Ainsworth studied law and worked in the publishing industry along with journalism and literature. William Harrison Ainsworth wrote more than 39 novels on various topics. William Harrison was educated at Manchester Grammar School. Some of his best and most well-known novels are The Tower of London (1840), Windsor Castle (1843), The Lancashire Witches (1848), and Old St. Paul's (1841). He was a well-trained lawyer, but he was uninterested in the profession, so he gave up and decided to devote himself to the world of writing. Ainsworth's first success as a writer came with his work "Rookwood" in 1834, and he last appeared in the year 1881.

CONTENTS

CHAPTER I.
POISON.

The execution of Lady Lake's criminal and vindictive project would not have been long deferred, after the defeat she had sustained from Lord Roos, but for her husband's determined opposition. This may appear surprising in a man so completely under his wife's governance as was Sir Thomas; but the more he reflected upon the possible consequences of the scheme, the more averse to it he became; and finding all arguments unavailing to dissuade his lady from her purpose, he at last summoned up resolution enough positively to interdict it.

But the project was only deferred, and not abandoned. The forged confession was kept in readiness by Lady Lake for production on the first favourable opportunity.

Not less disinclined to the measure than her father was Lady Roos, though the contrary had been represented to Sir Thomas by his lady; but accustomed to yield blind obedience to her mother's wishes, she had been easily worked upon to acquiesce in the scheme, especially as the fabricated confession did not appear to hurt her husband, for whom (though she did not dare to exhibit it) she maintained a deep and unchanging affection. So utterly heart-broken was she by the prolonged and painful struggle she had undergone, that she was now almost indifferent to its issue.

For some time her health had given way under the severe shocks she had endured; but all at once more dangerous symptoms began to manifest themselves, and she became so greatly indisposed that she could not leave her room. Extremely distressing in its effects, the attack resembled fever. Inextinguishable thirst tormented her; burning pains; throbbing in the temples; and violent fluttering of the heart. No alleviation of her sufferings could be obtained from the remedies administered by Luke Hatton, who was in constant attendance upon her; nor will this be wondered at, since we are in the secret of his dark doings. On the contrary, the fever increased in intensity; and at the end of four days of unremitting agony,—witnessed with cynical indifference by the causer of the mischief,—it was evident that her case was desperate.

From the first Lady Lake had been greatly alarmed, for with all her faults she was an affectionate mother, though she had a strange way of showing her affection; and she was unremitting in her attentions to the sufferer, scarcely ever quitting her bedside. After a few days, however, thus spent in nursing her daughter, she herself succumbed to a like malady. The same devouring internal fire scorched her up, and raged within her veins; the same unappeasable thirst tormented her; and unable longer to fulfil her task, she confided it to Sarah Swarton, and withdrew to another chamber, communicating by a side door, masked by drapery, with that of Lady Roos.

Devoted to her mistress, Sarah Swarton would have sacrificed her life to restore her to health; and she cared not though the fever might be infectious. The gentleness and resignation of the ill-fated lady, which failed to move Luke Hatton, melted her to tears; and it was with infinite grief that she saw her, day by day, sinking slowly but surely into the grave. To Lady Roos, the presence of Sarah Swarton was an inexpressible comfort. The handmaiden was far superior to her station, with a pleasing countenance, and prepossessing manner, and possessed of the soft voice so soothing to the ear of pain. But the chief comfort derived by Lady Roos from the society of Sarah Swarton, was the power of unbosoming herself to her respecting her husband, and of pouring her sorrows into a sympathising ear. Lord Roos had never been near his wife since her seizure—nor, that she could learn, had made any inquiries about her; but notwithstanding his heartless conduct, her great desire was to behold him once more before she died, and to breathe some last words into his ear; and she urged the wish so strongly upon her confidante, that the latter promised, if possible, to procure its accomplishment.

A week had now nearly elapsed—the fatal term appointed by Luke Hatton—and it could be no longer doubted that, if the last gratification sought by Lady Roos were to be afforded her, it must not be delayed.

The poor sufferer was wasted to a skeleton; her cheeks hollow; eyes sunk in deep cavities, though the orbs were unnaturally bright; and her frame so debilitated, that she could scarcely raise herself from the pillow.

Sarah Swarton accordingly resolved to set out upon her errand; but before doing so, she sought an interview with Lady Lake, for the purpose of revealing certain fearful suspicions she had begun to entertain of Luke Hatton. She would have done this before, but there was almost insuperable difficulty in obtaining a few words in private of her ladyship. The apothecary was continually passing from room to room, hovering nigh the couches of his patients, as if afraid of leaving them for a moment, and he seemed to regard Sarah herself with distrust. But he had now gone forth, and she resolved to take advantage of his absence to make her communication.

CHAPTER II.
COUNTER-POISON.

The physical tortures endured by Lady Lake were exceeded by her mental anguish. While the poison raged within her veins, the desire of vengeance inflamed her breast; and her fear was lest she should expire without gratifying it. Bitterly did she now upbraid herself for having delayed her vindictive project. More than once she consulted Luke Hatton as he stood beside her couch, with the habitual sneer upon his lips, watching the progress of his own infernal work, as to the possibility of renovating her strength, if only for an hour, in order that she might strike the blow. But he shook his head, and bade her wait. Wait, however, she would not, and she became at length so impatient, that he agreed to make the experiment, telling her he would prepare a draught which should stimulate her into new life for a short time, but he would not answer for the after consequences. This was enough. She eagerly grasped at the offer. Revenge must be had, cost what it would. And it was to prepare the potion which was to effect her brief cure that Luke Hatton had quitted her chamber, and left the coast clear for Sarah Swarton.

Startled by the abrupt entrance and looks of the handmaiden, Lady Lake anxiously inquired if all was well with her daughter.

"As well as it, seems ever likely to be with her, my lady," replied Sarah Swarton. "She is somewhat easier now. But has your ladyship courage to listen to what I have to tell you?"

"Have I ever shown want of courage, Sarah, that you should put such a question?" rejoined Lady Lake, sharply.

"But this is something frightful, my lady."

"Then do not hesitate to disclose it."

"Has your ladyship never thought it a strange illness by which you and my Lady Roos have been seized?" said Sarah, coming close up to her, and speaking in a low, hurried tone, as if afraid of being overheard, or interrupted.

"Why should I think it strange, Sarah?" returned Lady Lake, regarding her fixedly. "It is a dreadful and infectious fever which I have taken from my daughter; and that is the reason why Sir Thomas, and all others, except Luke Hatton and yourself, are forbidden to come near us. What we should have done without you, Sarah, I know not, for Luke Hatton tells me the rest of the household shun us as they would a pestilence. I trust you will escape the disorder, and if I am spared your devotion shall be adequately requited. As to Luke Hatton, he seems to have no fear of it."

"He has no reason to be afraid," replied Sarah, significantly. "This is no fever, my lady."

"How!" cried Lady Lake. "Would you set up your ignorance against the skill and science of Luke Hatton? Or do you mean to insinuate—"

"I insinuate nothing, my lady," interrupted Sarah; "but I beseech you to bear with fortitude the disclosure I am about to make to you. In a word, my lady, I am as certain as I am of standing here, that poison has been administered both to you and to my Lady Roos."

At this terrible communication, a mortal sickness came over Lady Lake. Thick damps gathered upon her brow, and she fixed her haggard eyes upon Sarah.

"Poisoned!" she muttered; "poisoned! If so, there is but one person who can have done it—but one—except yourself, Sarah!"

"If I had committed the crime, should I have come hither to warn you, my lady?" rejoined Sarah.

"Then it must be Luke Hatton."

"Ay," replied Sarah, looking round anxiously. "It is he. When he did not think I noticed him, I chanced to see him pour a few drops from a phial into the drink he prepares for your ladyship and my Lady Roos; and my suspicions being aroused by his manner as much as by the circumstance, I watched him narrowly, and found that this proceeding was repeated with every draught; with this difference merely, that the dose was increased in strength by one additional drop; the potion administered to your ladyship being some degrees less powerful than that given to my dear lady, and no doubt being intended to be slower in its effects. That it was poison, I am certain, since I have tested it upon myself, by sipping a small quantity of the liquid; and I had reason to repent my rashness, for I soon perceived I had the same symptoms of illness as those which distress your ladyship."

"Why did you not caution me sooner, Sarah?" said Lady Lake, horror-stricken by this narration.

"I could not do so, my lady," she replied. "It was only yesterday that I arrived at a positive certainty in the matter, and after my imprudence in tasting the drink, I was very ill—indeed I am scarcely well yet; and, to tell truth, I was afraid of Luke Hatton, as I am sure he would make away with me, without a moment's hesitation, if he fancied I had discovered his secret. Oh, I hope he will not come back and find me here."

"Who can have prompted him to the deed?" muttered Lady Lake. "But why ask, since I know my enemies, and therefore know his employers! Not a moment must be lost, Sarah. Let Sir Thomas Lake be summoned to me immediately. If he be at Theobalds, at Greenwich, or Windsor, let messengers be sent after him, praying him to use all possible dispatch in coming to me. I cannot yet decide what I will do, but it shall be something terrible. Oh, that I could once more confront the guilty pair! And I will do it—I will do it! Revenge will give me strength."

"I cannot undertake to bring the Countess hither, my lady," said Sarah. "But I may now venture to inform you that I am charged with a message from my dear lady to her cruel husband, with which I am persuaded he will comply, and come to her."

"Lure him hither, and speedily, by any means you can, Sarah," rejoined Lady Lake. "Before you go, help to raise me from my couch, and place me in that chair. It is well," she cried, as her wishes were complied with. "I do not feel so feeble as I expected. I was sure revenge would give me strength. Now give me my black velvet robe, and my coif. Even in this extremity I would only appear as beseems me. And hark ye, Sarah, open that drawer, and take out the weapon you will find within it. Do as I bid you quickly, wench. I may need it."

"Here it is, my lady," replied Sarah, taking out a dagger, and giving it to Lady Lake, who immediately concealed it in the folds of her robe.

"Now go," pursued the lady; "I am fully prepared. Let not a moment be lost in what you have to do. Do not give any alarm. But bid two of the trustiest of the household hold themselves in readiness without, and if I strike upon the bell to rush in upon the instant. Or if Luke Hatton should come forth, let him be detained. You understand?"

"Perfectly, my lady," replied Sarah, "and I make no doubt they will obey. I am sure it has only been Luke Hatton who, by his false representations, has kept them away, and I will remove the impression he has produced."

"Do not explain more than is needful at present," said Lady Lake. "We know not precisely how this plot may have been laid, and must take its authors by surprise. You were once more intimate than I liked with that Spanish knave, Diego. Breathe not a word to him, or all will be repeated to his master."

"Rest assured I will be careful, my lady. I have seen nothing whatever of Diego of late, and care not if I never behold him again. But what is to happen to my dear lady?"

"Leave her to me," replied Lady Lake. "I hope yet to be able to save her. Ha! here comes the villain. Away with you, Sarah, and see that my orders are obeyed."

The handmaiden did not require the command to be repeated, but hastily quitted the room, casting a terrified look at the apothecary, who entered it at the same moment.

Luke Hatton appeared greatly surprised on finding Lady Lake risen from her couch, and could not help exclaiming, as he quickly advanced towards her—"You up, my lady! This is very imprudent, and may defeat my plans."

"No doubt you think so," rejoined Lady Lake; "but knowing you would oppose my inclination, I got Sarah to lift me from the couch, and tire me during your absence. Have you prepared the mixture?"

"I have, my lady," he replied, producing a small phial.

"Give it me," she cried, taking it from him.

After examining the pale yellow fluid it contained for a moment, she took out the glass stopper, and, smelling at it, perceived it to be a very subtle and volatile spirit.

"Is this poison?" she demanded, fixing her eyes keenly upon Luke Hatton.

"On the contrary, my lady," he replied, without expressing any astonishment at the question, "it would be an antidote to almost any poison. It is the rarest cordial that can be prepared, and the secret of its composition is only known to myself. When I said your ladyship would incur great risk in taking it, I meant that the reaction from so powerful a stimulant would be highly dangerous. But you declared you did not heed the consequences."

"Nor do I," she rejoined. "Yet I would see it tasted."

"Your mind shall be made easy on that score in a moment, my lady," said Luke Hatton.

And taking a small wine-glass that stood by, he rinsed it with water and carefully wiped it; after which he poured a few drops of the liquid into it and swallowed them.

During this proceeding Lady Lake's gaze never quitted him for a second. Apparently satisfied with the test, she bade him return the phial to her.

"You had better let me pour it out for you, my lady," he replied, cleansing the glass as before. "The quantity must be exactly observed. Twenty drops, and no more."

"My hand is as steady as your own, and I can count the drops as accurately," she rejoined, taking the phial from him. "Twenty, you say?"

"Twenty, my lady," rejoined Hatton, evidently displeased; "but perhaps you had better confine yourself to fifteen, or even ten. 'T will be safer."

"You think the larger dose might give me too much strength—ha! What say you to fifty, or a hundred?"

"It must not be, my lady—it must not be. You will destroy yourself. It is my duty to prevent you. I must insist upon your giving me back the phial, unless you will consent to obey my orders."

"But I tell you, man, I will have a hundred drops of the cordial," she cried pertinaciously.

"And I say you shall not, my lady," he rejoined, unable in his anger to maintain the semblance of respect he had hitherto preserved, and endeavouring to obtain forcible possession of the phial.

But she was too quick for him. And as he stretched out his hand for the purpose, the dagger gleamed before his eyes.

"Back, miscreant!" she cried; "your over-eagerness has betrayed you. I now fully believe what I have hitherto doubted, that this is a counter-poison, and that I may safely use it. It is time to unmask you, and to let you know that your villanies are discovered. I am aware of the malignant practices you have resorted to, and that my daughter and myself would have been destroyed by your poisonous preparations. But I now feel some security in the antidote I have obtained; and if I do perish I have the satisfaction of knowing that I shall not die unavenged, but that certain punishment awaits you and your employers."

On this she poured out half the contents of the phial into the glass, saying as she drank it, "I reserve the other half for Lady Roos."

Luke Hatton, who appeared thunder-stricken, made no further effort to prevent her, but turned to fly. Lady Lake, however, upon whom the restorative effect of the cordial was almost magical, ordered him to stay, telling him if he went forth he would be arrested, on hearing which he sullenly obeyed her.

"You have not deceived me as to the efficacy of the potion," said the lady; "it has given me new life, and with returning vigour I can view all things as I viewed them heretofore. Now mark what I have to say, villain. You have placed me and my daughter in fearful jeopardy; but it is in your power to make reparation for the injury; and as I hold you to be a mere instrument in the matter, I am willing to spare the life you have forfeited, on condition of your making a full confession in writing of your attempt, to be 'used by me against your employers. Are you willing to do this, or shall I strike upon the bell, and have you bound hand and foot, and conveyed to the Gatehouse?"

"I will write that I was employed by the Countess of Exeter to poison you and my Lady Roos," replied Luke Hatton, stubbornly; "but I will do nothing more."

"That will suffice," replied Lady Lake, after a moment's reflection.

"And when I have done it, I shall be free to go?" he asked.

"You shall be free to go," she replied.

There were writing materials on an adjoining table, and, without another word, Luke Hatton sat down, and with great expedition drew up a statement which he signed, and handed to Lady Lake; asking if that was what she required?

A smile lighted up her ghastly features as she perused it.

"It will do," she said. "And now answer me one question, and you are free. Will this cordial have the same effect on my daughter as on me?"

"Precisely the same. It will cure her. But you must proceed more cautiously. Were she to take the quantity you have taken, it would kill her. Am I now at liberty to depart?"

"You are," replied Lady Lake.

So saying, she struck the bell, and immediately afterwards the door was opened; not, however, by the attendants, but by Sir Thomas Lake.

As the Secretary of State perceived that the apothecary avoided him, and would have passed forth quickly, he sternly and authoritatively commanded him to stay, exclaiming, "You stir not hence, till you have accounted to me for my daughter, who, I understand, is dying from your pernicious treatment. What ho, there! Keep strict watch without; and suffer not this man to pass forth!"

CHAPTER III.
SHOWING THAT "OUR PLEASANT VICES ARE MADE THE WHIPS TO SCOURGE US."

We must now request the reader to visit the noble mansion in the Strand, erected by Thomas Cecil, then Earl of Exeter, and bearing-his name; in a chamber of which Lord Roos and the Countess of Exeter will be found alone together—alone for the last time.

Very different was the deportment of the guilty pair towards each other from what it used to be. The glances they exchanged were no longer those of passionate love, but of undissembled hatred. Bitter reproaches had been uttered on one side, angry menaces on the other. Ever since the fatal order had been wrested from the Countess, her peace of mind had been entirely destroyed, and she had become a prey to all the horrors of remorse. Perceiving the change in her sentiments towards him, Lord Roos strove, by the arts which had hitherto proved so successful, to win back the place he had lost in her affections; but failing in doing so, and irritated by her reproaches, and still more by her coldness, he gave vent to his displeasure in terms that speedily produced a decided quarrel between them; and though reconciled in appearance, they never again were to each other what they had been.

As this was to be their final meeting, they had agreed not to embitter it with unavailing reproaches and recriminations. Lord Roos acquainted the Countess that he had decided upon travelling into Italy and Spain, and remaining abroad for a lengthened period; and the announcement of his intention was received by her without an objection. Perhaps he hoped that when put to this trial she might relent. If so, he was disappointed. She even urged him not to delay his departure, and concluded her speech with these words—

"Something tells me we shall meet no more in this world. But we are certain to meet hereafter at the Judgment Seat. How shall we regard each other then?"

"Trouble me not with the question," rejoined Lord Roos gloomily; "I have not come here to listen to sermons, and will brook no more reproaches."

"I do not mean to reproach you, William," she returned meekly; "but the thought of our dire offence rises perpetually before me. Would we could undo what we have done!"

"I tell you it is too late," rejoined Lord Roos harshly.

At this moment Diego suddenly presented himself, and apologizing for the abruptness of his entrance, accounted for it by saying that Sarah Swarton besought a word with his Lordship. She brought a message, he added, from Lady Roos, who was much worse, and not finding his Lordship at his own residence had ventured to follow him to Exeter House to deliver it.

"I will come to her anon," said Lord Roos carelessly.

"No, no; admit her at once, Diego," cried the Countess; "I would hear what she has to say." And the next moment Sarah Swarton being ushered into the room, she rushed up to her and eagerly demanded, "How fares it with your lady? Is there any hope for her?"

"None whatever," replied Sarah, shaking her head sadly. "She is past all chance of recovery."

"Then Heaven pardon me!" ejaculated the Countess, clasping her hands together, and falling upon her knees.

Sarah Swarton gazed at her in astonishment; while Lord Roos, rushing towards her, commanded her to rise.

"Take heed what you say and do, Countess," he whispered. "You will excite this woman's suspicions."

"Why should your ladyship implore Heaven's pardon because my poor dear lady is near her end?" inquired Sarah.

"I sue for it because I have caused her much affliction," replied the Countess.

"Your message, Sarah—your message?" interposed Lord Roos. "What have you to say to me?"

"My lady desires to see you once more before she expires, my lord," replied Sarah. "She would take leave of you; and—and—she has something to impart to you. You will not refuse her last request?"

"He will not—he will not, I am sure," cried the Countess, seeing him look irresolute.

"I did not expect to be seconded by you, my lady," observed Sarah, in increasing surprise.

"Would that I, too, might see her and obtain her forgiveness!" exclaimed the Countess, without heeding the remark.

"An idle wish, and not to be indulged," said Lord Roos.

A sudden idea appeared to strike Sarah, and she cried, "Your ladyship's desire may possibly be gratified. My poor lady desires to part in peace with all the world, even with those who have injured her. I will communicate your wishes to her, and it may be she will consent to see you."

"You shall have a reward well worthy of the service if you accomplish it," said the Countess. "Hasten to her with all speed, my Lord, and I will follow in my litter, ready to attend Sarah's summons."

"I like not the plan," rejoined Lord Roos. "You are wrong to go. Why need you see her?"

"Why?" she answered, regarding him fixedly. "Because it may be some little consolation to me afterwards."

"Then go alone," said Lord Roos savagely. "I will not accompany you."

"I do not ask you to accompany me, but to precede me," she replied. "Now, mark me, my Lord," she added in a low, firm tone, "and be assured I do not advance more than I will perform. If you refuse your wife's dying request, I will go back with Sarah and confess all to her."

Lord Roos looked as if he could have annihilated her, and muttered a terrible imprecation on her head.

"Threaten me—ay, and execute your threats hereafter if you will," continued the Countess in the same low decided tone, "but go you *shall* now."

Her manner was so irresistible that Lord Roos was compelled to obey, and he quitted the room without a word more, followed by Diego and Sarah Swarton, the latter of whom signed to the Countess that she might depend upon the fulfilment of her wishes.

They had not been gone many minutes before Lady Exeter entered her litter, and wholly unattended by page or serving-man, except those in charge of the conveyance, caused herself to be conveyed to Sir Thomas Lake's lodgings in Whitehall.

CHAPTER IV.
HOW THE FORGED CONFESSION
WAS PRODUCED.

Summoning up all his firmness for the interview with his lady, Lord Roos entered her chamber, attended by Sarah Swarton, and beheld her propped up by pillows, bearing evident marks in her countenance of the severe sufferings she had endured. She was emaciated in frame, and almost livid in complexion; hollow-cheeked and hollow-eyed; but still with a look of unaltered affection for him.

Having fulfilled her mission, Sarah left them alone together.

He took the thin fingers extended towards him, and pressed them to his lips, but scarcely dared to raise his eyes towards his wife, so much was he shocked by her appearance. It was with difficulty she gave utterance to the words she addressed to him.

"I thank you for coming to me, my Lord," she said; "but you will not regret your kindness. We are quite alone, are we not? My eyes are so dim that I cannot distinguish any object at the other end of the room—but I can see you plainly enough, my dear Lord."

"We are alone, Elizabeth," replied Lord Roos, in a voice of some emotion, after glancing around.

"Then I may speak freely," she continued. "What I predicted has occurred. You did not do well, my dear Lord, to take that phial from me and place it in other hands. Nay, start not! I know I am poisoned: I have known it from the first. But I have made no effort to save myself, for I was aware it was your will I should die."

"O, Elizabeth!" murmured her husband.

"I was aware of it," she repeated; "and as I have never voluntarily disobeyed you, I would not now thwart your purpose, even though I myself must be the sacrifice. It was to tell you this that I have sent for you. It was to forgive—to bless you."

And as she spoke she threw her arms round his neck, and he felt his cheek wet with her tears.

"This is more than I can bear," cried Lord Roos, in a voice suffocated by emotion. "I thought I had firmness for anything; but it deserts me entirely now. You are an angel of goodness, Elizabeth; as I am a demon of darkness. I do not deserve your forgiveness."

"You will deserve it, if you will comply with the request I am about to make to you," she rejoined, looking at him beseechingly.

"Whatever it be it shall be granted, if in my power," he rejoined earnestly. "I would redeem your life, if I could, at the price of my own. You have exorcised the evil spirit from me, Elizabeth."

"Then I shall die happy," she replied, with a smile of ineffable delight.

"But the request! What is it you would have me perform?" he asked.

"I would have you spare my mother," she replied. "I know she has been dealt with in the same way as myself; but I also know there is yet time to save her."

"It shall be done," said Lord Roos, emphatically. "Where is she?"

"In the adjoining chamber."

"Is Luke Hatton in attendance upon her?"

"In constant attendance," she rejoined. "That man has obeyed you well, my Lord. But take heed of him: he is a dangerous weapon, and may injure the hand that employs him. Strike gently upon that bell. He will attend the summons."

Lord Roos complied; when, to his astonishment and dismay, the curtains shrouding the entrance to the adjoining room were drawn aside, and Lady Lake stalked from behind them. Never before had she surveyed her son-in-law with such a glance of triumph as she threw upon him now.

"You were mistaken you see, Elizabeth," said Lord Roos to his lady. "Your mother needs no aid. She is perfectly well."

"Ay, well enough to confound you and all your wicked purposes, my Lord," cried Lady Lake. "You have not accomplished my destruction, as you perceive; nor shall you accomplish your wife's destruction, though you have well-nigh succeeded. Let it chafe you to madness to learn that I possess an antidote, which I have myself approved, and which will kill the poison circling in her veins, and give her new life."

"An antidote!" exclaimed Lord Roos. "So far from galling me to madness, the intelligence fills me with delight beyond expression. Give it me, Madam, that I may administer it at once; and heaven grant its results may be such as you predict!"

"Administered by you, my Lord, it would be poison," said Lady Lake, bitterly. "But you may stand by and witness its beneficial effects. They will be instantaneous."

"As you will, Madam, so you do not delay the application," cried Lord Roos.

"Drink of this, my child," said Lady Lake, after she had poured some drops of the cordial into a glass.

"I will take it from no hand but my husband's," murmured Lady Roos.

"How?" exclaimed her mother, frowning.

"Give it me, I say, Madam," cried Lord Roos. "Is this a time for hesitation, when you see her life hangs upon a thread, which you yourself may sever?"

And taking the glass from her, he held it to his wife's lips; tenderly supporting her while she swallowed its contents.

It was not long before the effects of the cordial were manifest. The deathly hue of the skin changed to a more healthful colour, and the pulsations of the heart became stronger and more equal; and though the debility could not be so speedily repaired, it was apparent that the work of restoration had commenced, and might be completed if the same treatment were pursued.

"Now I owe my life to you, my dear Lord," said Lady Roos, regarding her husband with grateful fondness.

"To him!" exclaimed her mother. "You owe him nothing but a heavy debt of vengeance, which we will endeavour to pay, and with interest. But keep calm, my child, and do not trouble yourself; whatever may occur. Your speedy restoration will depend much on that."

"You do not adopt the means to make me calm, mother," replied Lady Roos.

But Lady Lake was too much bent upon the immediate and full gratification of her long-deferred vengeance to heed her. Clapping her hands together, the signal was answered by Sir Thomas Lake, who came forth from the adjoining room with Luke Hatton. At the same time, and as if it had been so contrived that all the guilty parties should be confronted together, the outer door of the chamber was opened, and the Countess of Exeter was ushered in by Sarah Swarton.

On seeing in whose presence she stood, the Countess would have precipitately retreated; but it was too late. The door was closed by Sarah.

"Soh! my turn is come at last," cried Lady Lake, gazing from one to the other with a smile of gratified vengeance. "I hold you all in my toils. You, my Lord," addressing her son-in-law, "have treated a wife, who has ever shown you the most devoted affection, with neglect and cruelty, and, not content with such barbarous treatment, have conspired against her life, and against my life."

"Take heed how you bring any charge against him, mother," cried Lady Roos, raising herself in her couch. "Take heed, I say. Let your vengeance fall upon her head," pointing to the Countess—"but not upon him."

"I am willing to make atonement for the wrongs I have done you, Lady Roos," said the Countess, "and have come hither to say so, and to implore your forgiveness."

"You fancied she was dying," rejoined Lady Lake—"dying from the effects of the poison administered to her and to me by Luke Hatton, according to your order; but you are mistaken, Countess. We have found an antidote, and shall yet live to requite you."

"It is more satisfaction to me to be told this, Madam, than it would be to find that Luke Hatton had succeeded in his design, which I would have prevented if I could," said Lady Exeter.

"You will gain little credit for that assertion, Countess," remarked Sir Thomas Lake, "since it is contradicted by an order which I hold in my hand, signed by yourself, and given to the miscreant in question."

"O Heavens!" ejaculated the Countess.

"Do you deny this signature?" asked Sir Thomas, showing her the paper.

Lady Exeter made no answer.

"Learn further to your confusion, Countess," pursued Lady Lake, "that the wretch, Luke Hatton, has made a full confession of his offence, wherein he declares that he was incited by you, and by you alone, on the offer of a large reward, to put my daughter and myself to death by slow poison."

"By me alone!—incited by me!" cried Lady Exeter; "why, I opposed him. It is impossible he can have confessed thus. Hast thou done so, villain?"

"I have," replied Luke Hatton, sullenly.

"Then thou hast avouched a lie—a lie that will damn thee," said Lady Exeter. "Lord Roos knows it to be false, and can exculpate me. Speak, my Lord, I charge you, and say how it occurred."

But the young nobleman remained silent.

"Not a word—not a word in my favour," the Countess exclaimed, in a voice of anguish. "Nay, then I am indeed lost!"

"You are lost past redemption," cried Lady Lake with an outburst of fierce exultation, and a look as if she would have trampled her beneath her feet. "You have forfeited honour, station, life. Guilty of disloyalty to your proud and noble husband, you have sought to remove by violent deaths those who stood between you and your lover. Happily your dreadful purpose has been defeated; but this avowal of your criminality with Lord Roos, signed by yourself and witnessed by his lordship and his Spanish servant,—this shall be laid within an hour before the Earl of Exeter."

"My brain turns round. I am bewildered with all these frightful accusations," exclaimed the Countess distractedly. "I have made no confession,—have signed none."

"Methought you said I had witnessed it, Madam?" cried Lord Roos, almost as much bewildered as Lady Exeter.

"Will you deny your own handwriting, my Lord?" rejoined Lady Lake; "or will the Countess? Behold the confession, subscribed by the one, and witnessed by the other."

"It is a forgery!" shrieked the Countess. "You have charged me with witchcraft; but you practise it yourself."

"If I did not know it to be false, I could have sworn the hand was yours, Countess," cried Lord Roos; "and my own signature is equally skilfully simulated."

"False or not," cried Lady Lake, "it shall be laid before Lord Exeter as I have said—with all the details—ay, and before the King."

"Before the King!" repeated Lord Roos, as he drew near Lady Exeter, and whispered in her ear—"Countess, our sole safety is in immediate flight. Circumstances are so strong against us, that we shall never be able to disprove this forgery."

"Then save yourself in the way you propose, my Lord," she rejoined, with scorn. "For me, I shall remain, and brave it out."

The young nobleman made a movement towards the door.

"You cannot go forth without my order, my Lord," cried Sir Thomas Lake. "It is guarded."

"Perdition!" exclaimed Lord Roos.

Again Lady Lake looked from one to the other with a smile of triumph. But it was presently checked by a look from her daughter, who made a sign to her to approach her.

"What would you, my child?—more of the cordial?" demanded Lady Lake.

"No, mother," she replied, in a tone so low as to be inaudible to the others. "Nor will I suffer another drop to pass my lips unless my husband be allowed to depart without molestation."

"Would you interfere with my vengeance?" said Lady Lake.

"Ay, mother, I will interfere with it effectually unless you comply," rejoined Lady Roos, firmly. "I will acquaint the Countess with the true nature of that confession. As it is, she has awakened by her conduct some feelings of pity in my breast."

"You will ruin all by your weakness," said Lady Lake.

"Let Lord Roos go free, and let there be a truce between you and the Countess for three days, and I am content."

"I do not like to give such a promise," said Lady Lake. "It will be hard to keep it."

"It may be harder to lose all your vengeance," rejoined Lady Roos, in a tone that showed she would not be opposed.

Compelled to succumb, Lady Lake moved towards Sir Thomas, and a few words having passed between them in private, the Secretary of State thus addressed his noble son-in-law—

"My Lord," he said in a grave tone, "at the instance of my daughter, though much against my own inclination, and that of my wife, I will no longer oppose your departure. I understand you are about to travel, and I therefore recommend you to set forth without delay, for if you be found in London, or in England, after three days, during which time, at the desire also of our daughter—and equally against our own wishes—we consent to keep truce with my lady of Exeter; if, I say, you are found after that time, I will not answer for the consequences to yourself. Thus warned, my Lord, you are at liberty to depart."

"I will take advantage of your offer, Sir Thomas, and attend to your hint," replied Lord Roos. And turning upon his heel, he marched towards the door, whither he was accompanied by Sir Thomas Lake, who called to the attendants outside to let him go free.

"Not one word of farewell to me! not one look!" exclaimed his wife, sinking back upon the pillow.

"Nor for me—and I shall see him no more," murmured the Countess, compressing her beautiful lips. "But it is better thus."

While this was passing, Luke Hatton had contrived to approach the Countess, and now said in a low tone—"If your ladyship will trust to me, and make it worth my while, I will deliver you from the peril in which you are placed by this confession. Shall I come to Exeter House to-night?"

She consented.

"At what hour?"

"At midnight," she returned. "I loathe thee, yet have no alternative but to trust thee. Am I free to depart likewise?" she added aloud to Sir Thomas.

"The door is open for you, Countess," rejoined the Secretary of State, with mock ceremoniousness. "After three days, you understand, war is renewed between us."

"War to the death," subjoined Lady Lake.

"Be it so," replied the Countess. "I shall not desert my post."

And assuming the dignified deportment for which she was remarkable, she went forth with a slow and majestic step.

Luke Hatton would have followed her, but Sir Thomas detained him.

"Am I a prisoner?" he said, uneasily, and glancing at Lady Lake. "Her ladyship promised me instant liberation."

"And the promise shall be fulfilled as soon as I am satisfied my daughter is out of danger," returned Sir Thomas.

"I am easy, then," said the apothecary. "I will answer for her speedy recovery."

CHAPTER V.
A VISIT TO SIR GILES MOMPESSON'S HABITATION NEAR THE FLEET.

Allowing an interval of three or four months to elapse between the events last recorded, and those about to be narrated, we shall now conduct the reader to a large, gloomy habitation near Fleet Bridge. At first view, this structure, with its stone walls, corner turrets, ponderous door, and barred windows, might be taken as part and parcel of the ancient prison existing in this locality. Such, however, was not the fact. The little river Fleet, whose muddy current was at that time open to view, flowed between the two buildings; and the grim and frowning mansion we propose to describe stood on the western bank, exactly opposite the gateway of the prison.

Now, as no one had a stronger interest in the Fleet Prison than the owner of that gloomy house, inasmuch as he had lodged more persons within it than any one ever did before him, it would almost seem that he had selected his abode for the purpose of watching over the safe custody of the numerous victims of his rapacity and tyranny. This was the general surmise; and, it must be owned, there was ample warranty for it in his conduct.

A loop-hole in the turret at the north-east angle of the house commanded the courts of the prison, and here Sir Giles Mompesson would frequently station himself to note what was going forward within the jail, and examine the looks and deportment of those kept by him in durance. Many a glance of hatred and defiance was thrown from these sombre courts at the narrow aperture at which he was known to place himself; but such regards only excited Sir Giles's derision: many an imploring gesture was made to him; but these entreaties for compassion were equally disregarded. Being a particular friend of the Warden of the Fleet, and the jailers obeying him as they would have done their principal, he entered the prison when he pleased, and visited any ward he chose, at any hour of day or night; and though the unfortunate prisoners complained of the annoyance,—and especially those to whom his presence was obnoxious,—no redress could be obtained. He always appeared when least expected, and seemed to take a malicious pleasure in troubling those most anxious to avoid him.

Nor was Sir Giles the only visitant to the prison. Clement Lanyere was as frequently to be seen within its courts and wards as his master, and a similar understanding appeared to exist between him and the jailers. Hence, he was nearly as much an object of dread and dislike as Sir Giles himself, and few saw the masked and shrouded figure of the spy approach them without misgiving.

From the strange and unwarrantable influence exercised by Sir Giles and the promoter in the prison, they came at length to be considered as part of it; and matters were as frequently referred to them by the subordinate officers as to the warden. It was even supposed by some of the prisoners that a secret means of communication must exist between Sir Giles's habitation and the jail; but as both he and Lanyere possessed keys of the wicket, such a contrivance was obviously unnecessary, and would have been dangerous, as it must have been found out at some time by those interested in the discovery.

It has been shown, however, that, in one way or other, Sir Giles had nearly as much to do with the management of the Fleet Prison as those to whom its governance was ostensibly committed, and that he could, if he thought proper, aggravate the sufferings of its unfortunate occupants without incurring any responsibility for his treatment of them. He looked upon the Star-Chamber and the Fleet as the means by which he could plunder society and stifle the cry of the oppressed; and it was his business to see that both machines were kept in good order, and worked well.

But to return to his habitation. Its internal appearance corresponded with its forbidding exterior. The apartments were large, but cold and comfortless, and, with two or three exceptions, scantily furnished. Sumptuously decorated, these exceptional rooms presented a striking contrast to the rest of the house; but they were never opened, except on the occasion of some grand entertainment—a circumstance of rare occurrence. There was a large hall of entrance, where Sir Giles's myrmidons were wont to assemble, with a great table in the midst of it, on which no victuals were ever placed—at least at the extortioner's expense—and a great fire-place, where no fire ever burnt. From this a broad stone staircase mounted to the upper part of the house, and communicated by means of dusky corridors and narrow passages with the various apartments. A turnpike staircase connected the turret to which Sir Giles used to resort to reconnoitre the Fleet Prison, with the lower part of the habitation, and similar corkscrew stairs existed in the other angles of the structure. When stationed at the loophole, little recked Sir Giles of the mighty cathedral that frowned upon him like the offended eye of heaven. His gaze was seldom raised towards Saint Paul's, or if it were, he had no perception of the beauty or majesty of the ancient cathedral. The object of interest was immediately below him. The sternest realities of life were what he dealt with. He had no taste for the sublime or the beautiful.

Sir Giles had just paid an inquisitorial visit, such as we have described, to the prison, and was returning homewards over Fleet Bridge, when he encountered Sir Francis Mitchell, who was coming in quest of him, and they proceeded to his habitation together. Nothing beyond a slight greeting passed between them in the street, for Sir Giles was ever jealous of his slightest word being overheard; but he could see from his partner's manner that something had occurred to annoy and irritate him greatly. Sir Giles was in no respect changed since the reader last beheld him. Habited in the same suit of sables, he still wore the same mantle, and the same plumed hat, and had the same long rapier by his side. His deportment, too, was as commanding as before, and his aspect as stern and menacing.

Sir Francis, however, had not escaped the consequences naturally to be expected from the punishment inflicted upon him by the apprentices, being so rheumatic that he could scarcely walk, while a violent cough, with which he was occasionally seized, and which took its date from the disastrous day referred to, and had never left him since, threatened to shake his feeble frame in pieces; this, added to the exasperation under which he was evidently labouring, was almost too much for him. Three months seemed to have placed as many years upon his head; or, at all events, to have taken a vast deal out of his constitution. But, notwithstanding his increased infirmities, and utter unfitness for the part he attempted to play, he still affected a youthful air, and still aped all the extravagances and absurdities in dress and manner of the gayest and youngest court coxcomb. He was still attired in silks and satins of the gaudiest hues, still carefully trimmed as to hair and beard, still redolent of perfumes.

Not without exhibiting considerable impatience, Sir Giles was obliged to regulate his pace by the slow and tottering steps of his companion, and was more than once brought to a halt as the lungs of the latter were convulsively torn by his cough, but at last they reached the house, and entered the great hall, where the myrmidons were assembled—all of whom rose on their appearance, and saluted them. There was Captain Bludder, with his braggart air, attended by some half-dozen Alsatian bullies; Lupo Vulp, with his crafty looks; and the tipstaves—all, in short, were present, excepting Clement Lanyere, and Sir Giles knew how to account for his absence. To the inquiries of Captain Bludder and his associates, whether they were likely to be required on any business that day, Sir Giles gave a doubtful answer, and placing some pieces of money in the Alsatian's hand, bade him repair, with his followers, to the "Rose Tavern," in Hanging Sword Court, and crush a flask or two of wine, and then return for orders—an injunction with which the captain willingly complied. To the tipstaves Sir Giles made no observation, and bidding Lupo Vulp hold himself in readiness for a summons, he passed on with his partner to an inner apartment. On Sir Francis gaining it, he sank into a chair, and was again seized with a fit of coughing that threatened him with annihilation. When it ceased, he made an effort to commence the conversation, and Sir Giles, who had been pacing to and fro impatiently within the chamber, stopped to listen to him.

"You will wonder what business has brought me hither to-day, Sir Giles," he said; "and I will keep you no longer in suspense. I have been insulted, Sir Giles—grievously insulted."

"By whom?" demanded the extortioner.

"By Sir Jocelyn Mounchensey," replied Sir Francis, shaking with passion. "I have received a degrading insult from him to-day, which ought to be washed out with his blood."

"What hath he done to you?" inquired the other.

"I will tell you, Sir Giles. I chanced to see him in the court-yard of the palace of Whitehall, and there being several gallants nigh at hand, who I thought would take my part—ough! ough! what a plaguey cough I have gotten, to be sure; but 't is all owing to those cursed 'prentices—a murrain seize 'em! Your patience, sweet Sir Giles, I am coming to the point—ough! ough! there it takes me again. Well, as I was saying, thinking the gallants with whom I was conversing would back me, and perceiving Mounchensey approach us, I thought I might venture"—

"Venture!" repeated Sir Giles, scornfully. "Let not such a disgraceful word pass your lips."

"I mean, I thought I might take occasion to affront him. Whereupon I cocked my hat fiercely, as I have seen you and Captain Bludder do, Sir Giles."

"Couple me not with the Alsatian, I pray of you, Sir Francis," observed the extortioner, sharply.

"Your pardon, Sir Giles—your pardon! But as I was saying, I regarded him with a scowl, and tapped the hilt of my sword. And what think you the ruffianly fellow did? I almost blush at the bare relation of it. Firstly, he plucked off my hat, telling me I ought to stand bareheaded in the presence of gentlemen. Next, he tweaked my nose, and as I turned round to avoid him, he applied his foot—yes, his foot—to the back of my trunk-hose; and well was it that the hose were stoutly wadded and quilted. Fire and fury! Sir Giles, I cannot brook the indignity. And what was worse, the shameless gallants, who ought to have lent me aid, were ready to split their sides with laughter, and declared I had only gotten my due. When I could find utterance for very choler, I told the villain you would requite him, and he answered he would serve you in the same fashion, whenever you crossed his path."

"Ha! said he so?" cried Sir Giles, half drawing his sword, while his eyes flashed fire. "We shall see whether he will make good his words. Yet no! Revenge must not be accomplished in that way. I have already told you I am willing to let him pursue his present career undisturbed for a time, in order to make his fall the greater. I hold him in my hand, and can crush him when I please."

"Then do not defer your purpose, Sir Giles," said Sir Francis; "or I must take my own means of setting myself right with him. I cannot consent to sit down calmly under the provocation I have endured."

"And what will be the momentary gratification afforded by his death—if such you meditate," returned Sir Giles, "in comparison with hurling him down from the point he has gained, stripping him of all his honours, and of such wealth as he may have acquired, and plunging him into the Fleet Prison, where he will die by inches, and where you yourself may feast your eyes on his slow agonies? That is true revenge; and you are but a novice in the art of vengeance if you think your plan equal to mine. It is for this—and this only—that I have spared him so long. I have suffered him to puff himself up with pride and insolence, till he is ready to burst. But his day of reckoning is at hand, and then he shall pay off the long arrears he owes us."

"Well, Sir Giles, I am willing to leave the matter with you," said Sir Francis; "but it is hard to be publicly insulted, and have injurious epithets applied to you, and not obtain immediate redress."

"I grant you it is so," rejoined Sir Giles; "but you well know you are no match for him at the sword."

"If I am not, others are—Clement Lanyere, for instance," cried Sir Francis. "He has more than once arranged a quarrel for me."

"And were it an ordinary case, I would advise that the arrangement of this quarrel should be left to Lanyere," said Sir Giles; "or I myself would undertake it for you. But that were only half revenge. No; the work must be done completely; and the triumph you will gain in the end will amply compensate you for the delay."

"Be it so, then," replied Sir Francis. "But before I quit the subject, I may remark, that one thing perplexes me in the sudden rise of this upstart, and that is that he encounters no opposition from Buckingham. Even the King, I am told, has expressed his surprise that the jealous Marquis should view one who may turn out a rival with so much apparent complacency."

"It is because Buckingham has no fear of him," replied Sir Giles. "He knows he has but to say the word, and the puppet brought forward by De Gondomar—for it is by him that Mounchensey is supported— will be instantly removed; but as he also knows, that another would be set up, he is content to let him occupy the place for a time."

"Certes, if Mounchensey had more knowledge of the world he would distrust him," said Sir Francis, "because in my opinion Buckingham overacts his part, and shows him too much attention. He invites him, as I am given to understand, to all his masques, banquets, and revels at York House, and even condescends to flatter him. Such conduct would awaken suspicion in any one save the object of it."

"I have told you Buckingham's motive, and therefore his conduct will no longer surprise you. Have you heard of the wager between De Gondomar and the Marquis, in consequence of which a trial of skill is to be made in the Tilt-yard to-morrow? Mounchensey is to run against Buckingham, and I leave you to guess what the result will be. I myself am to be among the jousters."

"You!" exclaimed Sir Francis.

"Even I," replied Sir Giles, with a smile of gratified vanity. "Now, mark me, Sir Francis. I have a surprise for you. It is not enough for me to hurl this aspiring youth from his proud position, and cover him with disgrace—it is not enough to immure him in the Fleet; but I will deprive him of his choicest treasure—of the object of his devoted affections."

"Ay, indeed!" exclaimed Sir Francis.

"By my directions Clement Lanyere has kept constant watch over him, and has discovered that the young man's heart is fixed upon a maiden of great beauty, named Aveline Calveley, daughter of the crazy Puritan who threatened the King's life some three or four months ago at Theobalds."

"I mind me of the circumstance," observed Sir Francis.

"This maiden lives in great seclusion with an elderly dame, but I have found out her retreat. I have said that Sir Jocelyn is enamoured of her, and she is by no means insensible to his passion. But a bar exists to their happiness. Almost with his last breath, a promise was extorted from his daughter by Hugh Calveley, that if her hand should be claimed within a year by one to whom he had engaged her, but with whose name even she was wholly unacquainted, she would unhesitatingly give it to him."

"And will the claim be made?"

"It will."

"And think you she will fulfil her promise?"

"I am sure of it. A dying father's commands are sacred with one like her."

"Have you seen her, Sir Giles? Is she so very beautiful as represented?"

"I have not yet seen her; but she will be here anon. And you can then judge for yourself."

"She here!" exclaimed Sir Francis. "By what magic will you bring her hither?"

"By a spell that cannot fail in effect," replied Sir Giles, with a grim smile. "I have summoned her in her father's name. I have sent for her to tell her that her hand will be claimed."

"By whom?" inquired Sir Francis.

"That is my secret," replied Sir Giles.

At this juncture there was a tap at the door, and Sir Giles, telling the person without to enter, it was opened by Clement Lanyere, wrapped in his long mantle, and with his countenance hidden by his mask.

"They are here," he said.

"The damsel and the elderly female?" cried Sir Giles.

And receiving a response in the affirmative from the promoter, he bade him usher them in at once.

The next moment Aveline, attended by a decent-looking woman, somewhat stricken in years, entered the room. They were followed by Clement Lanyere. The maiden was attired in deep mourning, and though looking very pale, her surpassing beauty produced a strong impression upon Sir Francis Mitchell, who instantly arose on seeing her, and made her a profound, and, as he considered, courtly salutation.

Without bestowing any attention on him, Aveline addressed herself to Sir Giles, whose look filled her with terror.

"Why have you sent for me, Sir?" she demanded.

"I have sent for you, Aveline Calveley, to remind you of the promise made by you to your dying father," he rejoined.

"Ah!" she exclaimed; "then my forebodings of ill are realized."

"I know you consider that promise binding," pursued Sir Giles; "and it is only necessary for me to announce to you that, in a week from this time, your hand will be claimed in marriage."

"Alas! alas!" she cried, in accents of despair. "But who will claim it?—and how can the claim be substantiated?" she added, recovering herself in some degree.

"You will learn at the time I have appointed," replied Sir Giles. "And now, having given you notice to prepare for the fulfilment of an engagement solemnly contracted by your father, and as solemnly agreed to by yourself, I will no longer detain you."

Aveline gazed at him with wonder and terror, and would have sought for some further explanation; but perceiving from the inflexible expression of his countenance that any appeal would be useless, she quitted the room with her companion.

"I would give half I possess to make that maiden mine," cried Sir Francis, intoxicated with admiration of her beauty.

"Humph!" exclaimed Sir Giles. "More difficult matters have been accomplished. Half your possessions, say you? She is not worth so much. Assign to me your share of the Mounchensey estates and she shall be yours."

"I will do it, Sir Giles—I will do it," cried the old usurer, eagerly; "but you must prove to me first that you can make good your words."

"Pshaw! Have I ever deceived you, man? But rest easy. You shall be fully satisfied."

"Then call in Lupo Vulp, and let him prepare the assignment at once," cried Sir Francis. "I shall have a rare prize; and shall effectually revenge myself on this detested Mounchensey."

CHAPTER VI.
OF THE WAGER BETWEEN THE CONDE
DE GONDOMAR AND THE MARQUIS OF

Buckingham.

At a banquet given at Whitehall, attended by all the principal lords and ladies of the court, a wager was laid between the Conde de Gondomar and the Marquis of Buckingham, the decision of which was referred to the King.

The circumstance occurred in this way. The discourse happened to turn upon jousting, and the magnificent favourite, who was held unrivalled in all martial exercises and chivalrous sports, and who, confident in his own skill, vauntingly declared that he had never met his match in the tilt-yard; whereupon the Spanish Ambassador, willing to lower his pride, immediately rejoined, that he could, upon the instant, produce a better man-at-arms than he; and so certain was he of being able to make good his words, that he was willing to stake a thousand doubloons to a hundred on the issue of a trial.

To this Buckingham haughtily replied, that he at once accepted the Ambassador's challenge; but in regard to the terms of the wager, they must be somewhat modified, as he could not accept them as proposed; but he was willing to hazard on the result of the encounter all the gems, with which at the moment his habiliments were covered, against the single diamond clasp worn by De Gondomar; and if the offer suited his Excellency, he had nothing to do but appoint the day, and bring forward the man.

De Gondomar replied, that nothing could please him better than the Marquis's modification of the wager, and the proposal was quite consistent with the acknowledged magnificence of his Lordship's notions; yet he begged to make one further alteration, which was, that in the event of the knight he should nominate being adjudged by his Majesty to be the best jouster, the rich prize might be delivered to him.

Buckingham assented, and the terms of the wager being now fully settled, it only remained to fix the day for the trial, and this was referred to the King, who appointed the following Thursday—thus allowing, as the banquet took place on a Friday, nearly a week for preparation.

James, also, good-naturedly complied with the Ambassador's request, and agreed to act as judge on the occasion; and he laughingly remarked to Buckingham—"Ye are demented, Steenie, to risk a' those precious stanes with which ye are bedecked on the skill with which ye can yield a frail lance. We may say unto you now in the words of the poet—

'*Pendebant ter ti gemmata monilia collo;*'

but wha shall say frae whose round throat those gemmed collars and glittering ouches will hang a week hence, if ye be worsted? Think of that, my dear dog."

"Your Majesty need be under no apprehension," replied Buckingham. "I shall win and wear his Excellency's diamond clasp. And now, perhaps, the Count will make us acquainted with the name and title of my puissant adversary, on whose address he so much relies. Our relative chances of success will then be more apparent. If, however, any motives for secrecy exist, I will not press the inquiry, but leave the disclosure to a more convenient season."

"*Nunc est narrandi tempus,*" rejoined the King. "No time like the present. We are anxious to ken wha the hero may be."

"I will not keep your Majesty a moment in suspense," said De Gondomar. "The young knight whom I design to select as the Marquis's opponent, and whom I am sure will feel grateful for having such means of honourable distinction afforded him, is present at the banquet."

"Here!" exclaimed James, looking round. "To whom do you refer, Count? It cannot be Sir Gilbert Gerrard, or Sir Henry Rich; for—without saying aught in disparagement of their prowess—neither of them is a match for Buckingham! Ah! save us! We hae it. Ye mean Sir Jocelyn Mounchensey."

And as the Ambassador acknowledged that his Majesty was right, all eyes were turned towards the young knight, who, though as much surprised as any one else, could not help feeling greatly elated.

"Aweel, Count," said James, evidently pleased, "ye might hae made a waur choice—that we are free to confess. We begin to tremble for your braw jewels, Steenie."

"They are safer than I expected," replied Buckingham, disdainfully. But though he thus laughed it off, it was evident he was displeased, and he muttered to his confidential friend, Lord Mordaunt,—"I see through it all: this is a concerted scheme to bring this aspiring galliard forward; but he shall receive a lesson for his presumption he shall not easily forget, while, at the same time, those who make use of him for their own purposes shall be taught the risk they incur in daring to oppose me. The present opportunity shall not be neglected."

Having formed this resolution, Buckingham, to all appearance, entirely recovered his gaiety, and pressed the King to give importance to the trial by allowing it to take place in the royal tilt-yard at Whitehall, and to extend the number of jousters to fourteen—seven on one side, and seven on the other. The request was readily granted by the monarch, who appeared to take a stronger interest in the match than Buckingham altogether liked, and confirmed him in his determination of ridding himself for ever of the obstacle in his path presented by Mounchensey. The number of jousters being agreed upon, it was next decided that the party with whom Buckingham was to range should be headed by the Duke of Lennox; while Mounchensey's party was to be under the command of Prince Charles; and though the disposition was too flattering to his adversary to be altogether agreeable to the haughty favourite, he could not raise any reasonable objection to it, and was therefore obliged to submit with the best grace he could.

The two parties were then distributed in the following order by the King:—On the side of the Duke of Lennox, besides Buckingham himself, were the Earls of Arundel and Pembroke, and the Lords Clifford and Mordaunt; and while the King was hesitating as to the seventh, Sir Giles Mompesson was suggested by the Marquis, and James, willing to oblige his favourite, adopted the proposition. On the side of Prince Charles were ranked the Marquis of Hamilton, the Earls of Montgomery, Rutland, and Dorset, Lord Walden, and, of course, Sir Jocelyn Mounchensey. These preliminaries being fully adjusted, other topics were started, and the carouse, which had been in some degree interrupted, was renewed, and continued, with the entertainments that succeeded it, till past midnight.

Not a little elated by the high compliment paid to his prowess by the Spanish Ambassador, and burning to break a lance with Buckingham, Sir Jocelyn resolved to distinguish himself at the trial. Good luck, of late, had invariably attended him. Within the last few weeks, he had been appointed one of the Gentlemen of his Majesty's Bed-chamber; and this was looked upon as the stepping-stone to some more exalted post. Supported by the influence of De Gondomar, and upheld by his own personal merits, which by this time, in spite of all hostility towards him, had begun to be appreciated; with the King himself most favourably inclined towards him, and Prince Charles amicably disposed; with many of the courtiers proffering him service, who were anxious to throw off their forced allegiance to the overweening favourite, and substitute another in his stead: with all these advantages, it is not to be wondered at, that in a short space of time he should have established a firm footing on that smooth and treacherous surface, the pavement of a palace, and have already become an object of envy and jealousy to many, and of admiration to a few.

Possessing the faculty of adapting himself to circumstances, Sir Jocelyn conducted himself with rare discretion; and while avoiding giving offence, never suffered a liberty to be taken with himself; and having on the onset established a character for courage, he was little afterwards molested. It was creditable to him, that in a court where morality was at so low an ebb as that of James I., he should have remained uncorrupted; and that not all the allurements of the numerous beauties by whom he was surrounded, and who exerted their blandishments to ensnare him, could tempt him for a moment's disloyalty to the object of his affections. It was creditable, that at the frequent orgies he was compelled to attend, where sobriety was derided, and revelry pushed to its furthest limits, he was never on any occasion carried beyond the bounds of discretion. It was still more creditable to him, that in such venal and corrupt days he maintained his integrity perfectly unsullied. Thus severely tested, the true worth of his character was proved, and he came from the ordeal without a blemish.

The many excellent qualities that distinguished the newly-made knight and gentleman of the bed-chamber, combined with his remarkable personal advantages and conciliatory manner, considerably improved by the polish he had recently acquired, drew, as we have intimated, the attention of the second personage in the kingdom towards him. Struck by his manner, and by the sentiments he expressed, Prince Charles took frequent opportunities of conversing with him, and might have conceived a regard for him but for the jealous interference of Buckingham, who, unable to brook a rival either with the King or Prince, secretly endeavoured to set both against him. Such, however, was Sir Jocelyn's consistency of character, such his solidity of judgment and firmness, and such the respect he inspired, that he seemed likely to triumph over all the insidious snares planned for him. Things were in this state when the trial of skill in jousting was proposed by De Gondomar. The wily Ambassador might have—and probably had—some secret motive in making the proposal; but whatever it was, it was unknown to his *protégé*.

CHAPTER VII.
A CLOUD IN THE HORIZON.

But it must not be imagined that Sir Jocelyn's whole time was passed in attendance on the court. Not a day flew by that he did not pay a visit to Aveline. She had taken a little cottage, where she dwelt in perfect seclusion, with one female attendant, old Dame Sherborne,— the same who had accompanied her on her compulsory visit to Sir Giles Mompesson,—and her father's faithful old servant, Anthony Rocke. To this retreat, situated in the then rural neighbourhood adjoining Holborn, Sir Jocelyn, as we have said, daily repaired, and the moments so spent were the most delicious of his life. The feelings of regard entertained for him from the first by Aveline, had by this time ripened into love; yet, mindful of her solemn promise to her father, she checked her growing affection as much as lay in her power, and would not, at first, permit any words of tenderness to be uttered by him. As weeks, however, and even months, ran on, and no one appeared to claim her hand, she began to indulge the hope that the year of probation would expire without molestation, and insensibly, and almost before she was aware of it, Sir Jocelyn had become complete master of her heart. In these interviews, he told her all that occurred to him at court—acquainted her of his hopes of aggrandisement—and induced her to listen to his expectations of a brilliant future, to be shared by them together.

The severe shock Aveline had sustained in the death of her father had gradually worn away, and, if not free from occasional depression, she was still enabled to take a more cheerful view of things. Never had she seen Sir Jocelyn so full of ardour as on the day after the banquet, when he came to communicate the intelligence of the jousts, and that he was selected to essay his skill against that of Buckingham. The news, however, did not produce upon her the effect he expected. Not only she could not share his delight, but she was seized with anticipations of coming ill, in connection with this event, for which she could not account. Nor could all that Jocelyn said remove her misgivings; and, in consequence, their meeting was sadder than usual.

On the next day, these forebodings of impending calamity were most unexpectedly realised. A mysterious personage, wrapped in a long black cloak, and wearing a mask, entered her dwelling without standing upon the ceremony of tapping at the door. His presence occasioned her much alarm, and it was not diminished when he told her, in a stern, and peremptory tone, that she must accompany him to Sir Giles Mompesson's habitation. Refusing to give any explanation of the cause of this strange summons, he said she would do well to comply with it, — that, indeed, resistance would be idle as Sir Giles was prepared to enforce his orders; and that he himself would be responsible for her safety. Compelled to be satisfied with these assurances, Aveline yielded to the apparent necessity of the case, and set forth with him, attended by Dame Sherbourne. With what passed during her interview with the extortioner the reader is already acquainted. She had anticipated something dreadful; but the reality almost exceeded her anticipations. So overpowered was she by the painful intelligence, that it was with difficulty she reached home, and the rest of the day was occupied with anxious reflection. Evening as usual brought her lover. She met him at the door, where he tied his horse, and they entered the little dwelling together. The shades of night were coming on apace, and in consequence of the gloom he did not remark the traces of distress on her countenance, but went on with the theme uppermost in his mind.

"I know you have ever avoided shows and triumphs," he said; "but I wish I could induce you to make an exception in favour of this tilting-match, and consent to be present at it. The thought that you were looking on would nerve my arm, and make me certain of success."

"Even if I would, I cannot comply with your request," she replied, in an agitated tone. "Prepare yourself, Jocelyn. I have bad news for you."

He started; and the vision of delight, in which he had been indulging, vanished at once.

"The worst news you could have to tell me, would be that the claim had been made," he observed. "I trust it is not that?"

"It is better to know the worst at once. I have received undoubted information that the claim *will* be made."

A cry of anguish escaped Sir Jocelyn, as if a severe blow had been dealt him—and he could scarcely articulate the inquiry, "By whom?"

"That I know not," she rejoined. "But the ill tidings have been communicated to me by Sir Giles Mompesson."

"Sir Giles Mompesson!" exclaimed Sir Jocelyn, scarcely able to credit what he heard. "Your father would never have surrendered you to him. It is impossible he could have made any compact with such a villain."

"I do not say that he did; and if he had done so, I would die a thousand deaths, and incur all the penalties attached to the sin of disobedience, rather than fulfil it. Sir Giles is merely the mouth-piece of another, who will not disclose himself till he appears to exact fulfilment of the fatal pledge."

"But, be it whomsoever it may, the claim never can be granted," cried Sir Jocelyn, in a voice of agony. "You will not consent to be bound by such a contract. You will not thus sacrifice yourself. It is out of all reason. Your father's promise cannot bind you. He had no right to destroy his child. Will you listen to my council, Aveline?" he continued, vehemently. "You have received this warning, and though it is not likely to have been given with any very friendly design, still you may take advantage of it, and avoid by flight the danger to which you are exposed."

"Impossible," she answered. "I could not reconcile such a course to my conscience, or to my reverence for my father's memory."

"There is still another course open to you," he pursued, "if you choose to adopt it; and that is, to take a stop which shall make the fulfilment of this promise impossible."

"I understand you," she replied; "but that is equally out of the question. Often and often have I thought over this matter, and with much uneasiness; but I cannot relieve myself of the obligation imposed upon me."

"O Aveline!" cried Sir Jocelyn. "If you allow yourself, by any fancied scruples, to be forced into a marriage repugnant to your feelings, you will condemn both yourself and me to misery."

"I know it—I feel it; and yet there is no escape," she cried, "Were I to act on your suggestions, and fly from this threatened danger, or remove it altogether by a marriage with you—were I to disobey my father, I should never know a moment's peace."

There was a brief pause, interrupted only by her sobs. At length Sir Jocelyn exclaimed quickly, "Perhaps, we may be unnecessarily alarming ourselves, and this may only be a trick of Sir Giles Mompesson. He may have heard of the promise you have made to your father, and may try to frighten you. But whoever is put forward must substantiate his claim."

As those words were uttered, there was a slight noise in the apartment, and looking up, they beheld the dusky figure of Clement Lanyere, masked and cloaked, as was his wont, standing beside them.

"You here?" cried Sir Jocelyn, in astonishment.

"Ay," replied the promoter; "I am come to tell you that this is no idle fear,—that the claim *will* be made, and *will* be substantiated."

"Ah!" exclaimed Aveline, in a tone of anguish.

"You will not seek to evade it, I know, young mistress," replied the promoter; "and therefore, as you have truly said, there is no escape."

"Only let me know the claimant's name," cried Sir Jocelyn, "and I will engage he shall never fulfill his design."

"O no; this must not be—you must not resort to violence," said Aveline. "I will never consent to owe my deliverance to such means."

"You shall have all the information you require after the jousts on Thursday," said Lanyere; "and let the thought strengthen your arm in the strife, for if you fail, Aveline Calveley will have no protector in the hour of need."

With this, he departed as suddenly and mysteriously as he had come.

CHAPTER VIII.
WHITEHALL.

The Tilt-yard at Whitehall, where the jousting was appointed to take place, was situated on the westerly side of the large area in front of the old Banqueting House (destroyed by fire soon after the date of this history, and replaced by the stately structure planned by Inigo Jones, still existing), and formed part of a long range of buildings appertaining to the palace, and running parallel with it in a northerly direction from Westminster, devoted to purposes of exercise and recreation, and including the Tennis-court, the Bowling-alley, the Manage, and the Cock-pit.

A succession of brick walls, of various heights, and surmounted by roofs of various forms and sizes, marked the position of these buildings, in reference to Saint James's Park, which they skirted on the side next to King Street. They were mainly, if not entirely erected, in 1532 by Henry VIII., when, after his acquisition from Wolsey, by forfeiture, of Whitehall, he obtained by exchange from the Abbot and Convent of Westminister all their uninclosed land contiguous to his newly-acquired palace, and immediately fenced it round, and converted it into a park.

To a monarch so fond of robust sports and manly exercises of all kinds as our bluff Harry, a tilt-yard was indispensable; and he erected one on a grand scale, and made it a place of constant resort. Causing a space of one hundred and fifty yards in length and fifty in width to be inclosed and encircled by lofty walls, he fixed against the inner side large scaffolds, containing two tiers of seats, partitioned from each other like boxes in a theatre, for the accommodation of spectators. At the southern extremity of the inclosure he reared a magnificent gallery, which he set apart for his consort and the ladies in attendance upon her. This was decorated with velvet, and hung with curtains of cloth of gold. On grand occasions, when all the court was present, the whole of the seats on the scaffolds, previously described, were filled with bright-eyed beauties, whose looks and plaudits stimulated to deeds of high emprise the knights, who styled themselves their "servants," and besought "favours" from them in the shape of a scarf, a veil, a sleeve, a bracelet, a ringlet, or a knot of ribands. At such times Henry himself would enter the lists; and, in his earlier days, and before he became too unwieldy for active exertion, no ruder antagonist with the lance or sword could be found than he. Men indeed, existed in his days, very different in hardihood of frame and personal strength from the silken sybarites, enervated by constant riot and dissipation, who aped the deeds of arms of their grandfathers in the time of James the First.

But the tilt-yard was by no means neglected by Elizabeth. This lion-hearted queen encouraged a taste for chivalrous displays, and took almost as much delight in such exhibitions as her stalwart sire. During her long reign no festivity was thought complete unless jousting was performed. The name of the gallant Sir Philip Sidney need only be mentioned, to show that she possessed at least one perfect "mirror of chivalry" amongst her courtiers; but her chief favourites, Essex and Leicester, were both distinguished for knightly prowess. Many a lance was splintered by them in her honour. When the French Embassy arrived in London to treat of a marriage between Elizabeth and the Duc d'Anjou, and when a grand temporary banqueting-house, three hundred and thirty feet long, and covered with canvas, was improvised for the occasion, a magnificent tournament was given in the tilt-yard in honour of the distinguished visitors. Old Holinshed tells us, that—"the gallery or place at the end of the tilt-yard, adjoining to her Majesty's house at Whitehall, where, as her person should be placed, was called, and not without cause, the Castle or Fortress of Perfect Beauty, for as much as her highness should be there included." And he also gives a curious description of the framework used by the besiegers of the fortress. "They had provided," he says, "a frame of wood, which was covered with canvas, and painted outwardly in such excellent order, as if it had been very natural earth or mould, and carried the name of a rolling-trench, which went on wheels which way soever the persons within did drive it. Upon the top thereof were placed two cannons of wood, so passing well coloured, as they seemed to be, indeed, two fair field pieces of ordnance; and by them were placed two men for gunners, clothed in crimson sarcenet, with their baskets of earth for defence of their bodies by them. And also there stood on the top of the trench an ensign-bearer, in the same suit with the gunners, displaying his ensign, and within the said trench was cunningly conveyed divers kinds of most excellent music against the Castle of Beauty. These things thus all in readiness, the challengers approached, and came down the stable toward the tilt-yard." The challengers were the Earl of Arundel, Lord Windsor, Sir Philip Sidney, and Sir Fulke Greville; and the defenders were very numerous, and amongst them was the doughty Sir Harry Lee, who, as the "unknown knight," broke "six staves right valiantly." All the speeches made by the challengers and defenders are reported by Holinshed, who thus winds up his description of the first day's triumph:—"These speeches being ended, both they and the rest marched about the tilt-yard, and so going back to the nether end thereof, prepared themselves to run, every one in his turn, each defendant six courses against the former challengers, who performed their parts so valiantly on both sides, that their prowess hath demerited perpetual memory, and worthily won honour, both to themselves and their native country, as fame hath the same reported." And of the second day he thus writes:— "Then went they to the tourney, where they did very nobly, as the shivering of the swords might very well testify; and after that to the barriers, where they lashed it out lustily, and fought courageously, as if the Greeks and Trojans had dealt their deadly dole. No party was spared, no estate excepted, but each knight endeavoured to win the golden fleece, that expected either fame or the favour of his mistress, which sport continued all the same day." These pageantries were of frequent occurrence, and the pages of the picturesque old chronicler above-cited abound with descriptions of them. Yet, in spite of the efforts of Elizabeth to maintain its splendour undiminished, the star of chivalry was rapidly declining, to disappear for ever in the reign of her successor.

The glitter of burnished steel, the clash of arms, the rude encounter, and all other circumstances attendant upon the arena of martial sport, that had given so much delight to his predecessors, afforded little pleasure to James; as how should they, to a prince whose constitutional timidity was so great that he shuddered at the sight of a drawn sword, and abhorred the mimic representations of warfare! Neither were the rigorous principles of honour on which chivalry was based, nor the obligations they imposed, better suited to him. Too faithless by nature to adopt the laws of a Court of Honour, he derided the institution as obsolete. Nevertheless, as trials of skill and strength in the tilt-yard were still in fashion, he was compelled, though against his inclination, to witness them, and in some degree to promote them. The day of his accession to the throne—the 24th March—was always celebrated by tilting and running at the ring, and similar displays were invariably made in honour of any important visitor to the court.

Even in this reign something of a revival of the ancient ardour for knightly pastimes took place during the brief career of Prince Henry, who, if he had lived to fulfil the promise of his youth, would have occupied a glorious page in his country's annals, and have saved it, in all probability, from its subsequent convulsions and intestine strife. Inuring himself betimes to the weight of armour, this young prince became exceedingly expert in the use of all weapons—could toss the pike, couch the lance, and wield the sword, the battle-axe, or the mace, better than any one of his years. The tilt-yard and the tennis-court were his constant places of resort, and he was ever engaged in robust exercises—too much so, indeed, for a somewhat feeble constitution. Prince Henry indulged the dream of winning back Calais from France, and would no doubt have attempted the achievement if he had lived.

Of a more reflective cast of mind than his elder brother, and with tastes less martial, Prince Charles still sedulously cultivated all the accomplishments, proper to a cavalier. A perfect horseman, and well skilled in all the practices of the tilt-yard—he was a model of courtesy and grace; but he had not Prince Henry's feverish and consuming passion for martial sports, nor did he, like him, make their pursuit the sole business of life. Still, the pure flame of chivalry burnt within his breast, and he fully recognised its high and ennobling principles, and accepted the obligations they imposed. And in this respect, as in most others, he differed essentially from his august father.

The tilt-yard, and the various buildings adjoining it, already enumerated, were approached by two fine gates, likewise erected by Henry VIII., one of which, of extraordinary beauty, denominated the Cock-pit Gate, was designed by the celebrated painter, Hans Holbein. From an authority we learn that it was "built of square stone, with small squares of flint boulder, very neatly set; and that it had also battlements, and four lofty towers, the whole being enriched with bustos, roses, and portcullises." The other gate, scarcely less beautiful, and styled the Westminster Gate, was adorned with statues and medallions, and the badges of the royal house of Tudor carved in stone.

Viewed from the summit of one of the tall turrets of the Holbein Gate, the appearance of the palace of Whitehall, at the period of our history, was exceedingly picturesque and striking—perhaps more so than at any previous or subsequent epoch, since the various structures of which it was composed were just old enough to have acquired a time-honoured character, while they were still in tolerable preservation.

Let us glance at it, then, from this point, and first turn towards the great Banqueting House, which presents to us a noble and lengthened façade, and contains within a magnificent and lofty hall, occupyirg nearly its full extent, besides several other apartments of regal size and splendour. In this building, in former days, with a retinue as princely as that of the King himself, Wolsey so often and so sumptuously entertained his royal master, that he at last provoked his anger by his ostentation, and was bereft of his superb abode. Satisfied with our examination of the Banqueting House, we will suffer our gaze to fall upon the broad court beyond it, and upon the numerous irregular but picturesque and beautiful structures by which that court—quadrangle it cannot be called, for no uniformity is observed in the disposition of the buildings—is surrounded. Here the eye is attracted by a confused mass of roofs, some flat, turreted and embattled, some pointed, with fantastical gables and stacks of tall chimneys—others with cupolas and tall clock-towers—others with crocketed pinnacles, and almost all with large gilt vanes. A large palace is a city in miniature; and so is it with Whitehall. It has two other courts besides the one we are surveying; equally crowded round with buildings, equally wanting in uniformity, but equally picturesque. On the east it extends to Scotland Yard, and on the west to the open space in front of Westminster Hall. The state apartments face the river, and their large windows look upon the stream.

Quitting the exalted position we have hitherto assumed, and viewing Whitehall from some bark on the Thames, we shall find that it has a stern and sombre look, being castellated, in part, with towers like those over Traitor's Gate, commanding the stairs that approach it from the river. The Privy Gardens are beautifully laid out in broad terrace walks, with dainty parterres, each having a statue in the midst, while there is a fountain in the centre of the inclosure. In addition to the gardens, and separated from them by an avenue of tall trees, is a spacious bowling-green. Again changing our position, we discover, on the south of the gardens, and connected with the state apartments, a long ambulatory, called the Stone Gallery. Then returning to our first post of observation, and taking a bird's-eye view of the whole, after examining it in detail, as before mentioned, we come to the conclusion, that, though irregular in the extreme, and with no pretension whatever to plan in its arrangement, the Palace of Whitehall is eminently picturesque, and imposing from its vast extent. If taken in connection with Westminster Hall, the Parliament House, and the ancient Abbey—with the two towering gateways, on one of which we, ourselves, are perched—with the various structures appertaining to it, and skirting Saint James's Park, and with the noble gothic cross at Charing, we are fain to acknowledge, that it constitutes a very striking picture.

CHAPTER IX.
PRINCE CHARLES.

There is now great stir within the palace, and its principal court is full of horsemen, some of them apparelled in steel, and with their steeds covered with rich trappings, and all attended by pages and yeomen in resplendent liveries. Besides these, there are trumpeters in crimson cassocks, mounted on goodly horses, and having their clarions adorned with silken pennons, on which the royal arms are broidered. Then there are kettle-drummers and other musicians, likewise richly arrayed and well mounted, and the various pages, grooms, and officers belonging to the Prince of Wales, standing around his charger, which is caparisoned with white and gold.

Distinguishable even amidst this brilliant and knightly throng is Sir Jocelyn Mounchensey. Mounted upon a fiery Spanish barb, presented to him by the Conde de Gondomar, he is fully equipped for the jousts. The trappings of his steed are black and white velvet, edged with silver, and the plumes upon his helmet are of the same colours, mingled. He is conversing with the Spanish Ambassador, who, like all the rest, is superbly attired, though not in armour, and is followed by a crowd of lacqueys in jerkins and hose of black satin, guarded with silver.

An unusual degree of bustle proclaims the approach of some personage of extraordinary importance.

This is soon made known to be the Marquis of Buckingham. His arrival is announced by loud flourishes from the six mounted trumpeters by whom he is preceded. Their horses are caparisoned with orange-coloured taffeta, while they themselves are habited in gaberdines of the same stuff. After the trumpeters come four gentlemen ushers, and four pages, mounted on his spare horses, and habited in orange-coloured doublets and hose, with yellow plumes in their caps. To them succeed the grooms in mandilions, or loose sleeveless jackets, leading the Marquis's charger, which is to run in the lists—a beautiful dark bay jennet—trapped with green velvet, sewn with pearls, and pounced with gold. Next comes Buckingham himself, in a magnificent suit of armour, engraved and damaskeened with gold, with an aigret of orange feathers nodding on his casque. Thus apparelled, it is impossible to imagine a nobler or more chivalrous figure than he presents. Though completely cased in steel, his magnificent person seems to have lost none of its freedom of movement, and he bears himself with as much grace and ease as if clad in his customary habiliments of silk and velvet. For the moment he rides a sorrel horse, whose spirit is too great to allow him to be safely depended upon in the lists, but who now serves by his fire and impetuosity to display to advantage his rider's perfect management. Buckingham is followed by thirty yeomen, apparelled like the pages, and twenty gentlemen in short cloaks and Venetian hose. He acknowledges the presence of his antagonist and the Spanish Ambassador, with a courteous salutation addressed to each, and then riding forward, takes up a position beside the Duke of Lennox, who, mounted and fully equipped, and having his five companions-at-arms with him, is awaiting the coming forth of Prince Charles.

The Duke of Lennox is very sumptuously arrayed in armour, partly blue, and partly gilt and graven, and his charger is caparisoned with cloth of gold, embroidered with pearls. Besides this he has four spare horses, led by his pages, in housings equally gorgeous and costly. These pages have cassock coats, and Venetian hose, of cloth of silver, laid with gold lace, and caps with gold bands and white feathers, and white buskins. His rétinue consists of forty gentlemen and yeomen, and four trumpeters. His companions-at-arms are all splendidly accoutred, and mounted on richly-caparisoned chargers. The most noticeable figure amongst them, however, is that of Sir Giles Mompesson; and he attracts attention from the circumstance of his armour being entirely sable, his steed jet black, and his housings, plumes, and all his equipments of the same sombre hue.

At this juncture, a page, in the Prince's livery of white and gold, approaches Sir Jocelyn, and informs him that his highness desires to speak with him before they proceed to the tilt-yard. On receiving the summons the young knight immediately quits De Gondomar, and, following the page to the doorway leading to the state apartments, dismounts at the steps, leaving his steed in charge of his youthful companion.

On entering the vestibule he finds a large party assembled, comprising some of the fairest dames of court, and several noble gallants, who intend taking no other part than that of spectators in the approaching tilting-match. Most of them are known to Sir Jocelyn, and they eagerly crowd round him, fearing something may have occurred to interfere with the proceedings of the day. The young knight allays their apprehensions, and after experiencing the kindling influence always produced by the smiles of the fair, begins to ascend the great staircase, and has nearly reached the door at its head, communicating with the Stone Gallery, when it is thrown open by an usher, and Prince Charles comes forth.

The noble countenance of Prince Charles is stamped with the same gravity, and slightly touched with the same melancholy, which distinguished his features through life, but which naturally deepened as misfortune fell upon him. But as those dark days cannot now be discerned, and, as all seems brilliant around him, and full of brightest promise, this prophetic melancholy is thought to lend interest to his handsome features. He is attired in a suit of black armour of exquisite workmanship, lacking only the helmet, which is carried by a page—as are the *volante pièce*, the *mentonnière*, and the *grande-garde*, intended to be worn in the field. On seeing Sir Jocelyn, he pauses, and signs to his attendants to stand back.

"I have sent for you, Sir Jocelyn," he said, "to ascertain whether it is true that Sir Giles Mompesson is amongst the Duke of Lennox's party."

"It is perfectly true, your highness," replied Sir Jocelyn; "he is now in the court-yard."

A shade of displeasure crossed the Prince's noble countenance, and his brow darkened.

"I am sorry to hear it; and but that I should grievously offend the King, my father, I would forbid him to take part in the jousts," he cried. "Sir Giles deserves to be degraded from knighthood, rather than enjoy any of its honourable privileges."

"Entertaining these sentiments, if your highness will make them known to the King, he will doubtless order Sir Giles's immediate withdrawal from the lists," said Sir Jocelyn. "Most assuredly he is unworthy to enter them."

"Not so," rejoined the Prince. "I have already represented the matter to his Majesty, and trusted my remonstrances would be attended to. But I find they have proved ineffectual. Buckingham, it appears, has more weight than I have. Yet this notorious extortioner's insolence and presumption ought not to pass unpunished."

"They shall not, your highness," replied Sir Jocelyn. "I will so deal with him that I will warrant he will never dare show himself within the precincts of the palace again."

"Do nothing rashly," said the Prince. "You must not disguise from yourself that you may displease the King, and provoke Buckingham's animosity."

"I cannot help it," returned Sir Jocelyn. "I will insult him, if he crosses my path."

"I cannot blame you," said the Prince. "In your position I should do the same; and I am only restrained by the injunctions laid upon me by the King, from commanding his instant departure. But I must proceed towards the tilt-yard. We shall meet again anon."

With this he descended the staircase; and as soon as his train of gentlemen-ushers and pages had passed on, Sir Jocelyn followed, and making his way through the still-crowded vestibule, gained the door, and vaulted on the back of his steed.

CHAPTER X.
THE OLD PALACE-YARD OF WESTMINSTER.

The throng outside the gates of Whitehall felt their breasts dilate, and their pulses dance, as they listened to the flourishes of the trumpets and cornets, the thundering bruit of the kettle-drums, and other martial music that proclaimed the setting forth of the steel-clad champions who were presently to figure in the lists.

It was, in sooth, a goodly sight to see the long and brilliant procession formed by the fourteen knights, each so gallantly mounted, so splendidly accoutred, and accompanied by such a host of gentlemen ushers, pages, yeomen, and grooms, some on horseback, and some on foot; and the eye of the looker-on was never wearied of noticing the diversity of their habiliments,—some of the knights having cuirasses and helmets, polished as silver, and reflecting the sun's rays as from a mirror,—some, russet-coloured armour,—some, blue harness,—some, fluted,—some, corslets damaskeened with gold, and richly ornamented,—others, black and lacquered breastplates, as was the case with the harness of Prince Charles,—and one, a dead black coat of mail, in the instance of Sir Giles Mompesson. The arms of each were slightly varied, either in make or ornament. A few wore sashes across their breastplates, and several had knots of ribands tied above the coronals of their lances, which were borne by their esquires.

In order to give the vast crowd assembled in the neighbourhood of Whitehall, an opportunity of witnessing as much as possible of the chivalrous spectacle, it was arranged by Prince Charles that the line of the procession should first take its course through the Holbein Grate, and then, keeping near the wall of the Privy Garden, should pass beneath the King's Gate and draw up for a short time in the Old Palace-yard near Westminster-hall, where a great concourse was assembled, amidst which a space was kept clear by parties of halberdiers and yeomen of the guard.

The procession was headed by the Prince, and the stately step of his milk-white charger well beseemed his own majestic deportment. When the long train of gentlemen-ushers and pages accompanying him had moved on, so as to leave the course clear for the next comer and his followers, a young knight presented himself, who, more than any other in the procession, attracted the attention of the spectators. This youthful knight's visor was raised so as to disclose his features, and these were so comely, that, combined with his finely-proportioned figure, perfectly displayed by his armour, he offered an *ensemble* of manly attractions almost irresistible to female eyes. Nor did the grace and skill which he exhibited in the management of his steed commend him less highly to sterner judges, who did not fail to discover that his limbs, though light, were in the highest degree vigorous and athletic, and they prognosticated most favourably of his chances of success in the jousts.

When it became known that this *preux chevalier* was Sir Jocelyn Mounchensey, the chosen antagonist of Buckingham, still greater attention was bestowed upon him; and as his good looks and gallant bearing operated strongly, as we have stated, in his favour, many a good wish and lusty cheer were uttered for him.

The effect of all this excitement among the crowd on behalf of Mounchensey was to render Buckingham's reception by the same persons comparatively cold; and the cheers given for the magnificent favourite and his princely retinue were so few and so wanting in spirit, that he who was wholly unaccustomed to such neglect, and who had been jealously listening to the cheers attending Mounchensey's progress, was highly offended, and could scarcely conceal his displeasure. But if he was indignant at his own reception, he was exasperated at the treatment experienced by his ally.

Close behind him rode a knight in black armour, with a sable panache on his helm. Stalwart limbs and a manly bearing had this knight, and he bestrode his powerful charger like one well accustomed to the saddle; but though no one could gainsay his skill as a horseman, or his possible prowess as a man-at-arms, most thought he had no title to be there, and gave unmistakable evidence of their conviction by groans and hootings.

This black knight was Sir Giles Mompesson, and very grim and menacing was his aspect.

Ample accommodation for the knightly company and their attendants, as well as for the multitudes congregated to behold them was afforded by the broad area in front of Westminster Hall; nevertheless, as those in the rear could not see as well as those in front, every chance elevation offering a better view was eagerly seized upon. All the accessible points of Westminster Hall—its carved porch and windows—were invaded. So were the gates of the Old Palace hard by—so were the buttresses of the Abbey; and men were perched, like grotesque ornaments, on crocketed pinnacles and stone water-spouts. The tall and curiously-painted clock tower, resembling an Italian campanile, which then faced the portals of Westminster Hall, was covered with spectators. But the position most coveted, and esteemed the best, was the fountain at that time standing in the midst of the old palace-yard. This structure, which was of great antiquity and beauty, with a pointed summit supported by tall slender shafts, and a large basin beneath, formed a sort of pivot, round which the procession turned as it arrived upon the ground, and consequently formed the best point of view of all; and those were esteemed highly fortunate who managed to obtain a place upon it.

Amongst these lucky individuals were three of the reader's acquaintances, and we think he will scarce fail to recognise the saucy-faced apprentice with the cudgel under his arm, and the fair-haired, blue-eyed, country-looking maiden at his side, as well as the hale old rustic by whom they were attended. All three were delighted with their position, and Dick Taverner took full credit to himself for his cleverness in procuring it for them. As to pretty Gillian, nothing could please her better, for she could not only see all that was going forward, but everybody could see her—even Prince Charles himself; and she flattered herself that she attraeted no little attention. And now that the whole of the procession had come up, the picture was certainly magnificent, and well worth contemplation. Everything was favourable to the enjoyment of the spectacle. The day was bright and beautiful, and a sparkling sunshine lighted up the splendid accoutrements of the knights, the gorgeous caparisons of their steeds, and the rich habiliments of their attendants; while a gentle breeze stirred the plumes upon the helmets, and fluttered the bandrols on their lances. The effect was heightened by enlivening strains of minstrelsy, and the fanfares of the trumpeters. The utmost enthusiasm was awakened among the spectators, and their acclamations were loud and long.

At this juncture, Dick Taverner, who had been shouting as lustily as the rest, tossing his cap in the air, and catching it dexterously as it fell, held his breath and clapped his bonnet on his head, for an object met his eye which fixed his attention. It was the sombre figure of a knight accoutred in black armour, who was pressing his steed through the throng in the direction of the fountain. His beaver was up, and the sinister countenance was not unknown to the apprentice.

"Saints defend us!" he ejaculated. "Is it possible that can be Sir Giles Mompesson? What doth he here amidst this noble company? The villainous extortioner cannot surely be permitted to enter the lists."

"Hold your peace, friend, if you are wise," muttered a deep voice behind him.

"No, I will not be silent," rejoined the apprentice, without looking round at his cautioner, but keeping his eye fixed upon Sir Giles. "I will tell the felon knight my mind. I am not afraid of him. Harkye, my masters," he called, in a loud voice, to those around him. "Do you know who that black raven before you is? If not, I will tell you. He would peck out your eyes if he could, and devour you and your substance, as he has done that of many others. That bird of ill omen is Sir Giles Mompesson."

"Impossible!" cried a bystander, indignantly. "Yet, now I look again, 'tis certainly he."

"As certain as that we are standing here," said the apprentice; "and if you want further proof, behold, he is closing his visor. He thinks to hide himself from our notice; but the trick shall not avail him. A groan for the knavish extortioner, my masters—a deep groan for Sir Giles Mompesson!"

Thus enjoined, a great hooting was made by the bystanders, and Sir Giles's name was coupled with epithets that could not be very agreeable to his ear.

"You were best let him alone, fool," cried the deep voice behind Dick. "You will only bring yourself into trouble."

But the apprentice was not to be thus advised; and could not even be restrained by the entreaties of Gillian, who was sadly apprehensive that some mischief would befall him. So conspicuous did he make himself in the disturbance, that at last Sir Giles rode towards him, and singling him out, seized him with his gauntleted hand, and dragged him from the edge of the fountain. Dick struggled manfully to get free, but he was in a grasp of iron, and all his efforts at releasing himself were ineffectual. He called on those near him to rescue him, but they shrank from the attempt. Poor Gillian was dreadfully alarmed. She thought her lover was about to be sacrificed to Sir Giles's resentment on the spot; and, falling on her knees, she piteously besought him to spare his life.

"For shame, Gillian," cried Dick; "do not demean yourself thus. The caitiff knight dares not harm me for his life; and if he should maltreat me, I shall be well avenged by my patron, Sir Jocelyn Mounchensey. I would my voice might reach him—I should not long be kept here. To the rescue! Sir Jocelyn! to the rescue!" And he shouted forth the young knight's name at the top of his voice.

"Who calls me?" demanded Mounchensey, pressing through the throng in the direction of the outcries.

"I, your humble follower, Dick Taverner," roared the apprentice; "I am in the clutches of the devil, and I pray you release me."

"Ha! what is this?" cried Sir Jocelyn. "Set him free, at once, Sir Giles, I command you."

"What, if I refuse?" rejoined the other.

"Then I will instantly enforce compliance," thundered Mounchensey.

"If I release him it is because I must defend myself and punish your insolence," cried Sir Giles. And as he spoke, he thrust back the apprentice with such force that he would have fallen to the ground if he had not dropped into the arms of his kneeling mistress.

"Now, Sir Jocelyn," continued Sir Giles, fiercely; "you shall answer for this interference"—

"Hold!" interposed the authoritative voice of Prince Charles; "we must have no unseemly brawls here. To your places at once in the procession, Sir Knights. We are about to set forward to the tilt-yard."

With this, he gave the word to move on, and all further sound of disturbance was drowned by the trampling of steeds and the bruit of the kettle-drums, cornets, and trumpets.

Nowise disheartened by what had occurred, Dick Taverner would have followed with the stream, and carried his mistress and her grandsire along with him; but the former had been so much terrified by what had occurred, that dreading lest her lover's imprudence should get him into further scrapes, she positively refused to proceed any further.

"I have seen quite enough," she cried; "and if you have any love for me, Dick, you will take me away, and not expose yourself to further risk. If you are indeed bent on going on, I shall return with my grandsire."

"He will do well to follow your advice, young mistress," said the deep voice which had previously sounded in Dick's ears; "if he had taken mine, he would not have voluntarily thrust himself into the fangs of the tiger, from which it is well for him that he has escaped with a whole skin."

As this was said, Dick and his mistress turned towards the speaker, and beheld a tall man, masked, and muffled in a black cloak.

"Heaven shield us! 'tis the Enemy!" exclaimed Gillian, trembling.

"Not so, fair damsel," replied the disguised personage; "I am not the arch-enemy of man, neither am I enemy of yours, nor of Dick Taverner. Your froward lover neglected my previous caution, but I will give him another, in the hope that you may induce him to profit by it. Let him keep out of the reach of Sir Giles Mompesson's emissaries, or his wedding-day will be longer in coming than you both hope for. Nay, it may not come at all."

With these words, the man in the mask mingled with the crowd, and almost instantly disappeared, leaving the young couple, especially Gillian, in much consternation. So earnest was the maiden for instant departure, that Dick was obliged to comply; and as the whole of the thoroughfares about Whitehall were impassable, they proceeded to the river side, and took boat for London Bridge, at a hostel near which old Greenford had put up his horse.

CHAPTER XI.
THE TILT-YARD.

Meanwhile, the procession was pursuing its slow course towards the tilt-yard. It returned by the route it had taken in coming; but it now kept on the north side of King Street, which thoroughfare was divided in the midst by a railing, and deeply sanded.

Here, as in the area before Westminster-hall, not a wall, not a window, not a roof, but had its occupants. The towers of the two great gates were thronged—so were the roofs of the tennis-court and the manége, and the summit of the cock-pit; the latter, indeed, was a capital position inasmuch as it not only afforded an excellent view of the procession, but commanded the interior of the tilt-yard. No wonder, therefore, that great efforts should be made to obtain a place upon it, nor is it surprising that our old friend, Madame Bonaventure, who had by no means lost her influence among the court gallants, though she lacked, the support of Lord Roos, owing to the absence of that young nobleman upon his travels,—it is not surprising, we say, that she should be among the favoured individuals who had secured a position there. Undoubtedly, she would have preferred a seat amongst the court dames in the galleries of the tilt-yard, but as this was unattainable, she was obliged to be content; and, indeed, she had no reason to complain, for she saw quite as much as those inside, and was more at her ease.

From this exalted position, while listening to the inspiriting clangour of the trumpets, the clattering of arms, and the trampling and neighing of steeds, Madame Bonaventure could scrutinize the deportment of each knight as he issued from the lofty arch of the Holbein Gate, and rode slowly past her. She had ample time to count the number of his attendants before he disappeared from her view. As Sir Jocelyn Mounchensey approached, with his visor raised, and his countenance radiant with smiles at the cheers he had received, she recognised in him her former guest, and participating in the general enthusiasm, prevailing for the young knight, she leaned over the parapet, and addressed to him a greeting so hearty that it procured for her a courteous salutation in return. Enchanted with this, she followed with her eyes the graceful figure of Sir Jocelyn till it was lost to view—to re-appear a moment after in the tilt-yard.

Turning in this direction,—for all her interest was now centred in the young knight,—Madame Bonaventure allowed her gaze to pass over the entrance of the lists, and she goon espied him she sought, in conference with Prince Charles, and some other knights of his party. Near them was stationed Garter King-at-arms, apparelled in his tabard, and mounted on a horse covered with housings of cloth of gold. Glancing round the inclosure she perceived that all the foremost seats in the galleries and scaffolds set apart for the principal court dames were already filled, and she was quite dazzled with the galaxy of female loveliness presented to her gaze. Behind the court dames were a host of fluttering gallants in rich apparel, laughing and jesting with them on the probable issue of the contest they had come to witness.

She then looked round the arena. Stout barriers of wood were drawn across it, with openings at either end for the passage of the knights. At these openings were placed all the various officers of the tilt-yard, whose attendance was not required outside, including eight mounted trumpeters, four at one end of the field, and four at the other, together with a host of yeomen belonging to Prince Charles, in liveries of white, with leaves of gold, and black caps, with wreaths and bands of gold, and black and white plumes.

At the western extremity of the inclosure stood the royal gallery, richly decorated for the occasion with velvet and cloth of gold, and having the royal arms emblazoned in front. Above it floated the royal standard. Supported by strong oaken posts, and entered by a staircase at the side, this gallery was open below, and the space thus left was sufficiently large to accommodate a dozen or more mounted knights, while thick curtains could be let down at the sides to screen them from observation, if required. Here it was intended that the Prince of Wales and his six companions-at-arms should assemble, and wait till summoned forth from it by the marshals of the field. There was a similar place of assemblage for the Duke of Lennox and his knights at the opposite end of the tilt-yard; and at both spots there were farriers, armourers, and grooms in attendance, to render assistance, if needful.

On the right of the field stood an elevated platform, covered with a canopy, and approached by a flight of steps. It was reserved for the marshals and judges, and facing it was the post affixed to the barriers, from which the ring, the grand prize of the day, was suspended, at a height exactly within reach of a lance. Like the streets without, the whole arena was deeply sanded.

This was what Madame Bonaventure beheld from the roof of the cock-pit, and a very pretty sight she thought it.

All things, it will be seen, were in readiness, in the tilt yard, —and the arrival of the King seemed to be impatiently expected—not only by the knights who were eager to display their prowess, but by the court dames and the gallants with them, as well as by all the officials scattered about in different parts of the field, and enlivening it by their variegated costumes.

Suddenly loud acclamations resounding from all sides of the tilt-yard, accompanied by flourishes of trumpets, proclaimed the entrance of the royal laggard to the gallery. James took his place in the raised seat assigned to him, and after conferring for a few moments with the Conde de Gondomar, who formed part of the brilliant throng of nobles and ambassadors in attendance, he signified to Sir John Finett that the jousting might commence, and the royal pleasure was instantly made known to the marshals of the field.

The first course was run by Prince Charles, who acquitted himself with infinite grace and skill, but failed in carrying off the ring; and similar ill luck befell the Duke of Lennox. The Marquis of Hamilton was the next to run, and he met with no better success; and the fourth essay was made by Buckingham. His career was executed with all the consummate address for which the favourite was remarkable, and it appeared certain that he would carry off the prize; but in lowering his lance he did not make sufficient allowance for the wind, and this caused it slightly to swerve, and though he touched the ring, he did not bear it away. The course, however, was considered a good one by the judges, and much applauded; but the Marquis was greatly mortified by his failure.

It now came to Sir Jocelyn's turn, and his breast beat high with ardour, as he prepared to start on his career. Keeping his back to the ring till the moment of setting forward, he made a demi-volte to the right, and then gracefully raising his lance, as his steed started on its career, he continued to hold it aloft until he began to near the object of his aim, when he gently and firmly allowed the point to decline over the right ear of his horse, and adjusted it in a line with the ring. His aim proved so unerring that he carried off the prize, amid universal applause.

CHAPTER XII.
THE TILTING MATCH.

After all the other competitors for the prize had essayed a career within the arena, Sir Jocelyn's was held to be the best course run. The ring was again carried off both by the Earl of Pembroke and Lord Mordaunt; but in the opinion of the marshals of the field, neither of those noblemen displayed so much grace and skill as Mounchensey: and the decision was confirmed by the King.

The applauses which rang through the tilt-yard, on the announcement that our handsome young knight had gained the first course, increased the bitterness of Buckingham's feelings towards him; and he expressed his regrets in a low tone to Sir Giles Mompesson that the combat about to take place was not *à l'outrance* instead of being *à plaisance*.

Sir Giles smiled grimly in reply.

Some little time elapsed, during which preparations were made for the tilting-match, and great excitement pervaded the assemblage. The King laughingly inquired of the Spanish ambassador if he still felt secure of winning his wager, and was answered by De Gondomar that he had never had the slightest misgiving on the subject, but he was now better satisfied than ever that the result of the coming struggle would justify his expectations. In the ladies' gallery an unusual degree of interest was manifested in what was going forward; and many a wish was audibly expressed by many a fair dame in Mounchensey's favour.

At length, the trumpets sounded, and the cries of the heralds were heard, cheering on the combatants, as they prepared to dash furiously against each other, bidding them do their devoir bravely, since bright eyes looked down upon them. These stimulants to valorous display were scarcely needed, for the champions were eager to prove their prowess. Issuing one by one, from beneath their respective scaffolds, and curbing the impatience of their steeds till they received from the marshals permission to start, they rushed from their posts with lightning swiftness to meet with a crashing shock midway. Various successes attended the different combatants, but on the whole the advantage lay clearly on the side of the Duke of Lennox, none of whose party had sustained any material discomfiture; while on the side of Prince Charles, the Earls of Montgomery and Rutland had been unhorsed. The interest of the spectators was kept in breathless suspense to the last, it being arranged that the tilting-match should close with the conflict between Buckingham and Mounchensey.

Thus, when the trumpets sounded for the seventh and last time, and the two knights stationed themselves opposite each other, every eye was intently fixed upon them. Apparently, no two antagonists could be better or more equally matched than they were; and throughout the whole field it would have been in vain to search for another pair equally gifted by nature, both being models of manly beauty of feature and symmetry of frame. Indeed they might have been cast in the same mould, so nearly alike were they in shape and size; and if their armour had been similar, and their steeds corresponding in colour, they would have been undistinguishable, when apart. Buckingham in some respects presented the nobler figure of the two, owing to his flowing plumes, his embossed and inlaid armour, and the magnificent housings of his charger—but he was fully rivalled by the grace and chivalrous air of his antagonist.

As the Marquis, confident in his address, disdained the use of the *passe-guarde* and the *mentonnière*, Mounchensey abandoned those defences, though they were used by all the other knights, and placed his reliance in the strength of his breast-plate and gorget, and in the force of his right arm.

When summoned forth by the trumpets, the two champions executed demi-voltes with curvets, and then stood stock-still at either end of the barriers. Each then selected a lance from the bundle offered them by the esquires, and their choice of a weapon made, they carefully fastened down their visors, which up to this moment had been raised.

Seeing them in readiness, the heralds gave the signal for the encounter. Starting against each other like thunder-bolts, they met in mid-career. The shock was tremendous, and many a cry sprang from female lips, while bursts of applause arose from the hardier spectators.

Both lances were shivered, but the results of the strokes dealt on either side were widely different. Mounchensey maintained his seat firmly in the saddle, though his steed had been forced back upon its haunches by his opponent's blow, who had touched his gorget; and riding on with all the ease, vigour, and grace, our young knight had previously exhibited, he threw down the truncheon of his lance, and opened his gauntlet to show that his hand was wholly uninjured.

Very differently had it fared with Buckingham, whose defeat was unquestionable. Unhorsed and unhelmeted, he was rolled in the dust; and as he sprang to his feet, had the mortification of hearing the deafening cheers that greeted his adversary's triumph. Eager to hide his confusion, he vaulted upon the back of his steed, which was brought to him by an esquire, the animal's flanks still quivering and reeking from the terrible shock it had undergone, and dashed beneath the scaffold he had so lately quitted—his pride severely humbled.

While the crest-fallen favourite thus retired to recover himself, Sir Jocelyn rode slowly towards the royal gallery. Having now raised his visor, his features were fully revealed to view, and perhaps were never seen to such advantage as at this proud and happy moment. His emotions were indeed enviable—but one thing was wanting to complete his satisfaction—the presence of her, before whom, of all others, he was most eager to distinguish himself. What mattered it that scarves and kerchiefs were waved to him by some of the fairest dames in the land? What mattered it that his name was called aloud, and that gloves and knots of ribands fell at his feet, as he rode past the ladies' gallery? His heart was untouched by smile or glance, and he paused not to pick up one of the favours showered upon him.

But what means this sudden change in his demeanour? Why does he start and stop, and look inquiringly towards the back of the gallery? Whom does he discern amongst that bevy of beauties? Can it be Aveline? And if so, how comes she there?

As he pauses, all eyes are fixed upon her towards whom his gaze is directed. There is no difficulty in detecting the object of his regards, for her attire is simpler than that of all the glittering dames around her, and of a sadder hue. Her confusion also betrays her. She would not be seen by him she came to see. She would muffle up her features, but it is too late; and she is not only fully exposed to his view, but to that of a hundred other curious eyes. Though many a high-born damsel marvels at the young knight's insensibility to her own superior attractions, none can deny that the unknown maiden is exquisitely beautiful, and demands are eagerly made as to who she may be. No one can answer—and no clue is given by her companion, for the elderly dame by whom she is attended, and who resembles a duenna, is likewise unknown to all.

As soon as Sir Jocelyn recovers his surprise, he requests a favour from the lady of his love, and she cannot refuse him—for immediately all the dames in front of the gallery move aside, to let her advance.

With her pale cheeks crimsoned with blushes, and her dark eyes flashing with mingled emotions of shame and pleasure, Aveline steps forward—and having no other favour to bestow upon her knight, she gives him her kerchief, which he presses to his lips, and then with a graceful salutation moves forward on his course. This is no time for explanation—and he must be content with his happiness, without inquiring how it has been procured for him.

The incident, however, has been generally noticed, and causes a good deal of speculation and talk amongst the female portion of the assemblage. There is one individual, however, of the opposite sex, who witnesses it with sentiments different from those by which most other observers are affected. This is Sir Giles Mompesson. He, it appears, has not been unaware of Aveline's presence at the jousts, though he did not anticipate its revelation in this manner to Sir Jocelyn; and a bitter smile crosses his lips, as he watches the brief interview between the pair. He cares not what transports they indulge in now—nor what hopes they form for the future. He promises himself that he will effectually mar their bliss!

CHAPTER XIII.
THE FELON KNIGHT.

A few more bounds of his steed brought Sir Jocelyn to the royal gallery, where he dismounted, and leaving his steed in charge of an esquire, ascended the stairs in company with the marshals of the field, and presently found himself in the presence of the King. James received him very graciously. On the right of the monarch stood the Conde de Gondomar, who smiled on his *protégé* as he approached, and glanced at a silver coffer full of diamonds, pearls, emeralds, amethysts, and other precious stones, borne by an attendant in the gorgeous livery of the Marquis of Buckingham.

"We greet ye as victor, Sir Jocelyn," said James, as the young knight made a profound obeisance to him; "and it rejoices us to say ye hae demeaned yourself honourably and fairly in the field. How say ye, Sirs?" he added to the marshals and others. "Shall not the prize of the day be adjudged to Sir Jocelyn?"

"It must be so, of right, your Majesty," replied the foremost of them. "A better course at the ring could not be run than Sir Jocelyn hath performed, nor could greater 'vantage be gained in the jousts than he hath obtained over the Marquis of Buckingham. All has been done by him in accordance with the rules of honour, and without fraud or supercherie.

"Enough, gentlemen," said James. "Count, ye hae won your wager; and as to you, Sir Jocelyn, ye hae proved yourself a very mirror of chivalry—*exemplar antiquoe fortitudinis et magnanimitatis*—on the pattern of Bayard, the knight without fear and without reproach, and the like of whom we scarce expected to see in these latter days. You are right weel entitled to the prize ye hae gained, and which his Excellency so honourably assigns to you."

"With your Majesty's permission, I will add the diamond clasp which I staked against the Marquess's casket of gems," said De

Gondomar, "and will beseech Sir Jocelyn to wear it as a testimony on my part of his merit as a cavalier. It is scarcely too much to say for him, after his recent brilliant achievements, that he takes rank amongst the foremost of the distinguished knights encircling your Majesty's throne."

"He takes rank as the first and best," cried James, emphatically; "since he hath overcome Buckingham, who till this day hath held the chief place among our chivalry."

"Your Majesty overwhelms me by your commendations," replied Sir Jocelyn; "and I can only say, in reply, that my best energies shall be devoted to your service, whenever and howsoever called upon. As to your Excellency's gift," he added to De Gondomar, who had unfastened the glittering clasp and presented it to him, "I shall ever guard it, as a devotee in your own sunny land of Spain would the most precious relic."

The coffer containing the gems was then, upon a sign from the King, delivered to Sir Jocelyn, who, as he received it from the attendant, took a string of pearls from it and gave them to the marshal, requesting they might be offered as *largesse* to the heralds; and the officer promised that the request should be complied with. Having bestowed a similar boon upon each of the marshals, Mounchensey requested that the coffer might be placed in charge of his esquire— and his directions were complied with.

"Is all concluded?" demanded the King.

"The contest for the prize is necessarily decided," replied the marshal; "but there yet remains the combat with the sword on horseback, if it pleases Sir Jocelyn to engage in it."

"What saith our young knight?" demanded the King. "Is he willing to risk the laurels he hath so fairly won on another, and it may be more dangerous encounter? What he hath already done may fairly entitle him to decline further hazard, if he be so minded."

"I should ill deserve your Majesty's high commendations if I hesitated for a moment," replied Mounchensey; "but so far from feeling disinclination to the combat, I should regret if this opportunity for further distinction were denied me. With your Majesty's gracious permission, I will pray the marshals of the field to let it be proclaimed by the heralds and pursuivants-at-arms that I challenge any true knight to do battle with me with the sword, and on horseback."

"Ye will fight with a blunted blade, Sir Jocelyn," cried the King. "We maun hae nae risk of life. Our dear dog, Steenie, hath had his bonnie craig well-nigh broken, and we will hae nae mair mischief done."

"The laws of the tilt-yard, with which Sir Jocelyn is doubtless well acquainted," observed the marshal, "require that the edge of the sword shall be dull, as your Majesty hath stated, and that no blow shall be dealt with the point of the weapon. These conditions must be strictly observed."

"They shall be," replied Sir Jocelyn; "and I pray you now to do your devoir, and make the proclamation."

On this the marshal and his followers departed; and Sir Jocelyn, bowing reverently to the King, took his way after them, and descending the stairs, leaped on the back of his charger.

Soon after this, and while a sword, blunted in the manner prescribed, was girded round his waist by his esquire, the trumpets were sounded, and the challenge proclaimed by the marshal. It was immediately responded to by a blast from the opposite end of the arena, and a herald, stationed at this point, called out in a loud voice that the challenge was accepted. Again the excitement rose high among the spectators; again all eyes were directed towards Sir Jocelyn; and again many ardent aspirations were uttered by his numerous fair admirers for his success, — though none so fervent as that breathed by Aveline. Sir Jocelyn cast one glance towards that part of the ladies' gallery where he knew her to be placed, and then prepared for his last essay.

As yet, he knew not who was to be his antagonist; but when a knight in sable armour, and with a sable plume upon his helm, rode from beneath the scaffold, he discovered, to his great indignation, that it was Sir Giles Mompesson. After a moment's reflection, he resolved upon a course of action. When the signal for the combat was given by the marshal, and Sir Giles, sword in hand, dashed into the arena, Mounchensey rode towards him, but, without drawing his sword, and raising himself in the saddle, commanded him in a thundering voice to retire.

The impetuosity of Sir Giles's career carried him past his antagonist, but he now wheeled round, and regarded Mounchensey fiercely from beneath the bars of his helmet.

"Retire, said you?" he exclaimed; "not unless you acknowledge yourself defeated. In my turn, I bid you go back to the point you started from, and commence the combat in due form, or I shall hold you vanquished, and compel you to abase your crest."

"Hear me," cried Sir Jocelyn, "and let it be heard by all. I challenged any *true* knight to the combat, but you answer not to the description. I proclaim you publicly in this place as a false and felon knight, and declare you utterly unworthy of my sword. Back to your starting-place, and if the heralds do their duty, they will hack off your spurs, and drive you with shame from the lists."

"And think you I will tamely brook this insult?" roared Sir Giles; "draw your sword at once, and let it be a mortal combat between us."

"Never," replied Sir Jocelyn, disdainfully. "I will not stoop to the level of your infamy."

"Then stoop to earth," cried Sir Giles, aiming a terrible blow at him with his sword.

If the stroke had taken effect as intended, it would probably have made good Mompesson's threat, but Sir Jocelyn was too wary and too agile even for his powerful assailant. Before the sword could descend, he seized his adversary's wrist, and in another instant possessed himself of the blade. This he accomplished without injury, as the sword was blunted. Still maintaining his grasp of the weapon, he raised himself in his stirrups to give additional force to the blow, and with the pummel of the sword, struck Sir Giles a blow upon the brainpan with such violence, that he dropped from the saddle as if shot.

During this strange scene, not a word had been uttered by the spectators, who looked on with the greatest curiosity, wondering how it would end. As Sir Giles fell from his horse, and lay stretched in perfect insensibility on the ground, a tremendous shout was raised, and Sir Jocelyn was as much applauded as if he had performed an extraordinary feat—so universally was the extortioner detested.

Nor was there any sympathy manifested, when a few moments afterwards Sir Giles was raised from the ground by the pursuivants, and his helmet being removed, exhibited a countenance livid as death, with a stream of blood coursing slowly down the temples. Many would have been well-pleased if he had been killed outright, but the chirurgeon in attendance pronounced that he was only stunned by the blow.

CHAPTER XIV.
THE PRIVATE CABINET OF SIR
GILES MOMPESSON.

A small room, and rendered yet smaller by the numerous chests and strong boxes encroaching upon its narrow limits. In some cases these boxes are piled, one upon another, till they touch the ceiling. All of them look stout enough, yet many are further strengthened by iron hoops and broad-headed nails, and secured by huge padlocks. The door is cased with iron, within and without, and has a ponderous lock, of which the master of the room always keeps the key, and never trusts it out of his own hand.

This small chamber is the private cabinet of Sir Giles Mompesson.

No one is permitted to enter it without him. Though his myrmidons are fully aware of its existence, and can give a shrewd guess at its contents, only two of them have set foot within it. The two thus privileged are Clement Lanyere and Lupo Vulp. Neither the promoter nor the scrivener are much in the habit of talking over their master's affairs, even with their comrades, and are almost as habitually reserved as he is himself; still, from the few words let fall by them from time to time, the myrmidons have picked up a tolerable notion of the private cabinet, of its hidden cupboards in the walls, its drawers with secret springs; its sliding planks with hollows beneath them; its chests full of treasure, or what is the same thing as treasure, bonds, mortgage-deeds, and other securities; and its carefully concealed hoards of plate, jewels, and other valuables. Some of the least scrupulous among them—such as Staring, Hugh, Cutting Dick, and old Tom Wootton—have often discussed the possibility of secretly visiting it, and making a perquisition of its stores; but they have been hitherto restrained by their fears of their terrible and vindictive master.

On looking into the cabinet we find Sir Giles seated at a table, with a large chest open beside him, from which he has taken for examination sundry yellow parchments, with large seals attached to them. He is now occupied with a deed, on one of the skins of which the plan of an important estate is painted, and on this his attention becomes fixed. His countenance is cadaverous, and its ghastly hue adds to its grimness of expression. A band is tied round his head, and there is an expression of pain in his face, and an air of languor and debility in his manner, very different from what is usual with him. It is plain he has not yet recovered from the effects of the crushing blow he received at the jousts.

Opposite him sits his partner, Sir Francis Mitchell; and the silence that has reigned between them for some minutes is first broken by the old usurer.

"Well, Sir Giles," he inquires, "are you satisfied with your examination of these deeds of the Mounchensey property? The estates have been in the family, as you see, for upwards of two centuries—ever since the reign of Henry IV., in fact—and you have a clear and undisputed title to all the property depicted on that plan—to an old hall with a large park around it, eight miles in circumference, and almost as well stocked with deer as the royal chase of Theobald's; and you have a title to other territorial domains extending from Mounchensey Place and Park to the coast, a matter of twelve miles as the crow flies, Sir Giles,—and including three manors and a score of little villages. Will not these content you? Methinks they should. I' faith, my worthy partner, when I come to reckon up all your possessions, your houses and lands, and your different sources of revenue—the sums owing to you in bond and mortgage—your monopolies and your patents—when I reckon up all these, I say, and add thereunto the wealth hoarded in this cabinet, which you have not placed out at usance—I do not hesitate to set you down as one of the richest of my acquaintance. There be few whose revenue is so large as yours, Sir Giles. 'Tis strange, though I have had the same chance as yourself of making money, I have not a hundredth part of your wealth."

"Not a whit strange," replied Sir Giles, laying down the deed and regarding his partner somewhat contemptuously. "I waste not what I acquire. I have passions as well as yourself, Sir Francis; but I keep them under subjection. I drink not—I riot not—I shun all idle company. I care not for outward show, or for the vanities of dress. I have only one passion which I indulge,—Revenge. You are a slave to sensuality, and pamper your lusts at any cost. Let a fair woman please your eye, and she must be bought, be the price what it may. No court prodigal was ever more licentious or extravagant than you are."

"Sir Giles! Sir Giles! I pray you, spare me. My enemies could not report worse of me."

"Nay, your enemies would say that your extravagance is your sole merit, and that therein you are better than I," rejoined Sir Giles, with a sardonic laugh. "But I rejoice to think I am free from all such weaknesses. The veriest enchantress could not tempt me. I am proof against all female seductions. Think you the damsel lives who could induce me to give for her half these broad lands in Norfolk—this ancient hall, and its wide-spread domains? I trow not."

"Perchance I have given too much," cried the old usurer, eagerly; "if so, it is not too late to amend our contract. Between us, there should be fair dealing, Sir Giles."

"There is none other than fair dealing on my part," replied the extortioner sternly; "and the terms of our agreement cannot be departed from. What I have just said applies to your general mode of life; but you have better reason for your conduct in this instance than is usual with you, since you combine the gratification of revenge with the indulgence of your other passions. You obtain a fair young bride, and at the same time deprive the person whom you hate most of all others, of the mistress of his affections. This is as it should be. Vengeance cannot be too dearly purchased, and the more refined the vengeance, the higher must necessarily be the price paid for it. In no way can you so cruelly injure this detested Mounchensey, as by robbing him of his mistress. And the blow dealt by you, shall be followed by others not less severe on my part."

"Ay, ay, Sir Giles, you have to wipe out the outrage he inflicted upon you in the tilt-yard. As I am a true gentleman, that was worse than the indignity I endured from him in the court-yard of the palace. It must be confessed that the villain hath a powerful hand as well as a sharp tongue, and follows up his bitter words by bold deeds. The stroke he dealt you with his sword was like a blow from a sledge hammer, Sir Giles. He felled you from your horse as a butcher felleth an ox; and, in good truth, I at first thought the ox's fate had been yours, and that you would never rise again. Your helmet was dinted in as if by a great shot. And for twelve hours and upwards you were senseless and speechless;—But thanks to my care and the skill of Luke Hatton the apothecary who tended you, you have been brought round. After such treatment, I cannot wonder that you are eager for revenge upon Sir Jocelyn. How will you deal with him Sir Giles? How will you deal with him?"

"I will hurl him from the proud position he now holds," replied the other, "and immure him in the Fleet."

"While I revel in the bliss he panted to enjoy," cried the old usurer, chuckling. "Take it altogether, 'tis the sweetest scheme we ever planned, and the most promising, Sir Giles! But when am I to claim Aveline? when shall I make her mine?"

"You shall claim her to-morrow, and wed her as soon after as you list."

"Nay, there shall be no delay on my part, Sir Giles. I am all impatience. When such a dainty repast is spread out before me, I am not likely to be a laggard. But now, to the all-important point on which the whole affair hinges! How am I to assert my claim to her hand—how enforce it when made? Explain that to me, Sir Giles, I beseech you."

"Readily," replied the extortioner. "But before doing so let me give you a piece of information which will surprise you, and which will show you that my tenure of this great Norfolk property is not quite so secure as you suppose it. You are aware that Sir Ferdinando Mounchensey had a younger brother, Osmond—"

"Who disappeared when very young, and died, it was concluded," interrupted Sir Francis, "for he was never heard of more. And it was lucky for us he did so die, or he might have proved a serious obstacle to our seizure of these estates, for I remember it being stated at the time, by one of the judges, that had he been living, he might have procured a reversal of the Star-Chamber sentence upon Sir Ferdinando in his favour."

"Precisely so, and that judge's opinion was correct," said Sir Giles. "Now listen to me, Sir Francis. It is quite true that Osmond Mounchensey quitted his home when very young, owing to some family quarrel; but it is not true that he died. On the contrary, I have recently ascertained, beyond a doubt, that he is still alive. Hitherto, I have failed in tracing him out, though I have got a clue to him; but he has enveloped himself in so much mystery that he is difficult of detection. Yet I trust to succeed ere long; and my great business will be to prevent his re-appearance, which would be fraught with danger to us both. I have a scheme on foot in reference to him which will answer more than one purpose. You will learn it anon. And now, to give you the explanation you require in respect to Aveline."

And he stamped upon the floor.

"You are not about to invoke a spirit of darkness to our councils?" said Sir Francis, staring at him in astonishment and alarm.

"You will see," rejoined the extortioner with a grim smile.

After a brief pause, the door was almost noiselessly opened, and Clement Lanyere entered the chamber.

"What has Lanyere to do with the matter?" cried Sir Francis, suspiciously regarding the promoter, who was without his mask.

"You will hear," replied Sir Giles. "Be pleased to inform Sir Francis, good Lanyere, how you come to be in a position to demand the hand of fair Mistress Aveline Calveley?"

"He demand it! I understand you not, Sir Giles!" exclaimed the old usurer.

"Let him speak, I pray you, Sir Francis," returned the other. "You will the sooner learn what you desire to know."

CHAPTER XV.
CLEMENT LANYERE'S STORY.

"My tale shall be briefly told," said Lanyere. "You are aware, Sir Francis, that in the pursuit of my avocation I am often led into the most dangerous quarters of the metropolis, and at hours when the peril to any honest man is doubled. Adventures have not unfrequently occurred to me when so circumstanced, and I have been indebted to my right hand and my good sword for deliverance from many a desperate risk. Late one night, I chanced to be in the neighbourhood of Whitefriars, in a place called the Wilderness, when, hearing cries for help, accompanied by the clash of steel, I rushed towards a narrow court, whence the clatter and vociferations resounded, and perceived by the light of the moon, which fortunately happened to be shining brightly at the time, one man engaged with four others, who were evidently bent upon cutting his throat in order to take his purse. He defended himself gallantly, but the odds were too great, and he must have been speedily slain—for the villains swore with great oaths they would murder him if he continued to resist them—if I had not come to the rescue. I arrived just in time. They were pressing him hard. I struck down the point of a rapier which was within an inch of his breast—gave the swashbuckler who carried it a riposta he did not expect, and sent him off bowling—and then addressed myself to the others with such good effect, that in a brief space the stranger and I were alone together. I had been slightly wounded in the fray; but I thought nothing of it—a mere scratch. It seemed something more to the gentleman I had preserved. He expressed great concern for me, and bound his handkerchief round my arm. I was about to depart, but he detained me to renew his professions of gratitude for the service I had rendered him, and his earnest wish that he might be able to requite me. From his discourse, and from the texts of Scripture he mixed up with it, I knew him to be a Puritan; and I might have supposed him to be a preacher of the Gospel, had he not carried a sword, and borne himself so manfully in the encounter. However, he left me no doubt on the subject, for he told me he was named Hugh Calveley, and that he had served in the wars with more honour to himself than profit. He added, that if the knaves had succeeded in their design, and robbed and slain him, they would have deprived his daughter of her sole protector; and, indeed, of all means of subsistence, since the little they had would be lost with him. On hearing this, a thought struck me, and I said to him—'You have expressed an earnest desire to requite the service I have just been fortunate enough to render you, and as I am well assured your professions are not idly made, I shall not hesitate to proffer a request to you.' 'Ask what you will; if I have it to give, it shall be yours,' he replied. 'You make that promise solemnly, and before heaven?' I said. 'I make it solemnly,' he replied. 'And to prove to you that I mean it to be binding upon me, I will confirm it by an oath upon the Bible.' And as he spoke he took the sacred volume from his doublet, and reverently kissed it. Then I said to him—'Sir, you have told me you have a daughter, but you have not told me whether she is marriageable or not?' He started at the question, and answered somewhat sternly. 'My daughter has arrived at womanhood. But wherefore the inquiry? Do you seek her hand in marriage?' 'If I did so, would you refuse her to me?' A pause ensued, during which I observed he was struggling with deep emotion, but he replied at last, 'I could not do so after my solemn promise to you; but I pray you not to make the demand.' I then said to him: 'Sir, you cannot lay any restrictions upon me. I shall exact fulfilment of your promise. Your daughter must be mine.' Again he seemed to be torn by emotion, and to meditate a refusal; but after a while he suppressed his feelings, and replied. 'My word is plighted. She shall be yours.— Ay, though it cost me my life, she shall be yours.' He then inquired my name and station, and I gave him a different name from that by which I am known; in fact, I adopted one which chanced to be familiar to him, and which instantly changed his feelings towards me into those of warmest friendship. As you may well suppose, I did not think fit to reveal my odious profession, and though I was unmasked, I contrived so to muffle my hateful visage with my cloak, that it was in a great degree concealed from him. After this, I told him that I had no intention of pressing my demand immediately; that I would take my own means of seeing his daughter without her being conscious of my presence; and that I would not intrude upon her in any way without his sanction. I used some other arguments, which seemed perfectly to satisfy him, and we separated, he having previously acquainted me that he lived at Tottenham. Not many days elapsed before I found an opportunity of viewing his daughter, and I found her exquisitely beautiful. I had indeed gained a prize; and I resolved that no entreaties on his part, or on hers, should induce me to abandon my claim. I took care not to be seen by her, being sensible that any impression I might make would be prejudicial to me; and I subsequently learnt from her father that he had not disclosed to her the promise he had been rash enough to make to me. I had an interview with him—the third and last that ever took place between us—on the morning of the day on which he made an attempt upon the life of the King. I rode over to Tottenham, and arrived there before daybreak. My coming was expected, and he himself admitted me by a private door into his garden, and thence into the house. I perceived that his mind was much disturbed, and he told me he had passed the whole night in prayer. Without acquainting me with his desperate design, I gathered from what he said, that he meditated some fearful act, and that he considered his own life in great jeopardy. If he fell, and he anticipated he should fall, he committed his daughter to my care; and he gave me a written injunction, wherein, as you will find, his blessing is bestowed upon her for obedience to him, and his curse laid upon her in the event of a breach of duty; commanding her, by all her hopes of happiness hereafter, to fulfil the solemn promise he had made me—provided I should claim her hand within a twelvemonth of his death. The unfortunate man, as you know, died within two days of that interview, having, as I have since ascertained, reiterated the same solemn charge, and in terms equally impressive, to his daughter."

"A strange story truly," observed Sir Francis, who had listened attentively to the relation; "but though Aveline may consent to be bound by her father's promise to you, I see not how Lean enforce the claim."

"Hugh Calveley, when dying, disclosed no name to his daughter," said Sir Giles. "There is no name mentioned in the paper confided by him to Lanyere; and, possessed of that authority, you will represent the party entitled to make the claim, and can act as Lanyere would have acted."

"She will not resist the demand," said the promoter. "That I can avouch, for I overheard her declare as much to Sir Jocelyn."

"If such be the case, I am content," cried the old usurer. "Give me the authority," he added to Lanyere.

"I have it with me, Sir Francis," rejoined the promoter; "but Sir Giles will explain to you that there is something to be done before I can yield it to you."

"What does he require?" asked the old usurer, glancing uneasily at his partner.

"Merely all these title-deeds of the Mounchensey estates in exchange for that paper," replied Sir Giles.

"Not merely the deeds," said Lanyere; "but an assignment on your part, Sir Giles, and on yours, Sir Francis, of all your joint interest in those estates. I must have them absolutely secured to me; and stand precisely as you stand towards them."

"You shall have all you require," replied Mompesson.

"Amazement!" exclaimed Sir Francis. "Can you really mean to relinquish this noble property to him, Sir Giles? I thought I was assigning my share to you, and little dreamed that the whole estates would be made over in this way."

"I have told you, Sir Francis," rejoined the other, "that vengeance— ample, refined vengeance—cannot be too dearly purchased; and you will now perceive that I am willing to pay as extravagantly as yourself for the gratification of a whim. On no other terms than these would Lanyere consent to part with the authority he possesses, which while it will ensure you the hand of Aveline, will ensure me the keenest revenge upon Sir Jocelyn. I have therefore acceded to his terms. Thou hast got a rare bargain, Lanyere; and when the crack-brained Puritan gave thee that paper, he little knew the boon he bestowed upon thee."

"The exchange would, indeed, seem to be in my favour, Sir Giles," he said; "but you may believe me when I say, that though I gain these large estates, I would rather have had the damsel."

"Well, let the business be completed," said Sir Giles; "and that it may be so with all dispatch, do you, Lanyere, summon Lupo Vulp to us. You will find him in his chamber, and bid him bring with him the deed of assignment to you of the Mounchensey estates which he has already prepared, and which only requires my signature and that of Sir Francis."

"I obey you, Sir Giles," replied Lanyere, departing on the errand.

As soon as they were alone, the old usurer observed to his partner—"I am lost in astonishment at what you are about to do, Sir Giles. That I should make a sacrifice for a dainty damsel, whose charms are doubled because she should belong to an enemy, is not surprising; but that you should give up so easily a property you have so long coveted—I confess I cannot understand it."

A strange smile crossed the extortioner's countenance.

"And do you really think I would give it up thus, Sir Francis?" he said.

"But if we sign that deed—'tis his. How are you to get it back again?"

"Ask me not *how*—I have no time for explanation. Recollect what I told you of Osmond Mounchensey, and the possibility of his re-appearance."

"I will not seek to penetrate your scheme, Sir Giles," observed the old usurer; "but I would have you beware of Lanyere. He is cunning and determined."

"He will scarcely prove a match for me, I think," observed the extortioner—"but here he comes."

And as he spoke, the promoter again entered the chamber, followed by Lupo Vulp, with a parchment under his arm.

"Give me the deed, good Lupo," said Sir Giles, taking it from him. "It must be first executed by me—there!—and now your signature, Sir Francis," he added, passing the instrument to him. "Now thou shalt witness it, Lupo. 'Tis well!—'tis well!" he cried, snatching it back again, as soon as the scrivener had finished the attestation. "All is done in due form. This deed makes you Lord of Mounchensey, Lanyere." And he handed it to him.

"And this makes Sir Francis Mitchell ruler of the destiny of Aveline Calveley," rejoined Lanyere, giving a paper to the old usurer.

"This chest and its contents are yours also, Lanyere," pursued Sir Giles, putting in the deeds, and locking it. "Will it please you to take the key. From this moment we cease to be master and servant, and become equals and friends!"

"Equals, it may be, Sir Giles!" cried Lanyere, drawing himself up to his full height, and speaking with great haughtiness; "but never friends."

"Ha! what are we, then?" demanded the extortioner, fiercely. "Am I mistaken in you? Take heed. You are yet in my power."

"Not so, Sir Giles. I have nothing to apprehend from you now," replied Lanyere; "but you have much to fear from me."

So saying, and placing the parchment within his doublet, he hastily quitted the chamber.

"Perdition! have I been outwitted?" cried Sir Giles. "But he shall not escape me." And rushing after him, he called from the head of the great staircase—"What, ho! Captain Bludder!—and ye, Tom Wootton and Cutting Dick—let not Lanyere go forth. Stay him and take from him the deed which he hath placed in his doublet. Cut him down, or stab him if he resists."

But, though efforts were made to obey Sir Giles's commands, the promoter effected his retreat.

CHAPTER XVI.
SIR JOCELYN'S RUPTURE
WITH DE GONDOMAR.

Far and wide echoed the report of Sir Jocelyn's brilliant achievements at the jousts; and wherever he went, he was hailed as vanquisher of the hitherto-unconquered Buckingham. He bore his honours meekly, yet he did not escape calumny; for at a court, as everywhere else, distinguished success is certain to awaken a spirit of envy and detraction. These paltry feelings, however, were entirely confined to the disappointed of his own sex. By fairer and more impartial judges, who had witnessed his exploits, he was spoken of in terms of unmingled admiration; and at the grand revel at Whitehall that followed the jousts, many a soft glance told him how tenderly the gentle heart, whose feelings it betrayed, was inclined towards him. Faithful, loyal, and chivalrous, our young knight was as much proof against these lures, as against the ruder attacks of his armed opponents in the lists; and his constancy to the lady of his love remained entirely unshaken. Far rather would he have been with Aveline, in her humble dwelling, than in those superb festal halls, surrounded by all that was noble and beautiful—all that was dangerous and delusive. Far rather would he have received one smile from her, one kindly look, than all the blandishments showered upon him by these enchantresses.

Fain would he have avoided the banquet—but as the hero of the day, he was compelled to attend it. Indeed, he had to enact a principal part at the revel; and so well did he play it that compliments were lavished upon him, enough to have turned an ordinary head. Not from any desire for ostentatious display, but because Prince Charles had signified to him his wishes on the subject, he was arrayed in all the pearls and ornaments he had won from Buckingham; and more than one subtle courtier, anxious to stand well with him, flatteringly declared that they became him infinitely better than the

Marquis. Others, less favourably disposed, remarked that his gem-bedecked doublet was like the garment of Nessus, and would cause its wearer's destruction; and if they could have read Buckingham's secret thoughts, when he beheld his rival so adorned, they would have felt that the observation was not unwarranted. But, though fully determined upon revenge, Buckingham allowed neither look nor word to betray his purpose. On the contrary, he displayed more than his usual affability to Mounchensey, laughed at his own ill-luck, and even went so far as to say that Sir Giles Mompesson had been rightly served; adding, that he blamed himself for including him in his party, and was glad Sir Jocelyn had handled him so rudely.

Though our young knight might well doubt Buckingham's sincerity; he replied to all his courtly speeches in similar terms, and the greatest cordiality appeared to subsist between them. Enchanted with this show of friendship, the King endeavoured to promote it by keeping them near him throughout the evening, leading them to converse together, and fawning upon them, as was his way with those he highly favoured. All this could not fail to be satisfactory to Mounchensey; but he was far more pleased with the notice of Prince Charles, who treated him with marked consideration.

Next morning, in compliance with an invitation to that effect he had received at the revel, Sir Jocelyn repaired to Ely House, in Holborn, the residence of the Spanish Ambassador, and was at once admitted to his presence.

They were alone, and after a few preliminary observations upon the events of the previous day, De Gondomar remarked—"I think I have already afforded you abundant proof of my friendly feeling towards you, Sir Jocelyn. But I will not stop with what I have done. My power of serving you is greater than you may imagine it to be. I can lead you yet higher—and put you in a firmer position. In a word, I can place you on a level with Buckingham,—perchance above him,—if your ambition soars so high."

Mounchensey endeavoured to express his deep sense of gratitude to the ambassador, and regretted his small means of requiting the numerous and important favours he had received from him.

"I will tell you what to do," said De Gondomar. "You can procure me certain information which I desire to obtain. By my instrumentality you have, in some degree, already obtained the King's confidence, and ere long are sure to become the depositary of many important state secrets. These you shall communicate to me. And you must also use your best endeavours to win Prince Charles over to the Church of Rome."

"Is this proposal seriously made to me, Count?" demanded Mounchensey, looking at him with astonishment, mingled with displeasure.

"Unquestionably it is serious—perfectly serious," replied De Gondomar. "I ask you only to serve me as a certain young nobleman of your acquaintance served me before he was compelled to fly from England to avoid the consequences of a quarrel with his wife's family. Your opportunities will be greater than his, and therefore your service will be more valuable."

"I regret that such disloyalty should be laid to the charge of any English noble," said Sir Jocelyn sternly. "But think not, because Lord Roos played the spy and traitor, as your Excellency insinuates he did, that I will be guilty of like baseness. Up to this moment I have felt nothing but gratitude to you for the favours you have heaped upon me; but the feeling is changed to resentment when I understand they are to be purchased at the price of my honour. I cannot accede to your wishes, Count. You must seek out some other tool. I can be none in your hands."

"If this be real, and not affected indignation, Sir Jocelyn," said De Gondomar coldly, "it would seem that I have been altogether mistaken in you, and that I have been helping you up the ladder only to be kicked aside when you have gained a secure footing. But you have not reached the last step yet, and never will, unless I find you more reasonable. And allow me to ask you, if you are as scrupulous as you profess to be, how you came to bring a token to me from a hired spy—a token intended to let me know you were willing to undertake any secret service I might choose to confide to you? Have you changed your mind since then? or rather, do you not fancy yourself out of danger, and able to dispense with my assistance?"

"I have ever been of the same opinion, Count; have ever been influenced by the same feelings of loyalty and devotion to my sovereign, and of detestation of all treasonable practices. Had I been aware of the import of the ring I showed your Excellency on our first meeting, I would have hacked off my finger rather than have displayed it. Neither did I know the character of the man who confided it to me; though I ought to have distrusted him. He has played us both false, and for what end I cannot divine."

"I will solve the riddle for you, Sir: he thought to serve you," said De Gondomar; "and he has done so, and most effectually, though you are now unwilling to admit it. I have good reason to complain of him — you have none."

"I have more reason for complaint than your Excellency," rejoined Mounchensey. "He has placed me in a most painful and perplexing position."

"There you are right, Sir," said De Gondomar. "No matter how arrived at, you are in a position from which you cannot extricate yourself with honour. However disinclined you may be to act in concert with me, you have no other alternative. If I withdraw my support from you, your fall is inevitable. Think not I talk lightly. You are surrounded by enemies, though you discern them not. Buckingham's magnanimous conduct at the revel last night was feigned to mask his purposes towards you. He has not forgiven his defeat, and means to avenge it. You fancy yourself on the high road to preferment; but you are on the verge of disgrace and ruin. I alone can save you. Choose, then, between compliance with my wishes, coupled with present protection and future advancement, and the consequences certain to attend your refusal. Choose, I say, between my friendship and my enmity."

"My answer shall be as prompt and decisive as your proposal, Count," replied Sir Jocelyn. "I at once reject a friendship fettered with such conditions. And that I do not resent the affront put upon me in your dishonourable proposal, must be set down to the obligations you have imposed upon me, and which tie up my hands. But we are now quits; and if any further indignity be offered me, it will not be so lightly borne."

"*Perdone, vuestra merced!* — we are not quits," cried De Gondomar quickly. "The account between us is far from settled; nor will I rest content till you have paid me in full. But we had better break off this interview," he added, more calmly, "since no good is like to result from it. It is useless to reason with you; but you are wantonly throwing away a fairer opportunity than falls to the lot of most men, and will see your folly when too late."

"In taking my leave of your Excellency, as there are no terms henceforth to be observed between us, except those of hostility, I deem it right to state, that though I shall make no especial reference to yourself, I shall hold it my duty to acquaint his Majesty with the system of *espionage* introduced into the palace; and, above all, I shall take care to guard the Prince against the insidious snares laid for him."

"It is a pity so faithful a councillor as yourself should not be listened to," rejoined De Gondomar. "Yet, when I shut the doors of the palace against you—as I will do—you will find it difficult to obtain a hearing either from Prince or King. In spite of all your efforts to the contrary, I shall learn any state secrets I desire to know, and I have great hopes of winning over Charles Stuart to the faith for which his lovely and martyred ancestress died. One more word at parting, Sir Jocelyn. You will remember, when we first met, you were in danger from the Star-Chamber. It would be useless now to say how I saved you from the punishment your rashness had incurred—how, while aiding you with the King, I kept aloof your enemies, Mompesson and Mitchell, who were prepared to attach your person for contempt of that terrible court, and would have done so, if I had not prevented them. The warrant for your arrest still exists, and can be employed at any moment; so you will consider how long you can count upon your freedom, now that you have no strong arm to protect you."

"I have my own arm to trust to," rejoined Sir Jocelyn, resolutely, "and have no apprehensions."

"*Vaya usted con dios!*" said the Spaniard, bowing him out; "or I should rather say," he added to himself, "*Vaya mucho en mala hora!*"

CHAPTER XVII.
DISGRACE.

Sir Jocelyn was not without great uneasiness at the result of his interview with De Gondomar. Had it been possible, he would have avoided a rupture with so influential a personage—an event to be dreaded at any time, but especially so at a juncture like the present, when dangers menaced him on all sides, and the only question appeared to be, from what side the first blow would come. His chief anxiety, however, was for Aveline, whose position was one of such strange and imminent peril, against which he knew not how to guard her. He was still left in the same state of uncertainty as to who would be the claimant of her hand; for the mysterious personage in the mask had not appeared again, according to his promise, after the jousts. This suspense was terrible, and Sir Jocelyn found it so difficult of endurance, that he would have preferred the actual presence of the calamity by which he was threatened. His fears were, that the claim he so much dreaded would be made by Sir Giles Mompesson in person, and in that case he had determined forcibly to resist him. And this supposition might account for the delay—since he knew that Sir Giles was suffering severely from the effects of the blow he had dealt him in the tilt-yard.

De Gondomar's were not idle threats, as Sir Jocelyn soon found. On the next day, as he entered the palace, he was informed by the Lord Chamberlain that he was deprived of his office of Gentleman of the Bed-Chamber; and when he demanded the reason of his sudden dismissal, the Duke of Lennox, with a shrug of the shoulders, declared he was unable to afford him any information. But what the Duke refused was afforded by De Gondomar, who at that moment entered the corridor, in company with Buckingham and some other nobles, on his way to the presence-chamber. On seeing his late *protégé*, the ambassador halted for a moment, and with a smile of triumph said—"You owe your dismissal to me, Sir Jocelyn. I have made some few circumstances concerning you that had just come to my ears known to his Majesty; and as he does not choose to have spies about his person, he has released you from all further attendance upon him."

"In a word, he has forbidden your attendance again at the palace," added Buckingham, who had paused likewise, with an insulting laugh.

"I must to the King, your Grace," cried Sir Jocelyn to the Lord Chamberlain. "I will explain the falsehood of this charge to his Majesty, and show him who is the spy and traitor he has to fear."

"You cannot pass, Sir Jocelyn," said the Duke of Lennox, placing himself in his way, while two halberdiers advanced to bar his passage with their partizans. "I say not a word as to the cause of your disgrace; but I may tell you, that his Majesty is greatly offended with you, and that it would be highly imprudent to approach him in his present frame of mind, even were it permitted you to do so—which it is not. As I have said, you are deprived of your office, and enjoined to absent yourself from the palace, till it shall be his Majesty's pleasure to recall you."

"And that is not likely to be soon the case—eh, Count?" observed Buckingham, with a laugh.

"Not very likely indeed, Marquis," said the ambassador. "I much regret that I have been the means of introducing so unworthy a person to his Majesty; but I have made all the amends in my power."

"Must I tamely endure all these insults and calumnies, your Grace?" cried Sir Jocelyn furiously.

"If you will be guided by me, you will retire," rejoined the Duke of Lennox; "or the provocation you will receive may induce you to do some desperate act which may render your position worse, and put your restoration to the King's favour entirely out of the question."

While Sir Jocelyn was debating whether he should comply with the Duke's advice, the door of the presence-chamber was thrown open; and James, coming forth from it, marched slowly along the corridor.

Our young knight now fondly hoped that the King might deign to look upon him, and so enable him to plead his cause; and perhaps the Lord Chamberlain himself entertained similar expectations, for he did not insist upon Sir Jocelyn's withdrawal, but allowed him to remain within the corridor, though he was kept aloof by the halberdiers. But both were disappointed. James, no doubt, designedly, bestowed his most gracious marks of condescension on Buckingham and De Gondomar, and lingered for a few minutes to laugh and talk with them. After this, as he was passing Sir Jocelyn, he pretended to notice him for the first time, and observed, in a tone of reproof to the Lord Chamberlain, "What doth the spy here, my Lord Duke? I thought you had our orders concerning him. See they are better obeyed in future." And, when the young knight would have spoken, he interrupted him by an imperious gesture, crying out, "Not a word, Sir!—not a word! We will hear naught mair frae ye. We hae heard ower meikle already." And he passed on.

Thus was Mounchensey's disgrace accomplished by his enemies.

CHAPTER XVIII.
HOW SIR JOCELYN'S CAUSE WAS ESPOUSED BY THE 'PRENTICES.

Stung almost to madness by the sense of intolerable wrong, our young knight quitted Whitehall, never, as he imagined at the moment, to enter the palace again. Yet he was not humiliated by his disgrace, because he felt it to be wholly unmerited. His enemies had triumphed over him; but he would not have heeded the defeat, provided he could efface the foul stigma cast upon his reputation, and rebut the false charge brought against him by De Gondomar.

With a heart overflowing with rage and bitterness, and with a thousand wild projects passing through his brain, Sir Jocelyn took a boat at Whitehall stairs, and ordered the watermen to row down the river, without assigning any paticular place of landing. After awhile, he succeeded, to a certain extent, in controlling his angry emotions; and as the watermen rested on their oars for a moment, to inquire his destination, he looked round, and perceiving he was just opposite the Three Cranes in the Vintry, he desired to be put ashore there.

No better retreat wherein to recover his composure seemed to offer itself than Madame Bonaventure's comfortable house of entertainment; and thither, therefore, he proceeded, and at his request was shown into a private room overlooking the river. Scarcely was he installed within it, than the buxom hostess, who had caught sight of him as he mounted the stairs, entered, and in her blandest accents, and with her most bewitching smiles, begged to know his commands; declaring that all that her house possessed was at his service.

She was running on thus, but perceiving the young knight to be much disturbed, she instantly changed her tone, and expressed such genuine concern for him, that he could not fail to be moved by it. Without making her an entire confidante, Sir Jocelyn told her enough of what had occurred to make her comprehend his position; and highly indignant she was at the treatment he had experienced. She did her best to console him; and so far succeeded, that he was prevailed upon to partake of some delicacies which she caused Cyprien to set before him, together with a flask of the best vintage in her cellar; and the discussion of these good things, coupled with the hostess's assiduities, certainly operated as a balm upon his wounded feelings.

The repast over, the good-natured dame thought it best to leave him to himself; and drawing his chair to the open window, he began to ruminate upon the many strange events that had happened to him since he first beheld that fair prospect almost from the same place; and he was indulging in this retrospect, when his own name, pronounced in tones familiar to him, caught his ear, and looking forth, he perceived Dick Taverner, seated on a bench in front of the house, drinking in company with some half dozen other apprentices, his boon companions.

The conversation of these roysterers was held in so loud a key that it could not fail to reach his ears; and he soon ascertained that his own dismissal from court was the theme of their discourse, and that they rightly attributed it—doubtless owing to information derived from their hostess—to the instrumentality of De Gondomar. It was evidently Dick Taverner's design to rouse the indignation of his companions; and he had little difficulty in accomplishing his purpose, as they were all composed of very inflammable material, and prone to take fire on the slightest application of the match. Dick denounced the plotting and perfidious Spaniard as a traitor to the King and a subverter of the Protestant faith; and counselled vengeance upon him.

Finding Dick's suggestions eagerly caught up by his companions, and that the number of his listeners was momently increasing, while all were becoming excited by what the orator uttered, Sir Jocelyn, apprehensive that mischief might ensue, thought it right to interfere, and accordingly, leaning forward from the casement, he made himself known to the group below.

On seeing him, and learning who he was, the 'prentices began to shout and declaim vehemently against the Spanish ambassador; and instigated by Dick Taverner, who refused to listen either to the entreaties or commands of the young knight, the whole party seized their cudgels, and dispersing themselves in different directions, vociferated as they went—"Clubs! clubs!"

It was now as vain to arrest them as it would have been to stop the course of a conflagration; and Sir Jocelyn was deploring the damage which must necessarily be done to his cause by these injudicious friends, when Dick Taverner, with a look of exultation, and brandishing his cudgel, burst into the room, crying—"We have heard all from Madame Bonaventure. We have heard of De Gondomar's perfidy, and his Majesty's injustice. We will set you right. The bold London 'prentices have taken your cause in hand, and will avenge you. They will hang the treacherous Spaniard, and burn his house."

"Hark ye, my good friend, Dick Taverner," said Sir Jocelyn, "this must not be. Because I have been unjustly treated, and may perchance find it difficult, if not impossible, to obtain redress, it does not follow that you and your fellow 'prentices are to violate the law. These riotous proceedings will prejudice my cause rather than aid it; and if you have any regard for me you will use your influence with your comrades to check them ere mischief ensue."

"Impossible!" exclaimed Dick. "The matter has gone too far to be stopped now. You might as well attempt to turn back a mill-dam that has burst its bounds, as the headstrong London 'prentices when they have taken up their cudgels. Go through with the business they will. This is not the only quarrel we have with De Gondomar. We hate him for his insolence and arrogance, which have been often displayed towards us; We hate him because he is the sworn enemy of our religion, and would subvert it if he could. As regards myself, I have my own particular reasons for hating him. Do not you meddle with the affair, but leave its arrangement to us."

"But I *must* interfere," cried Sir Jocelyn; "if you act thus, in spite of all my remonstrances. I must regard you in the light of enemies rather than friends, and shall lend my help to quell the disturbance you will occasion. Be ruled by me, good Dickon, and desist from it. Call in your comrades, who are raging about like savage dogs broken loose."

"If they be dogs," rejoined Dick, with a laugh, "the Spanish ambassador is likely enough to become acquainted with their teeth. But I might whistle loudly enough to them before the staunch hounds would come back to me; and, in good sooth, I have no inclination to obey your commands in his instance, Sir Jocelyn."

So saying, and fearing he might be detained altogether if he waited longer, he darted out of the room, and presently afterwards was heard shouting along the wharf with the loudest of his riotous companions—"No Papists! No Spanish spies! Clubs!—clubs!"

Sir Jocelyn saw that a storm was roused which it would be very difficult to allay; but an effort must be made to do so, even if he were compelled to act against his friends; and he was about to follow the apprentice into the street, when he was prevented by the sudden entrance of a tall personage, wrapped in a black cloak, and masked, whom he at once recognised as the individual who had given him the token to De Gondomar.

"I am glad to have found you, Sir Jocelyn," said this personage. "I have been on the look-out for you to give you a warning. Avoid any place you have been in the habit of frequenting; and, above all, go not near Aveline's dwelling. The officers of the Star-Chamber are on the watch for you; and if found, your arrest is certain."

"I can place little reliance on aught you tell me, Sir," rejoined Sir Jocelyn, "after the trick you played me in causing me to deliver that ring to the Conde de Gondomar. Nothing you can say shall hinder me from going forth as I am accustomed to do; and it is my purpose to proceed ere long to the dwelling you specially caution me to avoid."

"You will repent your rashness, young Sir," said the other; "but I pray you not to go forth till you have heard certain disclosures which I have to make to you, and which I am well assured will induce you to alter your opinion of me."

"I can put no faith in the statements of a hireling, base enough to play the spy for an enemy of his country," rejoined Sir Jocelyn, scornfully. "Stand aside, Sir. Your employer, De Gondomar, is in danger from these hot-headed apprentices; and if you owe him any gratitude for past favours, you may find occasion for its display now."

"What! are you about to take part with your enemy and against your friends? These apprentices are about to redress your wrongs— in a lawless manner it is true—but the circumstances justify their conduct."

"No circumstances can justify outrage, and violation of the law," said Sir Jocelyn; "and if injury be attempted against De Gondomar, I must defend him."

"This is mere madness," cried the other. "Stay and hear what I have to say to you. It imports you much to know it."

"Not now," replied Sir Jocelyn, pushing past him. "On some other occasion."

"You are throwing life and liberty away, Sir Jocelyn, and to no purpose," cried the other. "He heeds me not," he added, in a tone of deep disappointment. "Imprudent that he is! he will thwart all the plans I have formed for his benefit, and at the very moment they have arrived at maturity. I must follow and protect him."

And he too rushed down the stairs, and made all the haste he could across the Vintry wharf after Sir Jocelyn, who was hurrying up a narrow thoroughfare communicating with Thames Street.

Here a numerous body of 'prentices were already collected, holding a consultation as to their plan of attack. After listening to a brief but stirring harangue from Dick Taverner, who got upon a horse-block for the purpose of addressing them, and recommended them to proceed to Ely House, in Holborn, the residence of the offending Ambassador, and there await his return from Whitehall; they approved of his proposal, and unanimously electing Dick as their leader, set forth on their expedition, gathering strength as they went along.

By the time they reached Blackfriars they numbered many hundreds. Little or no interruption was offered them on their route; and the slight hindrance they encountered from a detachment of the city-watch was speedily overborne. Skirting Bridewell, they traversed Shoe Lane, and ascending Holborn Hill, found themselves in the vicinity of Ely House, where they came to a halt, and arranged their forces.

CHAPTER XIX.
A NOBLE REVENGE.

Nothing could be pleasanter than the situation of the Spanish ambassador's residence, surrounded as it was by noble gardens; but its beauties seemed now likely to be devastated by the blind fury of the apprentices. Much mischief would indeed have been done in a very short time if it had not been for their leader. He authoritatively commanded them to refrain from the work of demolition till they had settled accounts with the ambassador himself, who might be expected each moment, as they had ascertained that he was on his way home from the palace. The information they had received proved to be correct; and ere many minutes elapsed, a magnificent litter, borne by eight stout varlets, and attended by several gentlemen and pages, in the well-known liveries of De Gondomar, was seen to pass through Holborn Bars and advance towards them.

Very soon, however, the bearers of the litter halted, surprised and alarmed at the sight of the crowd investing Ely House; but De Gondomar, who had no apprehension, commanded them to proceed, and they reluctantly obeyed. The 'prentices allowed the litter to come on till they could surround it, when they set up a loud shout, making it evident that mischief was intended.

On this the gentlemen and pages in attendance upon the ambassador drew their swords and put themselves into a posture of defence, endeavouring to keep off the crowd. But their resistance was of little avail. The 'prentices' clubs quickly shivered their weapons, and drove them back.

When he became aware of the jeopardy in which he stood, De Gondomar, anxious to gain time, in the hope that assistance might arrive, demanded of the leader of the furious-looking crew who had drawn aside the curtains of his litter, and ordered him in insolent tones to come forth, why they molested him. The individual appealed to replied that, having heard of his infamous usage of Sir Jocelyn Mounchensey, and of the false accusation he had brought against him to the King, they were determined to inflict upon his Excellency the punishment due to public and notorious slanderers.

"And by what right do you constitute yourselves my judges?" cried De Gondomar. "Take heed what you do—you may bring yourselves within reach of a halter."

"You hear what he says, brother 'prentices?" cried Dick Taverner. "He threatens to hang us, and no doubt if he could carry out his schemes, and bring back the Pope's authority, he would burn us in Smithfield, as they did the holy martyrs in Mary's days. He has charged a true and loyal subject of his Majesty with being a spy. In return we tell *him* he is the worst of spies—a spy employed by the Pope; and we will teach him the danger of his employment."

"Hands off, base varlets!" exclaimed De Gondomar, endeavouring to shake himself free from the rude grasp imposed upon him.

But, in spite of his resistance, he was dragged from the litter, while a shower of blows from the 'prentices cudgels fell upon his shoulders; and it is probable he would have experienced much severer treatment, if indeed he had escaped with life, if at this moment Sir Jocelyn Mounchensey, sword in hand and followed by Clement Lanyere, had not burst through the throng.

"Ha! as I suspected," cried De Gondomar. "You, Mounchensey, are the author and instigator of this outrage, and are come to see that your tools do their work properly."

"It is false," cried Dick Taverner. "Your Excellency judges of others by yourself. Sir Jocelyn would have checked us if he could."

"I cannot be expected to believe such an assertion as this," cried De Gondomar incredulously.

"Let my actions speak for me," cried Mounchensey. "Friends," he called out, "it is undoubtedly true that I have good ground of complaint against the Conde de Gondomar—that he has deeply injured me—and that I will compel him to make me reparation in due season—but I cannot permit outrage to be offered him; and if aught further be attempted, my arm will be raised in his defence."

"How! can this be possible!" exclaimed De Gondomar in surprise.

"Why, we are fighting Sir Jocelyn's battles, and he turns round upon us!" cried a burly 'prentice, while loud murmurs arose from the others, and the cudgels were again brandished menacingly.

"Leave him to us, Sir Jocelyn," said Dick Taverner.

"Ay, he had better not interfere, of he will come in for his share of the blows," roared several voices.

"I care not what befals me," shouted Mounchensey. "You shall not injure a hair of his Excellency's head while I stand by."

And as he spoke he warded off several blows aimed at the ambassador.

"I am with you, Sir Jocelyn," said Clement Lanyere, clearing a space around them with his long rapier, but avoiding, so far as possible, doing injury to the 'prentices.

At this critical juncture, and when it seemed likely that, owing to his chivalrous interference, Sir Jocelyn would share the ambassador's fate, he being fairly resolved, as he showed, to defend him with his life, a cry was raised that a body of the royal guards were approaching; and as the trampling of horse, accompanied by the clatter of swords, left no doubt of the fact, and as, moreover, the bold 'prentices felt no disposition to encounter regular soldiery, they instantly abandoned their prey and took to their heels, the chief part of them leaping the hedge which then grew along the north side of Holborn, and scouring off through the fields in every direction. Some half dozen were made prisoners by the guard; and amongst these, we regret to state, was the leader of the riotous assembly, Dick Taverner.

"Thou art likely to make acquaintance with the pillory and the cart's tail, if not with the hangman, friend," said the soldier who secured him, with a laugh.

"So I begin to fear," replied Dick. "Alack! and well-a-day! what will become of Gillian!"

"An that be thy mistress's name, friend, you should have thought of her before you engaged in this disturbance. You are likely now to part company with her for ever."

While Dick lamented the predicament in which he had placed himself, the Conde de Gondomar, freed from all apprehension, turned towards his deliverer, and proffering him his hand, said—"You have nobly revenged yourself, Sir Jocelyn. I trust we may be friends once more. I will make you ample reparation for the wrong I have done you."

But the young knight, folding his arms upon his breast, sternly replied—"When reparation is made, Count, I may accept your hand, but not till then."

"At least enter my house," urged the ambassador, "where you will be protected from arrest."

"Do not hesitate, Sir Jocelyn," subjoined Lanyere. "You are in great peril."

But the young knight haughtily refused.

"I will not owe an asylum to you, Count," he said, "till my name be cleared from reproach." And, with a proud salutation, he departed.

The Spanish ambassador shrugged his shoulders, and looked after him with mingled admiration and contempt. He then turned to the promoter, and said, "Come in with me, Lanyere. I have somewhat to say to you."

"I must pray your Excellency to excuse me just now," replied the other. "I have business on hand."

And bowing with nearly as much haughtiness as Sir Jocelyn, he followed in the course taken by the young knight.

CHAPTER XX.
A PLACE OF REFUGE.

After quitting De Gondomar, as before related, Sir Jocelyn hurried along Holborn with the intention of proceeding to Aveline's cottage, which was at no great distance from Ely House, though in a secluded situation, withdrawn from the road; and he was just about to strike into the narrow lane leading to it, when he was arrested by the voice of Clement Lanyere, who had followed him, unobserved.

"Stay, Sir Jocelyn, I beg of you," cried the promoter, coming quickly up to him; "you are rushing on certain destruction. You must not go nigh that cottage to-day; no, nor for several days to come. Foes are lying in ambush round it; and the only spectacle you will afford her you love will be that of your arrest."

There was an earnestness in the speaker's manner that could not fail to carry conviction of his sincerity to the breast of his hearer.

"By my soul, I speak the truth," said Lanyere, perceiving the impression he had made, "as you will find if you go many steps further. Place yourself in my hands, and I will save you."

"What motive can you have for acting thus?" demanded Sir Jocelyn. "What interest do you take in me?"

"Do not question me now: you shall have full explanation hereafter. Be satisfied I am a friend,—perchance your best friend. Come with me, and I will take you to a place of safety."

"But what is to happen to Aveline?" cried the young knight, in deep anxiety.

"I will endeavour to watch over her," replied the promoter; "and I trust no harm will befall her. At all events, you will deprive yourself of the power of rendering her any protection, if you are rash enough to go forward now."

Struck by the force of these remarks, our young knight felt he had no alternative but to submit to circumstances, and he accordingly agreed to accept the aid proffered him by his mysterious friend. But it was not without feelings of intense anguish that he turned away from the path leading to the little secluded cottage containing all he held dear, and followed his conductor, who seemed resolved to allow him no time for further hesitation, but proceeding at a rapid pace towards the west till he reached Broad Saint Giles's—then a rural village—and entered a small tavern, bearing the sign of "The Rose and Crown," the landlord of which appeared to have an understanding with the promoter, for at a sign from him, he immediately ushered his guests into a chamber up-stairs, and without saying a word, left them alone together.

"Here you will be secure and undisturbed," said Lanyere; "and all your wants will be cared for by my trusty ally, Barnabas Boteler; but, for your own sake, you must consent to remain a close prisoner, till I bring you word that you may go forth with safety. I must now leave you, having much to do, and must defer the explanations I design to give you to a more convenient season. Be not uneasy if you should not see me for a few days, as circumstances may prevent my coming to you. When I next appear, I trust it may be to bring you good tidings. Till then, farewell."

And without waiting for any reply from Sir Jocelyn, he hastily departed.

Left alone, our young knight did the best he could to reconcile himself to the strange situation in which he was placed. He was naturally full of anxiety, both on his own account, and on that of Aveline; yet, on calm reflection, he felt satisfied he had acted for the best, and that, in accepting the protection of the mysterious individual who seemed bent upon directing his fortunes, he had followed the dictates of prudence. Barnabas Boteler attended him in person, and suffered no one else to come near him; but though the worthy host seemed anxious to anticipate his wants in every particular, his manner was reserved, and, in Sir Jocelyn's opinion, he had something of the look of a jailor, and this notion was strengthened when he found himself locked in his room. Probably this was only done as a precautionary measure by the host; and as the window was at no great height from the ground, and he could descend from it when he chose, he gave himself no great concern about the matter.

In this way three days passed by without anything occurring to break the monotony of his wearisome confinement,—not even a visit from Clement Lanyere. To Sir Jocelyn's inquiries concerning him, the host professed utter inability to give a precise answer, but said that he might arrive at any moment. As he did not appear, however, on the fourth day, Sir Jocelyn's patience got quite worn out, and his uneasiness respecting Aveline having become insupportable, he determined, at all hazards, on visiting her cottage. Without acquainting the host with his intention, or asking to have the door unfastened, he opened the window which looked into a garden at the back of the house, and sprang from it. His furtive departure did not appear to be noticed, and he soon gained the road, and took the direction of Aveline's dwelling.

CHAPTER XXI.
THE ARREST.

As he approached the cottage a heavy presentiment of ill seized Sir Jocelyn. The place seemed to have lost its customary smiling air. No fair countenance beamed upon him from the casement; no light footsteps were heard hastening to the door; no one opened it to give him welcome. Could Aveline have fled'?—or had some dire misfortune happened to her. Suspense was worse than certainty of ill: and after a moment's hesitation, he raised the latch, and with trembling footsteps crossed the threshold.

She was gone—he could no longer doubt it. The disordered appearance of the chamber in which he found himself, with its furniture scattered about, seemed to tell of a struggle, and a forcible abduction. Nevertheless, though expecting no answer, he called forth her name in accents of wildest despair. She came not to his cries— neither she nor her companion, Dame Sherborne, nor her faithful attendant old Anthony Rocke. All were gone. The house was indeed desolate.

Still clinging to hope, he flew up-stairs, but could find no traces there of any of the inmates of the dwelling; and with a heart now completely crushed, he descended to the chamber he had just quitted. Here he found Clement Lanyere surveying the scene of confusion around him with a stern and troubled look. Sir Jocelyn instantly rushed up to him, and seizing him by the arm, fiercely demanded what had become of Aveline?

"She is in the hands of Sir Francis Mitchell," replied the promoter, shaking-him off; "and, for aught I know, may be wedded to him by this time."

"Wedded!" almost shrieked the young man. "Impossible! she would never consent—and he would not dare have recourse to violence."

"Though he might not, his partner, Sir Giles Mompesson, would have no such scruples," returned the promoter. "But perhaps you are right, and Aveline's determined resistance may intimidate them both so that they may abandon their design. I hope so for your sake, and for hers also—but I have my fears."

"You know more than you choose to avow, Sir," said Sir Jocelyn sternly,—"and as you value your life, I command you to speak plainly, and tell me what has happened, and where I shall find Aveline."

"So commanded by any other than yourself, Sir Jocelyn," rejoined the promoter, "I would *not* speak; but to you I say, as I have before declared, that Aveline is undoubtedly in the power of Sir Francis Mitchell, and that it will rest entirely with herself whether she escapes him or not."

"And you have caused me to be detained while she has been carried off," exclaimed Sir Jocelyn, furiously. "Fool that I was to trust you! You are in league with the villains."

"Think of me what you please, and say what you will—you shall not anger me," rejoined the promoter. "I discovered your flight from the place of refuge I had procured for you, and guessing where you had come, followed you hither. Your danger is not past. Vainly will you seek Sir Francis Mitchell. You will not find him,—but you *will* find a serjeant-at-arms with a Star-Chamber warrant for your arrest. To this you can offer no resistance; and what will follow? I will tell you:—immediate incarceration in the Fleet Prison. And when safely lodged there, how, may I ask, are you to liberate Aveline?"

"I must trust to chance," replied Sir Jocelyn. "I can no longer place any reliance upon you. Stand aside, and let me pass. I would not harm you."

"You cannot injure one whose intentions are friendly to you as mine are. Listen to me, and let what I have to say sink deeply into your breast. Do anything rather than render yourself amenable to the accursed tribunal I have named. Abandon mistress, friend, relative— all who are near and dear to you—if they would bring you within its grasp."

"And do you venture to give me this shameful council? Do you think I will attend to it?" cried Sir Jocelyn.

"I am sure you will, if you hear me out—and you *shall* hear me," the promoter exclaimed with so much authority that the young man, however impatient, could not refuse attention, to him. "Look me in the face, Sir Jocelyn! Regard me well! Behold these ineffaceable marks made by the heated iron, and the sharpened knife! How came they there? From a sentence of the Star-Chamber. And as my offence was the same as yours, so your sentence will correspond with mine. Your punishment will be the same as mine—branding and mutilation. Ha! I perceive I have touched you now."

"What was your offence, unhappy man?" asked Sir Jocelyn, averting his gaze from the hideous aspect which, now lighted up with mingled emotions of rage and despair, had become absolutely appalling.

"The same as your own, as I have said," replied the other;—"a few hasty words impugning the justice of this vindictive court. Better had I have cut out my tongue than have given utterance to them. But my case more nearly resembled yours than I have yet explained, for, like you, I had incurred the displeasure of Sir Giles Mompesson, and was by him delivered to these hellish tormentors. Acting under cover of the Star-Chamber, and in pursuance of its iniquitous decrees, he nailed me to the pillory, and so fast, that the ears through which the spikes were driven were left behind. Think how you would like that, Sir Jocelyn? Think what you would feel, if you stood there on that infamous post, a spectacle to the base and shouting rabble, with a paper fastened to your breast, setting forth your crimes, and acquainting all that you were a Star-Chamber delinquent?"

"Enough, Sir," interrupted Sir Jocelyn.

"Ay, enough—more than enough," rejoined the other; "but I cannot spare you the whole of the recital, however painful it may be to you. My own sufferings will be yours, if you heed not. So I shall go on. In robbing me of my ears, the executioner had only half done his work. He had still further to deface the image of his Maker,—and he hesitated not in his task. No savage in the wilds could have treated his deadliest enemy worse than he treated me; and yet the vile concourse applauded him, and not a word of pity escaped them. My sentence was fully carried out; my features for ever disfigured; and the letters of shame indelibly stamped upon my cheek. You may read them there now if you will look at me."

"You thrill me with horror," said Sir Jocelyn.

"Ay, mine is not a mirthful history, though that fiend in human form, Sir Giles, hath often laughed at it," rejoined the promoter. "It might make you shudder, and perchance move you to tears, if you could hear it all; but for the present, I shall confine myself to such portions of it as bear upon your own perilous position—and I therefore hold myself out as a lesson to you. Again, I bid you look upon this ravaged countenance, and say, if by any stretch of fancy you can persuade yourself it was once as comely as your own. You find it difficult to believe my words—yet such was the fact. Ay," he continued, in a tone of profoundest melancholy, "I was once proud of the gifts nature had vouchsafed me; too proud, alas! and I was punished for my vanity and self-boasting. In those days I loved—and was beloved in return—by a damsel beautiful as Aveline. After my horrible punishment, I beheld her no more. Knowing she must regard me with aversion, I shunned her. I desired not to be an object of pity. Bring this home to your own breast, Sir Jocelyn, and think how direful would be your lot to be driven for ever from her you love. Yet, such has been my case."

"I cannot bear the contemplation—it were madness," cried the young man.

There was a brief pause, after which Lanyere resumed his story.

"At the time of being cast into the Fleet Prison, my prospects were fair enough. When I came forth I was utterly ruined. Existence was a burden to me, and I should have ended my days by my own hand, if the insatiable desire of vengeance had not bound me to the world. For this alone I consented to live—to bear the agonies of blighted love— to endure the scorn and taunts of all with whom I was brought into contact. Nay, I attached myself to him who had so deeply wronged me, to ensure revenge upon him. My great fear was, lest I should be robbed of this precious morsel; and you may remember that I struck up your sword when it had touched his breast. He must die by no other hand than mine."

"Your vengeance has been tardy," observed Sir Jocelyn.

"True," replied the other. "I have delayed it for several reasons, but chiefly because I would have it complete. The work is begun, and its final accomplishment will not be long postponed. I will not destroy him till I have destroyed the superstructure on which he has built his fortunes—till all has crumbled beneath him—and he is beggared and dishonoured. I have begun the work, I say. Look here!" he cried, taking a parchment from his doublet. "You would give much for this deed, Sir Jocelyn. This makes me lord of a large property in Norfolk, with which you are well acquainted."

"You cannot mean the Mounchensey estates?" cried Sir Jocelyn. "Yet now I look at the instrument, it is so."

"I obtained this assignment by stratagem," said the promoter; "and I have thereby deprived Sir Giles of the most valuable portion of his spoils; and though; he thinks to win it back again, he will find himself deceived. My measures are too well taken. This is the chief prop of the fabric it has taken him so long to rear, and ere long I will shake it wholly in pieces."

"But if you have become unlawfully possessed of this property, as would appear to be the case by your own showing, you cannot hope to retain it," said the young knight.

"Trust me, Sir Jocelyn, I shall prove a better title to it than Sir Giles could exhibit," rejoined Lanyere; "but this is not a time for full explanation. If I carry out my schemes, you will not be the last person benefited by them."

"Again, I ask you, what possible interest you can feel in me?" demanded the young knight with curiosity.

"Next to myself, you have been most injured by Sir Giles, and even more than myself are you an object of dislike to him. These would suffice to excite my sympathy towards you; but I have other and stronger reasons for my friendly feeling towards you, which in due season you shall know."

"All your proceedings are mysterious," observed Sir Jocelyn.

"They must needs be so from the circumstances in which I am placed. I am compelled to veil them as I do my hateful features from the prying eyes of men: but they will be made clear anon, and you will then understand me and my motives better. Ha! what is this?" he suddenly exclaimed, as a noise outside attracted his attention. "Fly! fly! there is danger."

But the warning was too late. Ere the young man, who stood irresolute, could effect his retreat from the back of the cottage, the door was thrown open, and a serjeant-at-arms, with three attendants in black gowns and flat caps, and having black staves in their hands, entered the room.

Sir Jocelyn had partly drawn his sword, but restored it to the scabbard on a glance from Lanyere.

"Resistance must not be offered," said the latter, in a low tone. "You will only make a bad matter worse."

The serjeant-at-arms, a tall, thin man, with a sinister aspect, advanced towards the young knight, and touching him with his wand, said—"I attach your person, Sir Jocelyn Mounchensey, in virtue of a warrant, which I hold from the High Court of Star-Chamber."

"I yield myself your prisoner, Sir," replied Sir Jocelyn. "Whither am I to be taken?"

"You will be taken before the Lords of the Council in the first instance, and afterwards, in all probability, be consigned to the custody of the wardens of his Majesty's gaol of the Fleet," replied the serjeant-at-arms.

"I would fain know the nature of my offence?" said Sir Jocelyn.

"You will learn that when the interrogatories are put to you," replied the official. "But I am told you have disparaged the dignity of the High Court, and that is an offence ever severely punished. Your accuser is Sir Giles Mompesson."

Having said thus much, the serjeant-at-arms turned to the promoter, and inquired, "Are you not Clement Lanyere?"

"Why do you ask?" rejoined the other.

"Because if you are he, I must request you to accompany me to Sir Giles Mompesson."

"Lanyere is my name," replied the other; "and if I decline to attend you, as you request, it is from no disrespect to you, but from distaste to the society into which you propose to bring me. Your warrant does not extend to me?"

"It does not, Sir," replied the serjeant-at-arms. "Nevertheless—"

"Arrest him!" cried a voice at the back of the house,—and a window being thrown open, the face of Sir Giles Mompesson appeared at it— "Arrest him!" repeated the extortioner.

The serjeant-at-arms made a movement, as if of compliance; but Lanyere bent towards him, and whispered a few words in his ear, on hearing which the official respectfully retired.

"Why are not my injunctions obeyed, Sir?" demanded Sir Giles, furiously, from the window.

"Because he has rendered me good reason why he may not be molested by us — or by any one else," replied the officer, significantly.

Lanyere looked with a smile of triumph at the extortioner, and then turning to Sir Jocelyn, who seemed half disposed to make an attack upon his enemy, said in an under-tone, "Harm him not. Leave him to me."

After which he quitted the cottage.

Sir Giles then signed to the serjeant-at-arms to remove his prisoner, and disappeared; and the attendants, in sable cloaks, closing round Sir Jocelyn, the party went forth.

CHAPTER XXII.
THE OLD FLEET PRISON.

Mention is made of a prison-house standing near the River Fleet as early as the reign of Richard I.; and this was one of the oldest jails in London, as its first wardens, whose names are on record, Nathaniel de Leveland, and Robert his son, paid, in 1198, a fine of sixty marks for its custody; affirming "that it had been their inheritance ever since the Conquest, and praying that they might not be hindered therein by the counter-fine of Osbert de Longchamp," to whom it had been granted by the lion-hearted monarch.

The next warden of the Fleet, in the days of John, was Simon Fitz-Robert, Archdeacon of Wells,—probably a near relative of Robert de Leveland, as the wardship of the daughter of the said Robert, as well as the custody of the jail, was also committed to him. The freehold of the prison continued in the Leveland family for upwards of three centuries; until, in the reign of Philip and Mary it was, sold to John Heath for £2300—a large sum in those days, but not more than the value of the property, which from the way it was managed produced a large revenue to its possessor.

The joint wardens of the Fleet at the time of our history were Sir Henry Lello and John Eldred; but their office was executed by deputy in the person of Joachim Tunstall, by whom it was rented. As will naturally be supposed, it was the object of every deputy-warden to make as much as he could out of the unfortunate individuals committed to his charge; and some idea of the infamous practices of those persons may be gathered, from a petition presented to the Lords of the Council in 1586 by the then prisoners of the Fleet. In this it is stated that the warden had "let and set to farm the victualling and lodging of all the house and prison of the Fleet to one John Harvey, and the other profits of the said Fleet he had let to one Thomas Newport, the deputy there under the warden; and these being very poor men, having neither land nor any trade to live by, nor any certain wages of the said warden, and being also greedy of gain, did live by bribing and extortion. That they did most shamefully extort and exact from the prisoners, raising new customs, fines, and payments, for their own advantage. That they cruelly used them, shutting them up in close prisons when they found fault with their wicked dealings; not suffering them to come and go as they ought to do; with other abominable misdemeanours, which, without reformation, might be the poor prisoners' utter undoing."

In consequence of this petition, a commission of inquiry into the alleged abuses was appointed; but little good was effected by it, for only seven years later further complaints were made against the warden, charging him with "murders and other grave misdemeanours." Still no redress was obtained; nor was it likely it would be, when the cries of the victims of this abominable system of oppression were so easily stifled. The most arbitrary measures were resorted to by the officers of the prison, and carried out with perfect impunity. Their authority was not to be disputed; and it has been shown how obedience was enforced. Fines were inflicted and payment made compulsory, so that the wealthy prisoner was soon reduced to beggary. Resistance to the will of the jailers, and refusal to submit to their exactions, were severely punished. Loaded with fetters, and almost deprived of food, the miserable captive was locked up in a noisome subterranean dungeon; and, if he continued obstinate, was left to rot there. When he expired, his death was laid to the jail-fever. Rarely were these dark prison secrets divulged, though frequently hinted at.

The moral condition of the prisoners was frightful. As the greater portion of them consisted of vicious and disorderly characters, these contaminated the whole mass, so that the place became a complete sink of abomination. Drunkenness, smoking, dicing, card-playing, and every kind of licence were permitted, or connived at; and the stronger prisoners were allowed to plunder the weaker. Such was the state of things in the Fleet Prison at the period of our history, when its misgovernment was greater than it had ever previously been, and the condition of its inmates incomparably worse.

During the rebellion of Wat Tyler, the greater part of the buildings constituting the ancient prison were burnt down, and otherwise destroyed; and, when rebuilt, the jail was strengthened and considerably enlarged. Its walls were of stone, now grim and hoary with age; and on the side next to the Fleet there was a large square structure, resembling Traitor's Gate at the Tower, and forming the sole entrance to the prison. To this gate state-offenders were brought by water after committal by the Council of the Star-Chamber.

Nothing could be sterner or gloomier than the aspect of the prison on this side—gray and frowning walls, with a few sombre buildings peeping above them, and a black gateway, with a yawning arch, as if looking ready to devour the unfortunate being who approached it. Passing through a wicket, contrived in the ponderous door, a second gate was arrived at, and this brought the captive to the porter's lodge, where he was delivered up to the jailers, and assigned a room in one of the wards, according to his means of paying for it. The best of these lodgings were but indifferent; and the worst were abominable and noisome pits.

On entering the outer ward, a strange scene presented itself to the view. Motley groups were scattered about—most of the persons composing them being clad in threadbare doublets and tattered cloaks, and wearing caps, from which the feathers and ornaments had long since disappeared; but there were a few—probably new coiners— in somewhat better attire. All these wore debtors. Recklessness and effrontery were displayed in their countenances, and their discourse was full of ribaldry and profanity. At one side of this ward there was a large kitchen, where eating and drinking were constantly going forward at little tables, as at a tavern or cookshop, and where commons were served out to the poorer prisoners.

Near this was a large hall, which served as the refectory of the prisoners for debt. It was furnished with side benches of oak, and had two long tables of the same wood; but both benches and tables were in a filthy state, and the floor was never cleansed. Indeed, every part of the prison was foul enough to breed a pestilence; and the place was seldom free from fever in consequence. The upper part of the refectory was traversed by a long corridor, on either side of which were the dormitories.

The arrangements of the inner ward were nearly similar, and differed only from the outer, in so far that the accommodations were superior, as they had need to be, considering the price asked for them; but even here nothing like cleanliness could be found. In this ward was the chapel. At a grated window in the gate stood the poor debtors rattling their begging-boxes, and endeavouring by their cries to obtain alms from the passers-by.

Below the warden's lodgings, which adjoined the gate, and which were now occupied by the deputy, Joachim Tunstall, was a range of subterranean dungeons, built below the level of the Fleet. Frequently flooded by the river, these dungeons were exceedingly damp and unwholesome; and they were reserved for such prisoners as had incurred the censure of the inexorable Court of Star-Chamber. It was in one of the deepest and most dismal of these cells that the unfortunate Sir Ferdinando Mounchensey breathed his last.

Allusion has been previously made to the influence exercised within the Fleet by Sir Giles Mompesson. Both the wardens were his friends, and ever ready to serve him; their deputy was his creature, and subservient to his will in all things; while the jailers and their assistants took his orders, whatever they might be, as if from a master. Thus he was enabled to tyrannize over the objects of his displeasure, who could never be secure from his malice.

By the modes of torture he adopted through his agents, he could break the most stubborn spirit, and subdue the strongest. It was matter of savage satisfaction to him to witness the sufferings of his victims; and he never ceased from persecution till he had obtained whatever he desired. The barbarities carried out in pursuance of the atrocious sentences of the Court of Star-Chamber were to him pleasant spectacles; and the bleeding and mutilated wretches, whom his accusations had conducted to the pillory, when brought back to their dungeons, could not escape his hateful presence—worse to them, from his fiendish derision of their agonies, than that of the executioner.

CHAPTER XXIII.
HOW SIR JOCELYN WAS
BROUGHT TO THE FLEET.

After his arrest by the serjeant-at-arms, Sir Jocelyn was taken, in the first instance, to the Star-Chamber, where some of the Lords of the Council were sitting at the time, and examined respecting the "libellous language and false scandal" he had used in reference to the proceedings of that high and honourable court. The young knight did not attempt to deny the truth of the charge brought against him, neither did he express contrition, or sue for forgiveness; but though he demanded to be confronted with his accusers, the request was refused him; and he was told they would appear in due time. Several interrogatories were then addressed to him, which he answered in a manner calculated, in the judgment of his hearers, to aggravate the original offence. After this, he was required to subscribe the minutes of his confession, as it was styled; and a warrant for his committal to the Fleet Prison, and close confinement within it, was made out.

Consigned once more to the custody of the serjeant-at-arms, he was placed on board a barge, of ill-omened appearance, being covered with black cloth, like a Venetian gondola, and kept for offenders against the Star-Chamber. In this he was rowed down the Thames, and up the Fleet, to the entrance of the prison. The progress of the well-known sable barge up the narrow river having been noted by the passengers along its banks, as well as by those crossing Fleet Bridge, some curiosity was felt to ascertain whom it contained; and a crowd collected in front of the prison gate to witness the disembarkation.

When the young knight's title, and the nature of his offence, which latter did not appear so enormous in their eyes as in those of the Lords of the Council, became known to the bystanders, much sympathy was expressed for him; and it might have found a manifestation in more than words, but for the guard, who kept back the throng.

At this juncture, Sir Jocelyn heard his own name pronounced in familiar tones, and looking round for the speaker, perceived a person placed in a tub close beside him. The individual who occupied this singular and degrading position was the ill-starred Dick Taverner, who, it appeared, had made an attempt to escape from prison on the third day after he had been brought thither, and was punished, according to the custom of the place, by being bound hand and foot, set within a tub, and exposed to public gaze and derision.

"Alas! Sir Jocelyn!" ejaculated the apprentice, "but for you I should not have been here. I undertook a thankless office, and have been rightly served for my folly. We have both found our way to the Fleet, but I much doubt if either of us will find his way out of it. As for me, I liked the appearance of the place, and the society it seems to furnish, so little, that I resolved to make a clearance of it at once; and accordingly I managed to scramble up yonder lofty wall, in the hope of effecting my deliverance, without asking for a licence to go abroad from the warden; but, unfortunately, in dropping down from so great a height I sprained my ankle, and fell again into the hands of the Philistines—and here I am, like the Cynic philosopher in his tub."

Sir Jocelyn would have addressed a few words of consolation to the poor fellow, but at this moment the wicket was opened, and he was pushed through it by the attendants of the serjeant-at-arms, who were apprehensive of the crowd. The small aperture that had given him admittance to the prison was instantly closed, and all chance of rescue cut off.

The prisoner being thus effectually secured, the officials felt more easy; and smiling at each other, they proceeded deliberately to the porter's lodge, at the entrance of which stood a huge, powerfully-built, ill-favoured man, evidently chosen for the post of porter from his personal strength and the savageness of his disposition.

With a growl like that of a mastiff, to the black broad muzzle of which animal his own features bore a remarkable resemblance, the porter greeted the new comers, and ushered them into an apartment built of stone, octagonal in shape, with a vaulted roof, narrow windows like loopholes, and a great stone fireplace. Its walls, which resembled those of an ancient guardroom, were appropriately enough garnished with fetters; mixed up with which, as if to inspire greater terror among the beholders, were an executioner's heavy whip, with many knotted thongs, several knives, with strange blades, the purpose of which was obvious enough, and branding-irons.

As Sir Jocelyn was brought into the lodge by his guards, an elderly man, with a bald head and gray beard and moustaches, and possessing, in spite of his years, a most repulsive physiognomy, advanced to meet him. His doublet and hose were of murrey-colour; and his inflamed visage, blood-shot eyes, fiery nose, and blotchy forehead, were in keeping with the hue of his apparel. This was Joachim Tunstall, Deputy Warden of the Fleet.

Behind him were some half-dozen jailers, attired in garments of dark-brown frieze, and each having a large bunch of keys at his girdle. All of them were stout, hard-featured men, and bore upon their countenances the stamp of their vocation.

The warrant for Sir Jocelyn's committal to the Fleet was delivered by the serjeant-at-arms to the deputy-warden; and the latter having duly perused it, was conferring with one of the jailers as to where the prisoner should be conducted, when a side-door was suddenly opened, and Sir Giles Mompesson issuing from it, tapped the deputy-warden on the shoulder.

"You need not consider where the prisoner is to be lodged, Master Tunstall," he said, looking fixedly at Mounchensey all the while. "The dungeon he is to occupy is the darkest, the deepest and the dampest in the Fleet. It is that in which his father died. You know it well, Grimbald," he added, to one of the burliest of the jailers. "Take him thither at once, and I will go with you to see him safely bestowed.

"Pass on, Sir," he continued, with a smile of fiendish satisfaction, as Mounchensey was led forth by the jailer.

CHAPTER XXIV.
THE ABDUCTION.

Night had come on, and Aveline was anxiously expecting the arrival of her lover, when a loud knocking was heard at the door of the cottage; and before the summons could be answered by Anthony Rocke, two persons entered, and pushing past the old serving-man, who demanded their business, and vainly endeavoured to oppose their progress, forced their way into the presence of his mistress. Dame Sherborne was in an inner room, but, alarmed by the noise, she flew to the aid of her charge, and reached her at the same moment with the intruders. Her lamp threw its light full upon their countenances; and when she found who they were, she screamed and nearly let it fall, appearing to stand much more in need of support than Aveline herself.

The foremost of the two was Sir Giles Mompesson, and his usually stern and sinister features had acquired a yet more inauspicious cast, from the deathlike paleness that bespread them, as well as from the fillet bound round his injured brow. The other was an antiquated coxcomb, aping the airs and graces of a youthful gallant, attired in silks and velvets fashioned in the newest French mode, and exhaling a mingled perfume of civet, musk, and ambergris; and in him Aveline recognised the amorous old dotard, who had stared at her so offensively during the visit she had been forced to make to the extortioner.

Sir Francis's deportment was not a whit less impertinent or objectionable now than heretofore. After making a profound salutation to Aveline, which he thought was executed in the most courtly style, and with consummate grace, he observed in a loud whisper to his partner, "'Fore heaven! a matchless creature! a divinity! Introduce me in due form, Sir Giles."

"Suffer me to make known to you Sir Francis Mitchell, fair mistress," said Mompesson. "He is so ravished by your charms that he can neither eat, drink, nor sleep; and he professes to me, his friend and partner, that he must die outright, unless you take pity on him. Is it not so, Sir Francis? Nay, plead your own cause, man. You will do it better than I, who am little accustomed to tune my voice to the ear of beauty."

During this speech, the old usurer conducted himself in a manner that, under other circumstances, must have moved Aveline's mirth; but it now only excited her disgust and indignation. Sighing, groaning placing his hand upon his heart, languishingly regarding her, and turning up his eyes till the whites alone were visible, he ended by throwing himself at her feet, seizing her hand, and attempting to cover it with kisses.

"Deign to listen to me, peerless and adorable damsel!" he cried in the most impassioned accents he could command, though he wheezed terribly all the while, and was ever and anon interrupted by a fit of coughing. "Incline your ear to me, I beseech you. Sir Giles has in no respect exaggerated my sad condition. Ever since I beheld you I have been able to do nothing else than—ough! ough!—dwell upon your surpassing attractions. Day and night your lovely image has been constantly before me. You have driven sleep from my eyelids, and rest from my—(ough! ough!)—frame. Your lustrous eyes have lighted up such a fire in my breast as can never be extinguished, unless—(ough! ough! ough!)—plague take this cough! I owe it to you, fair mistress of my heart, as well as my other torments. But as I was about to say, the raging flame you have kindled in my breast will utterly consume me, unless—(ough! ough! ough!)"

Here he was well-nigh choked, and Sir Giles had to come to his assistance.

"What my worthy friend and partner would declare, if his cough permitted him, fair Mistress Aveline," urged the extortioner, "is that he places his life and fortune at your disposal. His desires are all centred in you, and it rests with you to make him the happiest or most miserable of mankind. Speak I not your sentiments, Sir Francis?"

"In every particular, good Sir Giles," replied the other, as soon as he could recover utterance. "And now, most adorable damsel, what say you in answer? You are too gentle, I am sure, to condemn your slave to endless tortures. Nay, motion me not to rise. I have that to say will disarm your frowns, and turn them into smiles of approval and assent. (O, this accursed rheumatism!" he muttered to himself, "I shall never be able to get up unaided!) I love you, incomparable creature—love you to distraction; and as your beauty has inflicted such desperate wounds upon my heart, so I am sure your gentleness will not fail to cure them. Devotion like mine must meet its reward. Your answer, divinest creature! and let it be favourable to my hopes, I conjure you!"

"I have no other answer to give," replied Aveline, coldly, and with an offended look, "except such as any maiden, thus unwarrantably and unseasonably importuned, would make. Your addresses are utterly distasteful to me, and I pray you to desist them. If you have any real wish to oblige me, you will at once free me from your presence."

"Your hand, Sir Giles—your hand!" cried the old usurer, raising himself to his feet with difficulty, "So, you are not to be moved by my sufferings—by my prayers, cruel and proud beauty?" he continued, regarding her with a mortified and spiteful look. "You are inflexible—eh?"

"Utterly so," she replied.

"Anthony Rocke!" cried Dame Sherborne, "show the gentlemen to the door—and bolt it upon them," she added, in a lower tone.

"Not so fast, Madam—not so fast!" exclaimed Sir Francis. "We will not trouble old Anthony just yet. Though his fair young mistress is indisposed to listen to the pleadings of love, it follows not she will be equally insensible to the controlling power of her father's delegated authority. Her hand must be mine, either freely, or by compulsion. Let her know on what grounds I claim it, Sir Giles."

"Your claim cannot be resisted, Sir Francis," rejoined the other; "and if you had followed my counsel, you would not have condescended to play the abject wooer, but have adopted the manlier course, and demanded her hand as your right."

"Nay, Sir Giles, you cannot wonder at me, knowing how infatuated I am by this rare and admirable creature. I was unwilling to assert my rights till all other means of obtaining her hand had failed. But now I have no alternative."

"Whence is your authority derived?" inquired Aveline, trembling as she put the question.

"From your dead father," said Sir Giles, sternly. "His last solemn injunctions to you were, that you should wed the man to whom he had promised you; provided your hand were claimed by him within a year after his death. With equal solemnity you bound yourself to fulfil his wishes. The person to whom you were thus sacredly contracted is Sir Francis Mitchell; and now, in your father's name, and by your father's authority, he demands fulfilment of the solemn pledge."

"O, this is wholly impossible!—I will not believe it!" almost shrieked Aveline, throwing herself into Dame Sherborne's arms.

"It is some wicked device to ensnare you, I am convinced," said the old lady, clasping her to her breast. "But we defy them, as we do the Prince of Darkness, and all his iniquities. Avoid thee, thou wicked old sinner!—thou worse than the benighted heathen! Get hence! I say, Sathanas!" she ejaculated to Sir Francis.

"Ay, I am well assured it is all a fabrication," said Anthony Rocke. "My master had too much consideration and tenderness for his daughter to promise her to a wretched old huncks like this, with one foot in the grave already. Besides, I knew he held both him and Sir Giles Mompesson in utter abomination and contempt. The thing is, therefore, not only improbable, but altogether impossible."

"Hold thy peace, sirrah!" cried Sir Francis, foaming with rage, "or I will cut thy scurril tongue out of thy throat. Huncks, indeed! As I am a true gentleman, if thou wert of my own degree, thou shouldst answer for the opprobrious expression."

"What proof have you that my father entered into any such engagement with you?" inquired Aveline, turning to Sir Francis. "Your bare assertion will scarcely satisfy me."

"Neither will it satisfy me," remarked Anthony. "Let him produce his proofs."

"You are acquainted with your father's handwriting, I presume, fair maiden?" rejoined Sir Francis. "And it may be that your insolent and incredulous serving-man is also acquainted with it. Look at this document, and declare whether it be not, as I assert, traced in Hugh Calveley's characters. Look at it, I say, thou unbelieving hound," he added, to Anthony, "and contradict me if thou canst."

"It is my master's writing, I am compelled to admit," replied the old serving-man, with a groan.

"Are you prepared to render obedience to your father's behests, maiden?" demanded Sir Giles, menacingly.

"O, give me counsel! What shall I say to them?" cried Aveline, appealing to Dame Sherborne. "Would that Sir Jocelyn were here!"

"It is in vain to expect his coming," rejoined Sir Giles, with a bitter laugh. "We have taken good care to keep him out of the way."

"There is no help then!" said Aveline, despairingly. "I must submit."

"We triumph," whispered Sir Giles to his partner.

"Talk not of submission, my dear young lady," implored Anthony Rocke. "Resist them to the last. I will shed my best blood in your defence. If my master did give them that paper he must have been out of his senses, and you need not, therefore, regard it as other than the act of a madman."

"Peace, shallow-pated fool!" cried Sir Giles. "And do you, fair mistress, attend to me, and you shall learn under what circumstances that contract was made, and how it becomes binding upon you. Deeply indebted to Sir Francis, your father had only one means of discharging his obligations. He did hesitate to avail himself of it. He promised you to his creditor, and obtained his own release. Will you dishonour his memory by a refusal?"

"O, if this tale be true, I have no escape from misery!" exclaimed Aveline. "And it wears the semblance of probability."

"I take upon me to declare it to be false," cried Anthony Rocke.

"Another such insolent speech shall cost thee thy life, sirrah!" cried Sir Giles, fiercely.

"Read over the paper again, my dear young lady," said Dame Sherborne. "You may, perhaps, find something in it not yet discovered, which may help you to a better understanding of your father's wishes."

"Ay, read it!—read it!" cried the old usurer, giving her the paper. "You will perceive in what energetic terms your father enjoins compliance on your part with his commands; and what awful denunciations he attaches to your disobedience. Read it, I say, and fancy he is speaking to you from the grave in these terms—'Take this man for thy husband, O my daughter, and take my blessing with him. Reject him, and my curse shall alight upon thy head.'"

But Aveline was too much engrossed to heed him. Suddenly her eye caught something she had not previously noticed, and she exclaimed,—"I have detected the stratagem. I knew this authority could never be committed to you."

"What mean you, fair mistress?" cried Sir Francis, surprised and alarmed. "My name may not appear upon the face of the document; but, nevertheless, I am the person referred to by it."

"The document itself disproves your assertion," cried Aveline, with exultation.

"How so?" demanded Sir Giles, uneasily.

"Why, see you not that he to whom my father designed to give my hand was named Osmond Mounchensey?"

"Osmond Mounchensey!" exclaimed Sir Giles, starting.

"This is pure invention!" cried Sir Francis. "There is no such name on the paper—no name at all, in short—nor could there be any, for reasons I will presently explain."

"Let your own eyes convince you to the contrary," she rejoined, extending the paper to him and revealing to his astounded gaze and to that of his partner, who looked petrified with surprise, the name plainly written as she had described it.

"How came it there?" cried Sir Giles, as soon as he could command himself.

"I cannot say," replied Sir Francis. "I only know it was not there when I—that is, when I received it. It must be Clement Lanyere's handiwork," he added in a whisper.

"I see not how that can be," replied the other, in a like low tone. "The alteration must have been made since it has been in your possession. It could not have escaped my observation."

"Nor mine," cried Sir Francis. "'T is passing strange!"

"Your infamous project is defeated," cried Aveline. "Let the rightful claimant appear, and it will be time enough to consider what I will do.—But I can hold no further discourse with you, and command your instant departure."

"And think you we mean to return empty-handed, fair mistress?" said Sir Giles, resuming all his wonted audacity. "Be not deceived. By fair means or foul you shall be the bride of Sir Francis Mitchell. I have sworn it, and I will keep my oath!"

"As I am a true gentleman, it will infinitely distress me to resort to extremities, fair mistress," said the old usurer, "and I still trust you will listen to reason. If I have put in practice a little harmless stratagem, what matters it? All is fair in love. And if you knew all, you would be aware that I have already paid so dearly for you that I cannot afford to lose you. Cost what it will, you must be mine."

"Never!" exclaimed Aveline, resolutely.

"You will soon alter your tone, when you find how little power of refusal is left you, fair mistress," said Sir Giles. "A litter is waiting for you without. Will it please you to enter it?"

"Not unless by force—and you dare to offer me violence," she replied.

"I advise you not to put our forbearance to the test," said Sir Giles.

"I should be grieved to impose any restraint upon you," subjoined Sir Francis; "and I trust you will not compel me to act against my inclinations. Let me lead you to the litter."

As he advanced towards her, Aveline drew quickly back, and Dame Sherborne uttered a loud scream; but her cries brought no other help than could be afforded by old Anthony Rocke, who, planting himself before his young mistress, menaced Sir Francis to retire.

But this state of things was only of brief duration. It speedily appeared that the two extortioners had abundant assistance at hand to carry out their infamous design. A whistle was sounded by Sir Giles; and at the call the cottage door was burst open by some half dozen of the myrmidons, headed by Captain Bludder.

Any resistance that the old serving-man could offer was speedily overcome. Knocked down by a pike, he was gagged and pinioned, and carried out of the house. The cries of Aveline and the elderly dame were stifled by scarves tied over their heads; and both being in a fainting condition from fright, they were borne to the litter which was standing at the door, and being shut up within it, were conveyed as quickly as might be to Sir Giles Mompesson's mansion, near the Fleet. Thither, also, was old Anthony Rocke taken, closely guarded on the way by two of the myrmidons.

CHAPTER XXV.
THE "STONE COFFIN."

A dreadful dungeon! the last and profoundest of the range of subterranean cells already described as built below the level of the river Fleet: a relict, in fact, of the ancient prison which had escaped the fury of Wat Tyler and his followers, when the rest of the structure was destroyed by them. Not inaptly was the dungeon styled the "Stone Coffin." Those immured within it seldom lived long.

A chill like that of death smote Sir Jocelyn, as he halted before the door of this horrible place. Preceded by Grimbald the jailer, with a lamp in one hand and a bunch of large keys in the other, and closely followed by the deputy-warden and Sir Giles Mompesson, our young knight had traversed an underground corridor with cells on one side of it, and then, descending a flight of stone steps, had reached a still lower pit, in which the dismal receptacle was situated. Here he remained up to the ankles in mud and water, while Grimbald unlocked the ponderous door, and with a grin revealed the interior of the cavernous recess.

Nothing more dank and noisome could be imagined than the dungeon. Dripping stone-walls, a truckle-bed with a mouldy straw-mattrass, rotting litter scattered about, a floor glistening and slippery with ooze, and a deep pool of water, like that outside, at the further end,—these constituted the materials of the frightful picture presented to the gaze. No wonder Sir Jocelyn should recoil, and refuse to enter the cell.

"You don't seem to like your lodgings, worshipful Sir," said Grimbald, still grinning, as he held up the lamp; "but you will soon get used to the place, and you will not lack company—rats, I mean: they come from the Fleet in swarms. Look! a score of 'em are making off yonder—swimming to their holes. But they will come back again with some of their comrades, when you are left alone, and without a light. Unlike other vermin, the rats of the Fleet are extraordinarily sociable—ho! ho!"

And, chuckling at his own jest, Grimbald turned to Sir Giles Mompesson, who, with Joachim Tunstall, was standing at the summit of the steps, as if unwilling to venture into the damp region below, and observed—"The worshipful gentleman does not like the appearance of his quarters, it seems, Sir Giles; but we cannot give him better,—and, though the cell might be somewhat more comfortable if it were drier, and perhaps more wholesome, yet it is uncommonly quiet, and double the size of any other in the Fleet. I never could understand why it should be called the 'Stone Coffin'—but so it is. Some prisoners have imagined they would get their death with cold from a single night passed within it—but that's a mistaken notion altogether."

"You have proof to the contrary in Sir Ferdinando Mounchensey, father of the present prisoner," said Sir Giles, in a derisive tone. "He occupied that cell for more than six months. Did he not, good Grimbald? You had charge of him, and ought to know?"

"One hundred and sixty days exactly, counting from the date of his arrival to the hour of his death, was Sir Ferdinando an inmate of the 'Stone Coffin,'" said the jailer, slowly and sententiously; "and he appeared to enjoy his health quite as well as could be expected—at all events, he did so at first. I do not think it was quite so damp in his days—but there couldn't be much difference. In any case, the worthy knight made no complaints; perhaps because he thought there would be no use in making 'em. Ah! worshipful Sir," he added to Sir Jocelyn, in a tone of affected sympathy which only made his mockery more offensive, "your father was a goodly man, of quite as noble a presence as yourself, though rather stouter and broader in the shoulders, when he first came here; but he was sadly broken down at the last—quite a skeleton. You would hardly have known him."

"He lost the use of his limbs, if I remember right, Grimbald?" remarked Sir Giles, willing to prolong the scene, which appeared to afford him infinite amusement.

"Entirely lost the use of 'em," replied the jailer. "But what of that? He didn't require to take exercise. A friend was permitted to visit him, and that was more grace than the Council usually allows to such offenders."

"It was far more than an offender like Sir Ferdinando deserved," said Sir Giles; "and, if I had known it, he should have had no such indulgence. Star-Chamber delinquents cannot expect to be treated like ordinary prisoners. If they do, they will be undeceived when brought here—eh, Master Tunstall?"

"Most true, Sir Giles, most true!" replied the deputy-warden. "Star-Chamber prisoners will get little indulgence from me, I warrant them."

"Unless they bribe you well—eh, Master Joachim?" whispered Sir Giles, merrily.

"Rest easy on that score, Sir Giles. I am incorruptible, unless you allow it," rejoined the other, obsequiously.

"My poor father!" ejaculated Sir Jocelyn. "And thou wert condemned without a crime to a death of lingering agony within this horrible cell! The bare idea of it is madness. But Heaven, though its judgments be slow, will yet avenge thee upon thy murderers!"

"Take heed what you say, prisoner," observed Grimbald, changing his manner, and speaking with great harshness. "Every word you utter against the decrees of the Star-Chamber, will be reported to the Council, and will be brought up against you; so you had best be cautious. Tour father was *not* murdered. He was immured in this cell in pursuance of a sentence of the High Court, and he died before his term of captivity had expired, that is all."

"O, the days and nights of anguish and despair he must have endured during that long captivity!" exclaimed Sir Jocelyn, before whose gaze a vision of his dying father seemed to pass, filling him with unutterable horror.

"Days and nights which will henceforth be your own," roared Sir Giles; "and you will then comprehend the nature of your father's feelings. But he escaped what you will *not* escape—exposure on the pillory, branding on the cheek, loss of ears, slitting of the nose, and it may be, scourging. The goodly appearance you have inherited from your sire will not be long left when the tormentor takes you in hand. Ha! ha!"

"One censured by the Star-Chamber must wear a paper on his breast at the pillory. You must not forget that mark of infamy, Sir Giles," said the deputy-warden, chuckling.

"No, no; I forget it not," laughed the extortioner. "How ingeniously devised are our Star-Chamber punishments, Master Joachim, and how well they meet the offences. Infamous libellers and slanderers of the State, like Sir Jocelyn, are ever punished in one way; but new crimes require new manner of punishment. You recollect the case of Traske, who practised Judaism, and forbade the use of swine's flesh, and who was sentenced to be fed upon nothing but pork during his confinement."

"I recollect it perfectly," cried Tunstall, "a just judgment. The wretch abhorred the food, and would have starved himself rather than take it; but we forced the greasy morsels down his throat. Ha! ha! You are merry, Sir Giles, very merry; I have not seen you so gleesome this many a day—scarcely since the time when Clement Lanyere underwent his sentence."

"Ah! the accursed traitor!" exclaimed Sir Giles, with an explosion of rage. "Would he had to go through it again! If I catch him, he shall—and I am sure to lay hands upon him soon. But to our present prisoner. You will treat him in all respects as his father was treated, Master Joachim—but no one must come nigh him."

"No one shall approach him save with an order from the Council, Sir Giles," replied the other.

"Not even then," said the extortioner decisively. "My orders alone must be attended to!"

"Hum!" ejaculated the deputy-warden, somewhat perplexed. "Well, I will follow out your instructions as strictly as I can, Sir Giles. I suppose you have nothing more to say to the prisoner, and Grimbald may as well lock him up."

And, receiving a nod of assent from the other, he called to the jailer to finish his task.

But Sir Jocelyn resolutely refused to enter the cell, and demanded a room in one of the upper wards.

"You shall have no other chamber than this," said Sir Giles, in a peremptory tone.

"I did not address myself to you, Sir, but to the deputy-warden," rejoined Sir Jocelyn. "Master Joachim Tunstall, you well know I am not sentenced by the Star-Chamber, or any other court, to confinement within this cell. I will not enter it; and I order you, at your peril, to provide me with a better chamber. This is wholly unfit for occupation."

"Do not argue the point, Grimbald, but force him into the cell," roared the extortioner.

"Fair and softly, Sir Giles, fair and softly," replied the jailer. "Now, prisoner, you hear what is said—are you prepared to obey?"

And he was about to lay hands rudely upon Sir Jocelyn, when the latter, pushing him aside, ran nimbly up the steps, and seizing Sir Giles by the throat, dragged him downward.

Notwithstanding the resistance of the extortioner, whose efforts at liberation were seconded by Grimbald, our young knight succeeded in forcing his enemy into the dungeon, and hurled him to the further end of it. During the struggle, Sir Jocelyn had managed to possess himself of the other's sword, and he now pointed it at his breast.

"You have constituted yourself my jailer," he cried, "and by the soul of him who perished in this loathsome cell, by your instrumentality, I will send you instantly to account for your crimes on High, unless you promise to assign me a different chamber!"

"I promise it," replied Sir Giles. "You shall have the best in the Fleet. Let me go forth, and you shall choose one for yourself."

"I will not trust you, false villain," cried Sir Jocelyn. "Give orders to the deputy-warden, and if he pledges his word they shall be obeyed, I will take it. Otherwise you die."

"Bid Master Tunstall come to me, Grimbald," gasped the extortioner.

"I am here, Sir Giles, I am here," replied the deputy-warden, cautiously entering the cell. "What would you have me do?"

"Free me from this restraint," cried Sir Giles, struggling to regain his feet.

Sir Jocelyn shortened his sword in order to give him a mortal thrust, but his purpose was prevented by Grimbald. With his heavy bunch of keys the jailer struck the young knight upon the head, and stretched him insensible upon the ground.

CHAPTER XXVI.
A SECRET FRIEND.

When Sir Jocelyn again became conscious, he found he had been transported to a different cell, which, in comparison with the "Stone Coffin," was clean and comfortable. The walls were of stone, and the pallet on which he was laid was of straw, but the place was dry, and free from the noisome effluvium pervading the lower dungeon. The consideration shown him originated in the conviction on the part of the deputy-warden, that the young man must die if left in his wounded state in that unwholesome vault, and so the removal took place, in spite of the objections raised to it by Sir Giles Mompesson, who would have willingly let him perish. But Master Tunstall dreaded an inquiry, as the prisoner had not yet been sentenced by the Council.

After glancing round his cell, and endeavouring recal the events that had conducted him to it, Sir Jocelyn tried to raise himself, but found his limbs so stiff that he could not accomplish his object, and he sank back with a groan. At this moment the door opened, and Grimbald, accompanied by a repulsive-looking personage, with a face like a grinning mask, advanced towards the pallet.

"This is the wounded man, Master Luke Hatton," said the jailer; "you will exert your best skill to cure him; and you must use dispatch, in case he should be summoned before the Council."

"The Council must come to him if they desire to interrogate him now," replied Luke Hatton; adding, after he had examined the injuries received by the young knight, "He is badly hurt, but not so severely as I expected. I will undertake to set him upon his legs in three days. I did as much for Sir Giles Mompesson, and he was wounded in the same manner."

"Why, this is the young knight who struck down Sir Giles at the jousts," said Grimbald. "Strange! you should have two mortal enemies to deal with."

"Is this Sir Jocelyn Mounchensey?" inquired Luke Hatton, with apparent curiosity. "You did not tell me so before."

"Perhaps I ought not to have told you so now," returned the other. "But do you take any interest in him?"

"Not much," replied the apothecary; "but I have heard his name often mentioned of late. You need not be uneasy about this young man being summoned before the Star-Chamber. The great case of the Countess of Exeter against Lady Lake comes on before the King and the Lords of the Council to-morrow or next day, and it will occupy all their attention. They will have no time for aught else."

"What think you will be the judgment in that case?" inquired Grimbald.

"I have my own opinion," returned the apothecary, with a significant smile; "but I care not to reveal it. I am a witness in the case myself, and something may depend on my evidence. You asked me just now whether I took any interest in this young man. I will tell you what surprised me to find him here. Sir Francis Mitchell has taken it into his head to rob him of his intended bride."

"Ah! indeed!" exclaimed the jailer, with a laugh. "The old dotard does not mean to marry her?"

"By my troth but he does—and the wedding is to be a grand one. I will tell you more about it anon."

At this moment Sir Jocelyn, who had hitherto remained with his eyes closed, uttered a cry of anguish, and again vainly endeavoured to raise himself.

"Aveline married to Sir Francis?" he cried. "Said you she was to be forced into a union with that hoary miscreant? It must be prevented."

"I see not how it can be, Sir Jocelyn," replied Luke Hatton, "since she is in the power of Sir Giles Mompesson. Besides which, the 'hoary miscreant,' as you style him, will take means to ensure her acquiescence."

"Means! what means?" demanded Sir Jocelyn, writhing in agony.

"A love-potion," replied Luke Hatton, calmly, "I am about to prepare a philter for her, and will answer for its effect. She will be the old knight's, and without opposition."

"Infernal villain! and that I should be lying here, unable to give her aid!"

And overcome by the intensity of his emotion, as well as by acute bodily suffering, Sir Jocelyn relapsed into insensibility.

He was not, however, suffered to remain long in this state. Stimulants applied by Luke Hatton soon restored him to consciousness. The first object his gaze fell upon was the apothecary, and he was about to vent his fury upon him in words, when the latter, cautiously raising his finger to his lips, said in a whisper—"I am a friend. Grimbald is only at the door, and a single exclamation on your part will betray me." He then leaned down, and bringing his lips almost close to the young knight's ear, whispered—"What I said before the jailer was correct. I have been applied to by Sir Francis for a philter to be administered to Mistress Aveline, and I have promised it to him; but I am secretly in the service of Clement Lanyere, and will defeat the old usurer's villainous designs."

Sir Jocelyn could not repress a cry of delight, and Grimbald entered the cell.

CHAPTER XXVII.
SHOWING HOW JUDGMENT WAS GIVEN BY
KING JAMES IN THE STAR-CHAMBER, IN THE

great cause of the Countess of Exeter against Sir Thomas and Lady Lake.

Five days had King James and the whole of the Privy Council been sitting within the Star-Chamber; and the great cause that had occupied them during the whole of that time was drawing to an end—little remaining for his Majesty to do in it, except to pronounce sentence.

The cause to which James and his Councillors had lent a hearing so long and patient, was no other than that of the Countess of Exeter against Sir Thomas Lake and his Lady. Throughout it, whether prompted or not as to the course he pursued, the Monarch displayed great sagacity and penetration. Prior to the trial, and when the preliminary statements had alone been laid before him, he determined personally to investigate the matter, and without acquainting any one with his design, while out hunting, he rode over to the Earl of Exeter's residence at Wimbledon—the place, it will be recollected, where the forged confession was alleged to have been signed by the Countess—and proceeded to examine the particular chamber indicated by Lady Lake and Sarah Swarton as the scene of the transaction. He was accompanied by Buckingham, and some other lords high in his favour. On examination it was found that the chamber was of such size, and the lower part of it, where Sarah was reported to have been concealed, was so distant from the large bay window, that any conversation held there must have been inaudible to her; as was proved, upon experiment, by the King and his attendants. But the crowning circumstance was the discovery made by James himself— for his courtiers were too discreet to claim any share in it—that the hangings did not reach within two feet of the floor, and consequently could not have screened a secret witness from view; while it was further ascertained that the arras had been entirely undisturbed for several years. On making this discovery, James rubbed his hands with great glee, and exclaimed—"Aha! my Lady Lake and her handmaiden may forswear themselves if they choose—but they will not convince me. Oaths cannot confound my sight."

This asseveration he repeated during the trial, at which he proffered his own testimony in favour of the plaintiff; and indeed it was evident from the first, however much he might seek to disguise it, that he was strongly biassed towards the Countess. Not content, however, with the discovery he had made at Wimbledon, James had secretly despatched a serjeant-at-arms to Rome, where Lord Roos had taken up his residence after leaving England, and obtained from him and from his confidential servant Diego, a statement incriminating Lady Lake, and denouncing the confession as a wicked forgery. Luke Hatton, moreover, who had gone over, as already intimated, to the side of the Countess, and who took care to hide his own complicity in the dark affair, and to give a very different colour to his conduct from what really belonged to it—Luke Hatton, we say, became a most important witness against the Lakes, and it was said to be owing to his crafty insinuations that the King conceived the idea of visiting Wimbledon as before-mentioned.

Notwithstanding all this, there were many irreconcileable contradictions, and the notoriously bad character of Lord Roos, his cruel treatment of his wife, and his passionate devotion to the Countess, led many to suspect that, after all, he and Lady Exeter were the guilty parties they were represented. Moreover, by such as had any knowledge of the man, Luke Hatton was not esteemed a credible witness; and it was generally thought that his testimony ought not to be received by the King, or accepted only with the greatest caution.

But the opinions favourable to Lady Lake and her husband underwent an entire change in the early part of the trial, when, to the surprise of all, and to the inexpressible dismay of her parents, Lady Roos, who had been included in the process by the Countess, made a confession, wherein she admitted that the document produced by her mother against Lady Exeter, was fabricated, and that all the circumstances said to be connected with it at the time of its supposed signature, were groundless and imaginary. The unfortunate lady's motive for making this revelation was the desire of screening her husband; and so infatuated was she by her love of him, that she allowed herself to be persuaded—by the artful suggestions, it was whispered, of Luke Hatton—that this would be the means of accomplishing their reconciliation, and that she would be rewarded for her devotion by his returning regard. If such was her belief, she was doomed to disappointment. She never beheld him again. Lord Roos died abroad soon after the trial took place; nor did his ill-fated lady long survive him.

Thus, it will be seen, all circumstances were adverse to the Lakes. But in spite of the difficulties surrounding her, and the weight of evidence, true or false, brought against her, no concession could be obtained from Lady Lake, and she stoutly protested her innocence, and retaliated in most forcible terms upon her accusers. She gave a flat contradiction to her daughter, and poured terrible maledictions on her head, ceasing them not until silenced by command of the King. The fearful charges brought by her ladyship against Luke Hatton produced some effect, and were listened to; but, as they could only be substantiated by herself and Sarah Swarton, they fell to the ground; since here again Lady Roos refused to be a witness against her husband.

Unwilling to admit his wife's criminality, though urged by the King to do so in order to save himself, Sir Thomas Lake was unable to make a successful defence; and he seemed so much bowed down by affliction and perplexity, that sympathy was generally felt for him. Indeed, his dignified deportment and reserve gave him some claim to consideration.

In this way was the trial brought to a close, after three days' duration.

Now, let a glance be cast round the room wherein the lords of the Council were deliberating upon their judgment.

It was the Star-Chamber.

Situated on the south-eastern side of Westminster Hall, near the river, this famous room,—wherein the secret councils of the kingdom were then held, and had been held during many previous reigns,—was more remarkable for the beauty of its ceiling than for size or splendour. That ceiling was of oak, richly carved and gilt, and disposed in squares, in the midst of which were roses, portculises, pomegranates, and fleurs-de-lys. Over the door leading to the chamber was placed a star, in allusion to its name, with the date 1602. Its walls were covered with ancient tapestry, and it had many windows looking towards the river, and filled with painted glass.

Though it would appear to be obvious enough, much doubt has been entertained as to the derivation of the name of this celebrated Court. "Some think it so called," writes the author of a learned treatise on its jurisdiction, before cited, "of *Crimen Stellionatus*, because it handleth such things and cases as are strange and unusual: some of *Stallen*. I confess I am in that point a Platonist in opinion, that *nomina naturâ fiunt potiùs quam vagâ impositone*. And so I doubt not but *Camera-Stellata* (for so I find it called in our ancient Year-books) is most aptly named; not because the Star-Chamber, where the Court is kept, is so adorned with stars gilded, as some would have it—for surely the chamber is so adorned because it is the seal of that Court, *et denominatio*, being *à praestantiori magis dignum trahit ad se minus*; and it was so fitly called, because the stars have no light but what is cast upon them from the sun by reflection, being his representative body, and, as his Majesty was pleased to say when he sat there in his royal person, representation must need cease when the person is present. So in the presence of his great majesty, the which is the sun of honour and glory, the shining of those stars is put out, they not having any power to pronounce any sentence in this Court—for the judgment is the King's only; but by way of advice they deliver their opinions, which his wisdom alloweth or disalloweth, increaseth or moderateth at his royal pleasure." This explanation, which seems rather given for the purpose of paying a fulsome compliment to James, in whose reign the treatise in question was written, is scarcely satisfactory; and we have little doubt that the name originated in the circumstance of the roof of the chamber being embellished with gilded stars. We are told in Strype's Stowe, that the Star-Chamber was "so called, either by derivation from the old English word *Steoran*, which signifieth to steer or rule, as doth the pilot of a ship; because the King and Council did sit here, as it were, at the *stern*, and did govern in the ship of the Commonwealth. Some derive in from *Stellio*, which signifies that starry and subtle beast so called. From which cometh the word *stellionatus*, that signifieth *cosenage*; because that crime was chiefly punishable in this Court by an extraordinary power, as it was in the civil law. Or, because the roof of this Court was garnished with gilded stars, as the room itself was starry, or full of windows and lights. In which respect some of the Latin Records name it *Camera Stellata;* the French *Chambre des Ètoiles;* and the English the Starred Chamber." The derivation of the name, we repeat, seems to us sufficiently simple and obvious; but as it has been matter of controversy, we have thought it worth while to advert to the circumstance.

To proceed. In a chair of state, elevated above the table round which the Lords of the Council were gathered, and having a canopy over it, sat the King, calmly watching them as they pursued their deliberations,—his own mind being completely made up as to the sentence he should pronounce—and ever and anon stealing a glance at Lady Lake and her husband, who were seated behind a bar that crossed the room below the Council-table. The defendants, or prisoners—for such in effect they were—were under the guard of a pursuivant and a serjeant-at-arms. A little behind them was Sarah Swarton; but, though faint and frightened, and scarcely able to sustain herself, she was not allowed a seat. On a raised bench at the side sat the beautiful Countess of Exeter, radiant with smiles and triumph. She was receiving the congratulations of several dames of high rank by whom she was accompanied. Amongst the Judges of the Court were the Lord Chancellor, who sat immediately under the King, with his mace and seal before him; the Lord Treasurer and the Keeper of the Privy Seal; the President of the Council; the Judges; the Archbishop of Canterbury, and eight bishops and other prelates; and all the dukes, marquises, earls, and barons composing the Privy Council, to the number of forty. Besides these, there were present Prince Charles, three of the lieger ambassadors, and many other distinguished persons. Though all had gone against her, Lady Lake's spirit was still undiminished, and she eyed the Council imperiously; but her husband's regards were fixed upon the ground, and his head rested upon his breast.

After some further time had been needlessly consumed by the Council in stating their opinions to the King, he prepared to deliver judgment. On this the defendants arose, and profound silence reigned throughout the Court as James addressed them.

The sentence was to this effect:—A fine of upwards of £22,000 was imposed upon Sir Thomas, with a further censure of imprisonment in the Tower, during the King's pleasure. Lady Lake was to be imprisoned with him. A public recognition of their offence, for reparation of the Countess's injured honour, was to be made by them, in the most ample manner His Majesty could devise. Sarah Swarton was adjudged to the Fleet. "Thence," ran the sentence, "to be whipped at the cart's tail to Westminster, and afterwards from the same place to Cheapside. At Cheapside to be branded with F.A. (signifying *false accusation*), one letter on either cheek. To do public penance in Saint Martin's Church. To be detained in the Fleet till they do weary of her; and then to be sent to Bridewell, there to spend and end her days."

When the poor handmaiden heard this severe sentence, she uttered a cry of despair, and fell down on the floor in a swoon.

Thereupon the delinquents were removed; and as Lady Lake withdrew, a look passed between her and the Countess, which, in spite of the assurance of the latter, made her turn pale, and tremble.

In a very remarkable letter, subsequently addressed by Lady Lake to her successful opponent in this great case, she said:—"I wish my submission could make you an innocent woman, and wash you as white as a swan; but it must be your own submission unto God, and many prayers, and tears, and afflictions, which, seeing you have not outwardly, examine your heart, and think on times past, and remember what I have written to you heretofore. The same I do now again, for I yet nothing doubt, but that, although the Lord Roos was sent away, and is dead, yet truth lives." The truth, however, was never fully brought to light; and that justice which the vindictive lady expected was denied her.

CHAPTER XXVIII.
THE TWO WARRANTS.

At the conclusion of the trial, James was observed to smile, and Buckingham, who had drawn near the chair of state, ventured to inquire what it was that entertained his Majesty.

"Our fancy has been tickled by a curious conceit," answered the King. "We discern a singular similitude between the case we hae just heard, and the transgression of our first parents."

"How so, your Majesty?" asked the favourite.

"As thus," replied James. "Sir Thomas Lake may be likened to our gude Father Adam, wha fell into sin frae listening to the beguilements of Eve—Mither Eve being represented by his dochter, my Lady Roos—and ye will own that there cannot be a closer resemblance to the wily auld serpent than we find in my Lady Lake."

"Excellent!" cried Buckingham, joining in the royal laughter; "but before your Majesty quits that seat, I must entreat you to perform that which I know you delight in—an act of justice."

"Anither act of justice, ye should say, my Lord," returned James in a tone of slight rebuke; "seeing we hae just delivered a maist memorable judgment in a case which has cost us five days of incessant labour and anxious consideration. But what is it ye require at our hands? In whose behalf are we to exercise our prerogative?"

"In that of Sir Jocelyn Mounchensey, my gracious Liege," replied Buckingham, "who has been committed to the Fleet for contempt of this high and honourable Court, and can only be released by your Majesty's warrant. As I was myself present on the occasion, when the intemperate expressions laid to his charge were used, I can affirm that he was goaded on by his enemies to utter them; and that in his calmer moments he must have regretted his rashness."

"Ye shall have the warrant, my Lord," said James, with a smile. "And it does ye meikle credit to have made the request. The punishment Sir Jocelyn has already endured is amply sufficient for the offence; and we hae nae fears of its being repeated. A single visit to the Fleet is eneuch for any man. But in respect to Sir Jocelyn, I am happy to say that his Excellency the Conde de Gondomar has quite set him right in our gude opinion; and has satisfactorily proved to us that the spy we suspected him to be was anither person, wha shall be nameless. Ha! here comes the Count himself," he exclaimed, as the Spanish Ambassador approached. "Your Excellency will be glad to hear, after the handsome manner you have spoken of him, that it is our intention to restore Sir Jocelyn to the favour he previously enjoyed. My Lord of Buckingham is to have a warrant for his release from the Fleet, and we shall trust to see him soon at Court as heretofore."

"While your Majesty is in this gracious mood," said De Gondomar, bending lowly, "suffer me to prefer a request respecting a person of very inferior consequence to Sir Jocelyn—but one in whom I nevertheless take an interest—and who is likewise a prisoner in the Fleet."

"And ye require a warrant for his liberation—ah, Count?"

"Your Majesty has said it," replied De Gondomar, again bending lowly.

"What is the nature of his offence?" demanded the King.

"A trifling outrage upon myself," returned the Ambassador;—"a mere nothing, your Majesty."

"Ah! I know whom you mean. You refer to that rascally apprentice, Dick Taverner," cried James. "Call ye his attack upon you a trifling outrage—a mere nothing, Count. I call it a riot—almost a rebellion— to assault an ambassador."

"Whatever it may be, I am content to overlook it," said De Gondomar; "and, in sooth, the knaves had received some provocation."

"Aweel, since your Excellency is disposed to view it in that light," rejoined James—"since ye display such generosity towards your enemies, far be it from us to oppose your wishes. The order for the 'prentice's release shall be made out at the same time as Sir Jocelyn's. My Lord of Buckingham will give orders to that effect to the Clerk of the Court, and we will attach our sign manual to the warrants. And now—have ye not done?" he continued, observing that Buckingham still lingered. "Have ye any mair requests to prefer?"

"I had some request to make on the part of the Prince, my Liege," replied the Marquis; "but his Highness, I perceive, is about to speak to you himself."

As he said this, Prince Charles, who had occupied a seat among the Council, drew near, and stepping upon the elevation on which the chair of state was placed, so as to bring himself on a level with his royal father, made a long and apparently important communication to him in a very low tone. James listened to what was said by his son with great attention, and seemed much surprised and indignant at the circumstances, whatever they were, related to him. Ever and anon, he could not repress a great oath, and, but for the entreaties of Charles, would have given vent to an explosion of choler, which must have betrayed the secret reposed to his keeping. Calming himself, however, as well as he could, he at length said, in a low tone—"We confide the matter to you, since you desire it, for we are assured our dear son will act worthily and well as our representative. Ye shall be clothed with our authority, and have power to punish these heinous offenders as ye see fit. We will confirm your judgments, whatever they be, and sae will our Preevy Council."

"I must have power to pardon, as well as to punish, my gracious Liege," said Charles.

"Ye shall hae baith," answered the King; "but the distinction is needless, since the ane is comprehended in the ither. Ye shall have our ain seal, and act as if ye were King yersel'—as ye will be ane of these days. Will that content ye?"

"Perfectly," replied Charles, gratefully kissing his royal father's hand. And, descending from the platform, he proceeded to join Buckingham and De Gondomar, with whom he held a brief whispered conference.

Meanwhile, the two warrants were made out, and received the royal signature; after which James quitted the Court, and the Council broke up.

The warrants having been delivered by the clerk to Buckingham, were entrusted by the latter to Luke Hatton, who, it appeared, was waiting for them in the outer gallery; and, after the latter had received some directions respecting them from the Marquis, he hastened away.

As he passed through New Palace-yard, Luke Hatton encountered a tall man muffled in a long black cloak. A few words were exchanged between them, and, the information gained by the individual in the cloak seemed perfectly satisfactory to him. So he went his way, while Luke Hatton repaired to the Fleet Prison.

There he was at once admitted to the ward wherein Sir Jocelyn was confined, and announced to him the glad tidings of his restoration to freedom. By this time Sir Jocelyn was perfectly recovered from the injuries he had received from the jailer, during his struggle with Sir Giles Mompesson, so that there was no obstacle to his removal, and his natural wish was to quit the prison at once; but such cogent reasons were assigned by Luke Hatton for his remaining there for another day, that he could not but acquiesce in them. Indeed, when all the circumstances were explained to him, as they were, by the apothecary, he could not but approve of the plan, which, it appeared, was about to be acted upon in the next day for the punishment of his enemies; and it then became evident why Sir Giles should not be made acquainted with his release, which must be the case if the warrant were immediately acted upon. Neither the deputy-warden nor the jailer—both of whom, as he knew, were the extortioner's creatures— were to be informed of it till the last moment. Certain disclosures respecting Clement Lanyere, which were made by Luke Hatton to the young knight, affected him very deeply, and plunged him for a long time in painful thought.

Quitting the cell of the more important prisoner, Luke Hatton proceeded to that of the apprentice, whom he acquainted with his good fortune, holding out to him certain prospects of future happiness, which drove poor Dick nearly distracted. At the suggestion of his new friend, the 'prentice wrote a letter to Gillian Greenford, conjuring her, by the love she bore him, and by their joint hopes of a speedy union, implicitly to comply with the directions of the bearer of the note—whatever they might be: and, armed with this, Luke Hatton quitted the Meet, and, procuring a horse, rode off, at a rapid pace, to Tottenham.

CHAPTER XXIX.
THE SILVER COFFER.

Within Sir Giles Mompesson's vast and gloomy mansion, it has been said there were certain rooms which, from their size and splendour, formed a striking contrast to the rest of the habitation. Never used,—except on extraordinary occasions, when their owner gave a grand entertainment with some ulterior object,—these apartments, notwithstanding their magnificence, partook in some degree of the chilling and inhospitable character of the house. Even when brilliantly lighted up, they wanted warmth and comfort; and though the banquets given within them were sumptuous and profuse, and the wine flowed without stint, the guests went away dissatisfied, and railing against their ostentatious host. Thus, though the stone walls were hung with rich tapestry, the dust had gathered thickly upon its folds, while portions of the rugged masonry were revealed to view. The furniture was massive, but cumbrous and ill-assorted; and the gilded ceiling and Venetian mirrors, from want of care, had become tarnished and dim.

Such as they were, however, these apartments were assigned to Aveline, when she was forcibly brought to the extortioner's habitation, as before narrated. Allowed to range within them at pleasure, she was kept strictly within their limits. The doors were constantly guarded by one or other of the myrmidons; and any communication with the external world was impossible, because the windows were partially grated, and looked into a court-yard. Beyond this, she was subjected to no restraint; and her own attendants, Dame Sherborne and old Anthony Rocke, were suffered to remain with her.

Had it not been for her exposure to the annoyance of frequent from Sir Francis Mitchell, and her anxiety about Sir Jocelyn, Aveline would not have found her confinement so intolerable. But the enamoured old usurer persecuted her at all hours, and she could never be free from the intrusion, since the doors could not be shut against him. Sometimes, he came accompanied by his partner, though more frequently alone, but ever with the same purpose,—namely, that of protesting the violence of his passion, and seeking to soften her obduracy. As may be well supposed, his pleadings, however urged, were wholly ineffectual, and excited no other feelings, except those of detestation, in her bosom. Such a state of things could not endure for ever; and her only hope was, that finding all his efforts to move her fruitless, he would in time desist from them. Not that she was without other fearful apprehensions, which were shared by her attendants.

Nearly a fortnight had thus passed by, when, one day, during which she had seen nothing of her tormentor, and was rejoicing at the circumstance, the repast usually served at noon was brought in by a fresh serving-man. Something in this person's manner, and in the meaning glance he fixed upon her attracted her attention; otherwise, he was a man of singularly unprepossessing appearance. She addressed a few words to him, but he made no reply, and became suddenly as reserved as his predecessor had been. This deportment, however, it presently appeared, was only assumed. While placing a flask of wine on the table, the man said in a low tone—"I am a friend of Sir Jocelyn. Constrain yourself, or you will betray me. Sir Francis is watching us from an eyelet-hole in the door. Drink of this," he added, pouring wine into a goblet.

"Is it medicated?" she asked in a whisper, regarding him anxiously.

"It is supposed to be so," he answered, with a scarcely perceptible smile. "Drink, I say. If you do not, you will mar my project. 'Tis well!" he added, as she raised the goblet to her lips. "A few words must explain my design. Sir Francis will fancy you have swallowed a love-potion. Take care not to undeceive him, for on that belief rests your safety. When he presents himself, as he will do shortly, do not repulse him as heretofore. Smile on him as kindly as you can; and though the task of duping him may be difficult and distasteful to you, shrink not from it. The necessity of the case justifies the deception. If he presses his suit, no longer refuse him your hand."

"I cannot do it," murmured Aveline, with a shudder.

"You MUST," rejoined Luke Hatton—for it was he—"or incur worse dangers. Provoked by your resistance, Sir Francis has lost all patience, and is determined to accomplish his purpose. Knowing my skill as a brewer of philters, he has applied to me, and I have promised him aid. But have no fear. Though employed by him, I am devoted to you, and will effect your deliverance—ay, and avenge you upon your persecutors at the same time—if you follow my instructions exactly. Raise the goblet to your lips again. Quaff its contents without apprehension—they are perfectly harmless. Force smiles to your features—give tenderness to your tones, and softness to your glances—and all will be won."

And with a grin, which, though intended to encourage her, somewhat alarmed Aveline, he took up the flask of wine and departed.

As her singular adviser had predicted, it was not long before the old usurer made his appearance, evidently full of eagerness to ascertain whether any change had been wrought in her disposition towards him by the wonder-working draught. Dissembling her aversion as well as she could, and assuming looks very foreign to her feelings, she easily succeeded in persuading him that the philter had taken effect, and that all obstacles to his happiness were removed. Transported with rapture, he fell upon his knees, and besought her to crown his felicity by consenting to their union on the following day. Bewildered by various emotions, yet still managing to play her part, she returned an answer, which he construed into an affirmative; and now quite beside himself with delight, the amorous old dotard left her.

The alteration in Aveline's manner and deportment towards her persecutor, did not escape the notice of her attendants, and greatly perplexed them. Dame Sherborne ventured to remonstrate with her, hoping she could not be in earnest; and old Anthony Rocke bluntly told her he would rather see her in her grave than the bride of such a hoary reprobate as Sir Francis. Aware that her actions were watched, Aveline thought it best to dissemble, even with her attendants; and they were both convinced she was either bewitched or had lost her senses; and in either case bitterly deplored her fate.

Nor must it be supposed that Aveline herself was without much secret misgiving, however skilfully and courageously she might act her part. The appearance of Luke Hatton, as we have more than once remarked, was calculated to inspire distrust in all brought in contact with him; and with no other proofs of his sincerity except such as were furnished by the circumstances, she might well entertain suspicion of him. While professing devotion, he might intend to betray her. In that event, if driven to extremity, she resolved to liberate herself by the only means that would then be left her.

In the evening, Luke Hatton paid her a second visit; and cn this occasion comported himself with as much caution as at first. He applauded her conduct towards Sir Francis, whom he stated to be most effectually duped, and counselled her to persevere in the same course; adding, with his customary sardonic grin, that grand preparations were making for the wedding-feast, but he thought the cook's labours likely to be thrown away.

Next day, Aveline found all her counsellor had told her was correct. Several of the rooms, hitherto thrown open to her—in especial the great banquetting-chamber—were now closed; and it was evident from the sounds that reached her ear—footsteps hurrying to and fro, loud impatient voices, and noises occasioned by the removal of furniture, and the placing of chairs and tables, together with the clatter of plates and dishes—that preparations for a festival were going on actively within them. Nothing could equal the consternation and distress exhibited by Dame Sherborne and old Anthony Rocke; but, faithful to her scheme, Aveline (however she desired it) did not relieve their anxiety.

At noon, Luke Hatton came again. He seemed in great glee; and informed her that all was going on as well as could be desired. He counselled her to make two requests of Sir Francis. First, that he should endow her with ten thousand marks, to be delivered to her before the nuptials; secondly, that she should be permitted to shroud her features and person in a veil during the marriage ceremony. Without inquiring the meaning of these requests, which, indeed, she partly conjectured, Aveline promised ready compliance; and her adviser left her, but not till he had once more proffered her the supposed philter, and caused her to place the cup containing it to her lips.

Ere long, he was succeeded by Sir Francis, arrayed like a bridegroom, in doublet and hose of white satin, thickly laid with silver lace, and a short French mantle of sky-blue velvet, branched with silver flowers, white roses in his shoes, and drooping white plumes, arranged à l'Espagnolle, in his hat. Besides this, he was trimmed, curled, oiled, and would have got himself ground young again, had such a process been practicable.

But though he could not effect this, he did the next thing to it, and employed all the restoratives suggested by Luke Hatton. He bathed in milk, breakfasted on snail-broth, and swallowed a strange potion prepared for him by the apothecary, which the latter affirmed would make a new man of him and renovate all his youthful ardour. It certainly had produced an extraordinary effect; and when he presented himself before Aveline, his gestures were so extravagant, and his looks so wild and unpleasant, that it was with the utmost difficulty she repressed a scream. His cheeks were flushed, as if with fever, and his eyes dilated and burning with unnatural lustre. He spoke almost incoherently, tossing his arms about, and performing the antics of a madman. The philter; it was clear, had been given him, and he was now under its influence.

Amid all this strange frenzy, so alarming to Aveline, he dwelt upon nothing but his inextinguishable passion, and never for a moment withdrew his fevered gaze from her. He told her he would be her slave for life, proud to wear her chains; and that she should be absolute mistress of his house and all his possessions. On this she mustered up resolution to prefer the requests she had been counselled to make; and Sir Francis, who was in no mood to refuse her anything, at once acceded to them. He laughed at the notion of the veil—said it was a delicate fancy, and quite charmed him—but as to the ten thousand marks, they were utterly unworthy of her acceptance, and she should have thrice the amount delivered to her in a silver coffer before the ceremony. With these, and a great many other professions, he released her from his presence, which had become well-nigh insupportable.

After a while, a magnificent bridal-dress of white satin, richly trimmed with lace, together with a thick white veil of the largest size, calculated to envelope her whole person, were brought her by a young damsel, who told her she was engaged to serve her as tire-woman; adding, that "she hoped she would be able to satisfy her ladyship, as she had already served the Countess of Exeter in that capacity."

"Why do you call me 'ladyship' child?" said Aveline, without looking at her. "I have no right to any such title."

"But you soon will have," replied the young tire-woman; "as the bride of Sir Francis, you must needs be my Lady Mitchell."

Checking the rejoinder that rose to her lips, Aveline cast her eyes, for the first time, on the speaker; and then, to her great surprise, perceived it to be her village acquaintance, Gillian Greenford. A significant glance from the blue eyes of the pretty damsel impressed her with the necessity of caution, and seemed to intimate that Gillian herself was likewise in the plot. And so it presently appeared she was; for when the damsel had an opportunity of talking quite in private to her new mistress, she informed her of the real motive of her coming there.

"I am engaged, by one who wishes you well, to take your place, sweet Mistress Aveline, and to be married in your stead to Sir Francis Mitchell," she said.

"And have you really consented to such an arrangement?" rejoined Aveline. "Is it possible you can sacrifice yourself thus?"

"I am not to be sacrificed," returned the damsel quickly. "If it were so, I would never have agreed to the scheme. But I am told I shall get a fortune, and—"

"Oh, then the ten thousand marks are for you!" interrupted the other. "I now see the meaning of that part of the plan. But what else do you hope to accomplish?"

"The deliverance of my unfortunate lover, Dick Taverner, from the Fleet," she answered.

"But how is your marrying this wicked old usurer to effect your object?" inquired Aveline. "You may save me by the proposed stratagem; but you will destroy your own happiness, and all your lover's hopes."

"No, no, I shall not," replied Gillian, hastily; "I can't tell how it's to be managed, but I am quite sure no harm will happen to me, and that Dick's restoration to liberty will be the reward of the service—if such it may be called—that I am about to render you. He wrote to me so himself."

"At least, tell me by whom you are engaged, and I can then judge of the probability of the rest happening in the way you anticipate?"

"Do not question me further, sweet mistress," replied the damsel, "for I am bound to secrecy. But thus much I may declare—I am the agent of one, who, for some purposes of his own—be they what they may—is determined to counteract all Sir Francis's vile machinations against you, as well as those of his partner, Sir Giles Mompesson, against your lover, Sir Jocelyn Mounchensey. Ah! you understand me now, I perceive, sweet mistress! You have been guarded by this unseen but watchful friend, during the whole of your confinement in this dreadful habitation; and he has kept an equal watch over your lover in the Fleet."

"What! Is Sir Jocelyn a prisoner in the Fleet?" exclaimed Aveline. "I knew it not!"

"He is; but the period of his deliverance approaches," replied Gillian. "The secret friend I spoke of has bided his time, and the hour is at hand when full measure of revenge will be dealt upon those two wicked oppressors. He has long worked towards it; and I myself, am to be an humble instrument towards the great end."

"You astonish me!" cried Aveline, greatly surprised at the change in the damsel's manner as well as by what she said.

"Do not perplex yourself, fair mistress," pursued Gillian. "All will be speedily made known to you. But now, no more time must be lost, and we must each assume the character we have to enact. As I am to be the bride, and you the tire-woman, you must condescend to aid me in putting on these rich robes and then disguise yourself in my rustic attire. We are both pretty nearly of a size, so there is little risk of detection in that particular; and if you can but conceal your features for a short while, on Sir Francis's entrance, the trick will never be discovered. All the rest has been arranged; and I am a mere puppet in the hands of others, to be played as they direct. Bless us! how beautiful this dress is, to-be-sure!—what satin!—and what lace! The Countess of Exeter has just such another. Have you heard that her ladyship has gained her cause against those wicked Lakes, who conspired against her? But what am I saying—when I know you cannot have heard of it! Well, then, it occupied five days in the Star-Chamber; and Sir Thomas and his lady are sent to the Tower, and Sarah Swarton to the Fleet. Poor creature! she is to be whipped and branded, and to do penance in Saint Martin's church. Dreadful! but I won't think of it. I wonder how this dress will become me! How astounded Dick Taverner would be, if he could only see me in it! Mayhap he will—there's no saying. And now, fair mistress, may I crave your aid?"

While Gillian was thus running on, she had partially disrobed herself, and very soon afterwards was decked out in the rich attire, the effect of which upon her own person she was so desirous of ascertaining. When her toilet was complete, she could not help running up to a mirror, and on seeing the reflection of her well-formed figure now displayed to unwonted advantage, she clapped her hands and cried out with girlish delight.

Allowing her to gratify her feelings of vanity by the contemplation of her pretty person for a few minutes, Aveline felt it necessary to recal her to her situation, and her own transformation into the tire-woman was speedily effected,—Gillian's dress fitting her exactly. The light-hearted damsel was quite as much pleased with this change as with the other—and vowed that Aveline looked far better in the rustic gown, than she herself did in the silken attire.

But time pressed; and as Sir Francis might surprise them, they hastened to complete their arrangements. Gillian's comely features, as well as her sumptuous robe, had to be obscured by the envious veil; and as it was thrown over her, she could not help heaving a sigh. Aveline then put on the muffler which had been worn by the country damsel, and their disguises were complete.

Not a minute too soon. At this juncture a tap was heard at a door communicating with the adjoining apartment, and the voice of the old usurer was heard inquiring whether his bride was ready. An answer in the affirmative was given by Aveline, and, with a throbbing heart and faltering steps, Gillian prepared to obey the summons.

The door was thrown open, and mustering up all her resolution, she passed through it. Both Sir Francis and his partner were waiting to receive her. The latter was richly attired, but had not changed the sombre hue of his habiliments, even for the anticipated ceremonial, being clad, as usual, in black. In this respect he offered marked contrast to the gay apparel of the antiquated bridegroom, as well as by the calmness of his deportment and the stern gravity of his looks. Behind them stood Luke Hatton, bearing a heavy silver coffer, of antique workmanship.

"What means this veil?" cried Sir Giles, gazing suspiciously at Gillian as she emerged from the inner room, followed cautiously by Aveline, who was wrapped in the muffler. "Why are the bride's features thus hidden?"

"A mere whim, Sir Giles—a pleasant fancy," replied the old usurer. "But she must have her way. I mean to indulge her in everything."

"You are wrong," rejoined the extortioner. "Make her feel you will be her master. Bid her take it off."

"On no account whatever, Sir Giles. I have only won her by submission, and shall I spoil all at the last moment, by opposing her inclinations? Of a truth not."

"Who is the maiden with her?" demanded Sir Giles, scrutinizing Aveline, with a keen glance. "Why does she wear a muffler? Is that a whim, likewise?"

"Perchance it is," replied Sir Francis; "but I have given no consent to it. She is only the tire-woman."

"Come, mistress, unmuffle. Let us see your face," cried Sir Giles, striding towards the terrified maiden, who thought discovery was now inevitable.

But Luke Hatton interposed to save her.

"Prevent this rudeness," he whispered, plucking Sir Francis's cloak. "Prevent it instantly. If her whim be thwarted, I will not answer for the consequences."

"Desist, Sir Giles—desist, I pray you!" cried the old usurer, in alarm. "It is my bride's wish that her attendant be not interfered with—and mine too."

"Well, be it as you will," replied the extortioner, testily. "But I would not permit the impertinence were I in your case. The bride must raise her veil when she stands before the priest."

"She shall do as she pleases," replied Sir Francis, gallantly. "If she desires to hide her blushes, I will not put any compulsion upon her to disclose them. Come, fair mistress," he added, taking the trembling hand of the veiled maiden, "the priest awaits us in the further chamber, where the ceremony is to take place, and where several of the noble and illustrious guests who have consented to grace our nuptials are already assembled. Some of the most illustrious personages in the land will be present—the Marquis of Buckingham, and perhaps Prince Charles himself. His Excellency the Spanish Ambassador has promised to come. Let us on, then. Yet, ere we proceed further, I have to request your acceptance of that silver coffer. The thirty thousand marks within it constitute your dowry."

As he spoke Luke Hatton advanced, and, holding the coffer towards the veiled damsel, so that she could touch it, said—"Place your hand upon this silver box, and take possession of it, fair mistress. I am a witness that Sir Francis Mitchell has freely bestowed it, with its contents, upon you. It will remain in my custody till you require me to deliver it up to you.

CHAPTER XXX.
HOW THE MARRIAGE WAS INTERRUPTED.

After the presentation of the silver casket, as before described, the whole of the bridal party, with the exception of Aveline, who contrived to remain behind, passed on into the adjoining chamber, where the priest was understood to be in waiting to perform the marriage ceremony.

Apprehensive of the consequences of the discovery which must inevitably be soon made, Aveline would have flown back to her own room, but was deterred, from the strange noises and confusion she heard within it. Uncertain how to act, she at last resolved upon attempting an escape from the house, and was hurrying forward, in the hope of gaining the corridor unperceived, but the sound of voices outside again drove her back; and, in this new dilemma, she had nothing left but to take refuge behind the tapestry covering the walls, which being fortunately loose and hanging upon the ground, effectually concealed her.

Scarcely was she screened from observation in this manner, when the door was thrown open, and a crowd of young gallants— evidently, from their bearing and the richness of their attire, of high rank—entered the apartment. Without exposing herself, Aveline was enabled, through the folds of the tapestry, to command a view of what was going forward. The youthful nobles—for such they were—who had just come in, were laughing loudly; and their jests were chiefly at the expense of the old usurer, whose marriage they had been invited to attend.

After looking round for a moment, as if in search of some one to direct them whither to go, the foremost of them clapped his hands, whereupon the thick curtains which, in lieu of a door, guarded the entrance to the other room, were drawn aside, and disclosed a group of persons collected together within that chamber. In the midst of them were the bride and bridegroom—the former still enveloped in her veil—together with the priest and his assistant. At this sight, the band of youthful nobles set up a shout of laughter, and rushed tumultuously forward, while the curtains, dropping to their place, closed upon the scene.

Presently the outer door again opened, and this time to admit three persons, all of whom were magnificently dressed, and apparently of yet higher rank than those who had preceded them. As they were masked, their features could not be discerned; but they were all distinguished by rare personal grace. One of them, indeed, was remarkable for symmetry of figure, and his finely-proportioned limbs were arrayed in habiliments of the most splendid material, adorned with pearls and precious stones, and richly embroidered. Yet he did not seem to hold the chief place among them: that, by common consent, seemed accorded to a young man clad in black velvet, who, by the majesty of his deportment and the gravity of his manner, appeared to exercise a certain sway over his companions, and to be treated by them, when he spoke, with marked respect. The third individual was habited in a Spanish-cloak of murrey-velvet, lined with cloth of silver, branched with murrey-flowers, and wore a chain of gold, richly set with precious stones, round his neck, from which depended the order of the Golden Fleece.

There was something in the presence of these three important personages that gave Aveline a feeling of security, such as she had not experienced since her forcible detention by the two extortioners, and she almost felt inclined to throw herself at the feet of the one who appeared to be the principal of them, and solicit his protection. But before she could execute her half-formed design, the party had approached the entrance of the nuptial chamber; and the curtain being raised for their admittance, excluded them, the next moment, from her view.

All now appearing quiet, she again ventured from her hiding-place, and speeded towards the door communicating with the gallery. But her departure was unexpectedly interrupted by the sudden entrance of another masked personage, tall in stature, and habited entirely in black; and in him she could not fail to recognise the messenger employed by Sir Giles Mompesson to bring her, in the first instance, to his habitation. Circumstances had subsequently occurred to induce her to change her opinion respecting this mysterious individual. Nevertheless, his appearance at this juncture would have caused her to utter a cry of terror, if she had not been reassured by the timely appearance of one upon whom she had reliance, and who raised his finger to his lips in token of silence. This was Luke Hatton, who, at the very moment that Lanyere appeared, issued from the chamber where the marriage ceremony was being performed.

"Be not alarmed, fair maiden," said Lanyere, in a low voice, "you are in no danger; and all your troubles, I trust, are well-nigh ended. I thought you were in the marriage-chamber. Give me your hand. You must assist at the mock ceremonial taking place within there. I have no time for explanations; and indeed they are needless, since all will be speedily made clear to you. Divest yourself, I pray you, of this muffler. It is part of my plan that your features should now be revealed. You will understand why, anon."

With this, he led her quickly towards the entrance of the inner chamber; and, pushing aside the curtain, advanced a few steps beyond it, still holding her by the hand, and followed by Luke Hatton.

The apartment, which was of considerable size and splendidly furnished, was full of wedding-guests, grouped around that portion of it which was railed off for the accommodation of those more immediately connected with the ceremonial, amongst whom, as a matter of course, was Sir Giles Mompesson.

Somewhat apart from the others were the three important persons who had arrived last; and the most exalted among them was seated on a raised chair, contemplating the scene, while his companions stood near him. They had now taken off their masks; and, even in that agitating moment Aveline recognised in the trio the Marquis of Buckingham, the Conde de Gondomar, and Prince Charles. All the rest of the company remained standing; and some of the young nobles formed a small semicircle behind the royal chair.

Lanyere's entrance with his fair companion could not have been better timed. They arrived at the particular juncture when Sir Francis, having presented the wedding-ring to the priest was in the act of receiving it back from him, in order that it might be placed upon the finger of the bride; and the noise made by the promoter, who still wore his vizard, drew all eyes upon him, and upon the damsel by whom he was accompanied.

A smile of intelligence passed between Prince Charles and Buckingham; and some remark was made by the latter, to which the Prince replied by a gesture, seeming to intimate that the interruption was not altogether unexpected by him. De Gondomar's looks also betrayed that he was likewise in the secret.

Others of the company laughed as if in anticipation of a jest; but the majority looked surprised—but none so much so as Sir Giles Mompesson. As his eye fell upon the dark and ominous figure of Lanyere, and shifted from him to Aveline, he appeared transported with rage; and dashing the ring from the hand of the astonished bridegroom (who, having his back toward the newcomers, was unaware of what was going forward), exclaimed—"Proceed no further! We have been deceived! Look there!"

"Where? where?" cried Sir Francis. "What is the matter, Sir Giles? You quite terrify me with your fierce looks. Help me to pick up the ring, and let the ceremony go on."

"It is well for you that it is *not* completed," replied Sir Giles, almost black in the face with choler. "You know not whom you are about to wed. But we will soon see. Off with your veil, minion! Off with it, I say!"

"Sir Giles, I will not permit this liberty," cried the old usurer. "You shall not touch her. Whom should it be but my own dear, delectable Aveline?"

"Look round, I say, and credit your own eyes, since you doubt my assertions!" roared Sir Giles.

"Ten thousand furies!" ejaculated Sir Francis, as he complied with the injunction. "Why, there she is, in good truth, when I thought she was by my side. Whom, then, have I been about to take to my bosom?"

"It matters not," replied Sir Giles. "She you desired to wed is yonder, and must take the other's place. That is—but I forget," he added, suddenly checking himself, and lowering his tone, "naught can be done, except according to rule, in this presence. Your vanity must needs be gratified by bringing together all this courtly company to witness your marriage. And now they will only mock you."

"S'death! you are right, Sir Giles," rejoined the old usurer. "I am become a mere laughing-stock to my guests. But at least I will see my false bride's features. You hear what I say, Madam," he added to Gillian—"let me behold your face without more ado."

As he uttered the command, the damsel threw off her veil, and stood blushing, half-smiling and half-abashed, before the assemblage. Her natural charms, heightened by her attire, and by the peculiar situation in which she was placed, elicited general admiration.

"As I live, 'tis the pretty tirewoman from Tottenham, engaged by Luke Hatton to attend on Aveline," cried Sir Francis; "but, 'fore Heaven, I have gained by the exchange. I like her better than the other, and will go through with the ceremony. Proceed, Sir Priest."

At this declaration there was a shout of laughter from the assemblage; but the merriment was increased, when Do Gondomar, stepping up to the bride, said, "I forbid the marriage. She belongs to me."

"But my claim is paramount to that of your Excellency," cried the old usurer.

"I cannot admit it," rejoined the other. "Let the damsel decide for herself."

"Then I will accept neither," said Gillian. "Dick Taverner is already master of my heart, and no one but he shall have my hand. I have been brought here to play a part, on the clear understanding that nothing serious was to come of it."

"And nothing serious shall come of it, fair maiden," said Prince Charles. "I promise that on my princely faith."

"Then, indeed, I am easy," replied Gillian, inclining herself reverentially towards the royal speaker.

At this juncture, Sir Giles Mompesson, who had been hitherto restrained by the presence of the royal guest from any violent measures, was advancing with menacing looks towards Lanyere, when the attention of Charles being directed to his movements by Buckingham, the Prince instantly arose, and in a tone of authority not to be disputed, said—

"Not a step further, Sir Giles. I will take care that all needful explanations be given."

"But your Highness cannot be aware that this is a heinous offender and traitor," rejoined Sir Giles, pointing to Lanyere. "I was about to take means to prevent his escape."

"He has no intention of escaping," rejoined Charles; "and I forbid any one to leave this apartment without my permission."

"Will your Highness suffer me to relieve this fair creature from the embarrassing position in which she is placed," said De Gondomar. "The youth she has mentioned, and to whom she declares her affections are given, was confined in the Fleet Prison for an attack on me; but, on my representation of the matter to the King, your father, his Majesty's gracious consent was immediately accorded for his liberation."

"I am aware of it, Count," replied Prince Charles.

"But your Highness may not be aware that the poor fellow is without," pursued the Ambassador. "Will it please you to allow him to be brought in?"

The Prince assented, on which De Gondomar signed to Luke Hatton, who seemed waiting for the order, and, disappearing for a moment, returned with the apprentice.

Though evidently prepared for the scene that awaited him, and not overburthened with modesty, Dick Taverner could not help exhibiting considerable confusion; but the sight of his mistress somewhat restored him, and he pressed towards her. Sir Francis, however, stepped between them, exclaiming—"Get hence, base varlet—she is my wife."

"No such thing!" cried Gillian—"the ceremony has only been half performed. I am *not* married. I am yours—and yours only, dear, sweet Dickon."

"You never shall be his—you are mine—" exclaimed the old usurer—"I implore his Highness the Prince to let the marriage go forward."

"Nay, I shall not allow any compulsion to be placed on the damsel's inclinations," replied Charles, unable to repress a smile. "She must choose for herself."

"In that case, your Highness, my choice is soon made," replied Gillian, taking her lover's hand.

"And honest Dickon need not be under any alarm at such part of the marriage as has already taken place," observed De Gondomar. "It has been a mock ceremonial throughout. This is no priest, but one of my Lord of Buckingham's grooms employed for the occasion."

"Then I have been a dupe all this time!" cried Sir Francis furiously. "O, purblind dolt that I am!"

But he met with no commiseration from the assemblage, who only laughed at his rage and absurd grimaces.

"Kneel and thank his Highness for his goodness," said De Gondomar to the young couple; "and then, if he will give you leave to do so, depart at once. Stay not a moment longer than you can help it in this house, or in the neighbourhood."

"Most assuredly I will not, your Excellency," returned Dick. "It is much too near the Fleet to be agreeable to me. I have to offer my heartfelt thanks to your Excellency for your kindly consideration of me, and I own that I have scarcely deserved it at your hands."

"Render your thanks, as I have said, to his Highness, who is alone entitled to them, good fellow," said the Ambassador. "Take Gillian home to her grandsire—and wed her as soon as you can. She will need no dowry," he added in a low tone—"for she is already provided with thirty thousand marks."

"Honestly come by, I hope, your Excellency?" inquired Dick.

"Ay, ay—thou suspicious blockhead. Do as I have bidden thee, and get hence. More remains to be done to which thou art a hindrance."

On this, the young couple prostrated themselves before Prince Charles, who graciously gave his hand to Gillian to kiss, and then motioning them to rise, they were allowed to quit the room.

Luke Hatton saw them safe out of the house, and very well it was he accompanied them, for they had many obstacles to encounter. Before quitting them, the apothecary delivered up the silver casket to Dick, bidding him take good care of it, as it contained his intended wife's dowry.

Meanwhile, Sir Giles Mompesson, who had with difficulty controlled his impatience during the incidents previously described, advanced towards Prince Charles, and with a profound reverence, said—"Will it please your Highness to terminate this idle scene, which, though apparently amusing to the company assembled, is by no means so entertaining to Sir Francis and myself?"

"You shall have your wish, Sir," rejoined Charles in a stern tone and with a freezing look, that seemed of ill augury to the extortioner—"It is my intention to terminate the scene. Stand forth, Clement Lanyere and let me hear what you have to declare in reference to this man."

Hereupon, the promoter, consigning Aveline to the care of a gentleman who advanced towards her for the purpose, and respectfully took her hand, stepped forward, and, removing his mask, confronted his enemy.

CHAPTER XXXI.
ACCUSATIONS.

By this time a very different complexion had been imparted to the scene. The interruption of the marriage ceremony, and the perplexities of the old usurer, tricked out of his intended bride, and bereft even of her substitute, had afforded abundant amusement to the company, who, so far from feeling pity for the sufferer, seemed vastly to enjoy his mortification and disappointment. But all laughter died away, and every tongue became suddenly mute, as Prince Charles, assuming the severe look and dignified deportment of a judge, commanded Clement Lanyere to stand forward, and prefer the charges he had to make against Sir Giles Mompesson.

All eyes were fixed upon the extortioner and his accuser; and though etiquette prevented the company from advancing too near the royal seat, a dense semicircle was formed in front of it, in the midst of which stood the two principal actors in the drama about to take place, together with the discomfited Sir Francis Mitchell.

Sir Giles Mompesson was not without great misgivings. He saw that his case was already prejudged by the Prince; and the glance of inquiry with which he had consulted his patron, the Marquis of Buckingham, and which was answered by a cold, menacing regard, convinced him that little support was to be expected in that quarter. Nevertheless, though he felt himself in considerable jeopardy, he allowed no look or gesture indicative of uneasiness to escape him; and the courage that had borne him through many a trial still remained unshaken. Not so Sir Francis Mitchell. He also perceived the perilous position in which he and his partner were placed, and his abject manner showed how thoroughly he was daunted. Look wherever he would, he found no sympathy: every one derided his distress.

But far more than the two extortioners did their accuser command attention. As he cast off his mask and displayed his appalling features, a thrill of surprise and horror pervaded such of the assemblage as had never seen them before. But the feeling was speedily lost in wonder. Drawing himself up to his full height, so that his lofty figure towered above those with whom he was confronted, he seemed to dart lightning glances against them. Even Sir Giles could not bear his scathing looks, and would have shielded himself from them if he could. Though fearful to behold, Lanyere's countenance had a terrible purpose impressed upon it which none could mistake. The effect produced by his appearance upon the spectators was shared even by Prince Charles, and a few minutes elapsed before the silence was broken. At length, the Prince again spoke:—

"I sit here," he said, "as the representative of the Majesty of England—clothed with the authority of my royal father, and prepared to exercise it, as he would do were he present in person. But though this seat is erected into a tribunal before which accusations against wrong-doers can be brought, and sentence upon them pronounced; still, whatever charges are now made, and against whomsoever they may be preferred, those charges will have to be repeated to the Lords of the Council of the Star-Chamber, before whom the accused will be taken; and any judgment now given will have to be confirmed by that high and honourable Court. Of late, the course of justice has been too often baffled and turned aside by the craft and subtlety of certain powerful and audacious offenders. Hence it has been the wish of the King's Highness, in order that the laws may no longer be broken with impunity, that certain preliminary inquiries and investigations should be made on the spot itself, where it is alleged that the crimes and misdemeanours have been committed; and, according to the evidence afforded, such measures as may be deemed fitting taken against the wrong-doers. All present have witnessed this mock ceremonial, and have laughed at its conclusion, but mirth will be changed to indignation, when it is known that the intended marriage was the result of a vile conspiracy on the part of Sir Giles Mompesson and Sir Francis Mitchell, against a young, virtuous, and unprotected maiden, whose beauty had inflamed the breast of the elder, and it might have been expected from that circumstance, the wiser of the two. Into the details of their infamous scheme, it will not be necessary now to enter; and it may suffice to say, that the devoted attachment of the damsel to another was wholly disregarded, while the basest means were employed to induce her consent to a match so abhorrent to her feelings, as must have been that with Sir Francis. Failing in this, however, the two conspirators went yet further. They forcibly carried off the maiden from her own dwelling, and detained her against her will within this house, till by their arts they imagined they had gained their point—and that a love-potion would accomplish all for them, that their persuasions and fair promises were unable to effect. But the damsel was guarded from all ill by an unseen friend—and the weapons of the conspirators were turned against themselves. You have witnessed how they have been duped, and, as no mischief has resulted from this infamous endeavour, the mortification they have endured may be taken as part punishment of the offence. Stand forward, fair Mistress Aveline Calveley, and substantiate what I have just declared."

Thus adjured, the maiden approached within a few paces of the Prince, and having made a lowly salutation, said,—

"All that your Highness has advanced concerning me is correct."

"Enough, fair mistress," rejoined Charles. "How say you, Sirs," he continued, in a stern tone, to the two extortioners. "Do you confess your guilt, and sue for pardon? If so, down on your knees before this injured damsel, and implore her forgiveness!"

A prey to violent terror, the old usurer instantly adopted the supplicatory posture recommended by the Prince; but Sir Giles refused compliance.

"Having committed no offence, I sue for no pardon," he said, with his wonted audacity. "I repel the charge with indignation; and, in my turn, accuse Clement Lanyere and Luke Hatton of a conspiracy against me. This damsel is but their tool, as I will show, if your Highness will deign to give ear to me."

"It were mere waste of time to listen to idle fabrications," replied Charles. "The evidence against you is complete, and my opinion upon it is formed. But what saith the maiden herself? Is she willing that any grace be shown her persecutors?"

"The redress I have already obtained at the hands of your Highness is amply sufficient," replied Aveline. "Great as has been the misery these two persons have occasioned me, and grievously as they have sought to injure me, I seek no further satisfaction; but would implore your Highness to pardon them. Their own thoughts will be punishment enough."

"Amply sufficient—for nothing can be more bitter," cried the old usurer, while a scornful smile curled Sir Giles's lips.

"Spoken as I expected you would speak, fair maiden," said Charles; "and, were there nothing else against them, I might listen to your kindly intercessions. But other and darker disclosures have to be made; and when you have heard all, even your compassionate breast may be steeled against them. Retire for a moment; but do not leave the room. Your presence may yet be needed."

And bowing graciously to Aveline, she withdrew under the care of the gentleman who had brought her forward, but still remained a spectatress of the scene.

"And now to proceed with the investigation," pursued Charles. "What have you to allege against the two persons before you?" he added, to Clement Lanyere.

"Were I to relate all their enormities, most gracious Prince," replied the promoter, "the recital would be too painful for your hearing, and that of this noble assemblage. But I will, in a word, declare that there is no kind of outrage, oppression, and extortion of which they have not been guilty. Their insatiable greediness has been fed by constant plunder; and, alike cruel and rapacious, nothing but the ruin and absolute destruction of their victims would content them. Merciless as creditors, they have ground their unfortunate debtors to the dust. The tears of the widow they have robbed of her husband and her means of existence—the despair of the orphan, whose fair prospects they have blighted—have failed to move them. Utterly unscrupulous as to the means of obtaining possession of property, they have forged wills, deeds, and other documents. Their ingenuity has been taxed to devise new means of unjust gain; and, imposing upon the King's Majesty by false representations, they have succeeded in obtaining his letters patent for certain monopolies, which they have so shamefully abused, as to bring his sovereign authority into discredit."

"Hold!" cried Sir Giles Mompesson. "To the first—vague and general accusations brought against me and my co-patentee, by this branded traitor, who, having been publicly punished for falsehood and libel, cannot be received as a witness, I have deigned no answer, conceiving such accusations cannot be for a moment entertained by you, most gracious Prince. But to this specific charge, I give a flat denial; and demand proof of it. I appeal to the most noble Marquis of Buckingham, through whose interest Sir Francis Mitchell and myself obtained those patents for the licences of inspection of inns and hostelries, as well as for the manufacture of gold and silver lace, whether he has ever heard aught to our disparagement in our conduct of them?"

"Do not appeal to me, Sir," replied Buckingham, coldly.

"Sir Giles has demanded proof of my charge, and I am prepared to produce it," said Lanyere. "As to the vagueness of my accusations, your Highness will judge of that when the full catalogue of the offences of these two extortioners, with the damnatory proofs of them, shall be laid before you. This memorial, signed by nearly the whole of the sufferers from their exactions, perpetrated by means of the monopolies, will satisfy your Highness of the truth of my statement— but I have also a witness to call."

"A witness!—here!" muttered Sir Giles, uneasily. "This must be a deeply-concerted scheme."

"Before you bring forward any one," said Charles, addressing Lanyere, "Sir Giles must be set right on one point in which he is in error. Your credibility is not to be disputed, and I accept your testimony against him."

"Your Highness!" cried the extortioner.

"Peace, Sir! you shall be heard anon," said Charles. "Produce your witness," he added to Lanyere.

At a sign from the promoter, Luke Hatton, who was standing near the doorway, stepped behind the tapestry, and almost immediately reappearing with Madame Bonaventure, led her towards the Prince, before whom she prostrated herself.

"Arise, Madame," said Charles, graciously. "Your features are not unfamiliar to me. Methinks you are the hostess of the French ordinary at the tavern of the Three Cranes, in the Vintry."

"Tour Highness is in the right—I am Madame Bonaventure, at your Highness's service," replied the hostess, enchanted at this recognition on the part of the Prince. "My lord of Buckingham, I am well persuaded, will condescend to speak to the merits and respectability of my establishment."

"In sooth will I, good hostess," replied the Marquis. "I can give your Bordeaux my heartiest commendation. 'Tis the best in London."

"Nay, I can speak to it myself—and to the good order of the house too; having visited the tavern incognito," remarked the Prince, smiling.

"Is it possible!" exclaimed Madame Bonaventure, rapturously. "Have I been so greatly honoured? Mon Dieu!—and not to be aware of it!"

"I must remind you of the cause of your appearance here, Madame Bonaventure," said Lanyere.

"You are required to depose before his Highness as to the exactions you suffered from Sir Giles and his partner."

"His Highness shall hear all from me," rejoined the hostess. "I should have been reduced to beggary had I submitted to their extortionate usage. I bore it as long as I could, but when absolute ruin stared me in the face, I had recourse to a noble friend who helped me in my extremity and delivered me by a, stratagem."

"It was a fraudulent scheme," cried Sir Giles;—"a fraud upon his Majesty, as well as upon those who enjoyed the privileges conferred by his letters patent."

"That I can contradict, Sir," said Buckingham, "since I myself was present on the occasion, and stated in the hearing of the large company then assembled,—several of whom are now before us,—that his Majesty relinquished all share of the ruinous fine of three thousand marks imposed by you and your co-patentee upon this good woman."

"And I trust you added, my Lord, that the King's Highness would never knowingly consent to have his exchequer enriched by such shameful means," said Charles, with a look of indignation. "These monopolies were not granted by his Majesty for the wrongful profit of their holders; and, since they have been turned to such iniquitous use, I will take upon me to declare that they shall all be suppressed. Do you attempt to deny," he continued to Sir Giles, "that this outrageous fine was imposed?"

"It were useless to deny it," replied the extortioner, with a malicious look at Buckingham; "but the noble Marquis has not always disapproved so strongly of my proceedings. Nay, I can show that he himself has been secretly a party to like transactions."

"Ah, villain!" exclaimed Buckingham,—"do you venture to calumniate your protector? I shall leave you to the fate you so richly merit. Your foul and false assertions cannot affect me; but they are not likely to improve your case with his Highness, who, though aware of its impotency, will perceive the extent of your malice. If you dared, I doubt not you would likewise assert that his Majesty himself was cognisant of your frauds and oppressions, and approved them."

"I do assert, and will maintain it—ay, and prove it, too—that the King's Highness was aware how these monopolies were managed, and derived a considerable revenue from them," said Sir Giles.

"You hear him, Prince," remarked Buckingham, with a disdainful smile.

"I would not have believed in such matchless effrontery had I not witnessed it," replied Charles. "You may retire, Madame," he added to the hostess, who, with a profound reverence, withdrew. "Have you aught further to declare, or any other witnesses to produce?" he continued to Lanyere.

"I have both, your Highness," replied the promoter.

"What more false accusations have you to bring against me?" demanded Sir Giles, folding his arms upon his breast, and fixing his keen gaze upon Lanyere.

"His Highness shall hear," replied the promoter. "I have a multitude of cases which I could adduce in support of my charges—all of which will be mentioned in due season—but I shall now content myself with one, and from it the nature of the rest may be inferred. But let me premise that, in the greater part of these cases, and in all the more important of them, where grievous and irreparable wrong has been committed, the engine employed by these crafty and dangerous men has been the Star-Chamber."

"The Star-Chamber!" exclaimed Charles, bending his brows.

"Your Highness will now perceive the drift of this cunning knave's argument," said Sir Giles. "Through me and my partner, all whose actions will bear the strictest scrutiny, he would covertly attack that high and honourable Court, whose dignity we have ever been most zealous to maintain; and his motive for doing so is because he has incurred its censure. When I have heard his precise charges, I will reply to them—ay, one by one—if he will bring forward the multitude of cases he affirms he can produce against me. But meanwhile I can fearlessly declare my innocence of the wrong imputed to me. If I have been to blame in those monopolies, I am not the only one in fault, as time will show. Nay, there are greater culprits than I"—looking hard at Buckingham, who regarded him disdainfully—"but I deny that I have done more than I can fully justify. As regards other matters, and the way in which my wealth has been acquired, I have acted only with caution, prudence, and foresight. Is it my fault that there are so many persons who, from various causes, will have money, no matter what they pay for it? If they apply to me under such circumstances, and ruin ensues to them, am I to blame? I lend monies as a usurer—all men know it. 'Tis my vocation, and that of my partner; and my answer is his answer. We have done nothing beyond the law; and the law, which has hitherto supported us, will support us still. To affirm that we have employed the highest court of the kingdom as an instrument of oppression and extortion is an assertion too monstrous to obtain a moment's credit. The Star-Chamber is too jealous of its honour not to resent the imputation; and such a charge will not escape its censure."

"Nevertheless, at whatever risk, I repeat the accusation," rejoined Lanyere; "and my words will not be forgotten by his Highness, and by all others who hear them. I assert that Sir Giles Mompesson has subtly and designedly perverted the practice of that high and honourable Court, causing it to aid his schemes of rapacity and injustice, and using it as a means of stifling the cries of his victims, and working out his purposes of vengeance. Hitherto, he has succeeded in masking his designs with so much skill that they have escaped detection; but when the mischief he has done under the mask of justice, and the wrongs and cruelties he has perpetrated in the name of the law shall be fully made known, no punishment will be deemed commensurate to his crimes. It is chiefly he and his partner who, by their evil doings, have brought the Star-Chamber into disrepute, and made it a terror to all just men, who have dreaded being caught within the toils woven around it by these infamous wretches; and the Court will do well to purge itself of such villanies, and make a terrible example of those who have so dishonoured it."

"The Star-Chamber will never desert its faithful servants, and such we have been," said Sir Giles.

"Say rather the serpents it has nourished in its bosom," rejoined Lanyere. "But to my case. Years ago, a gentleman possessed of noble estates in Norfolk, was unfortunate enough to have some dealings with these two usurers, who thus becoming acquainted with his circumstances, marked him for their prey. He borrowed a large sum of money from them. The loan was not obtained for himself, but for a younger brother"—here the voice of the promoter was choked with emotion, and a few moments elapsed before he could proceed—"I have said that the money was borrowed, not for himself, but for a younger brother, whose recklessness and extravagance had plunged him deeply in debt. Would that his too generous relative had left him to his fate, and allowed him to rot in a dungeon! But he rescued him from it, only to take his place in the end. From this sad epoch may all the unfortunate gentleman's calamities be dated. Certain title-deeds and other instruments had to be deposited with Sir Giles and his partner, as security for repayment of the sum borrowed. They were never returned. On the contrary, under one plea or another, all the deeds relating to the property were obtained from its unsuspecting owner; and then a mortgage deed covering the whole estates was forged by them."

"'Tis false!" exclaimed Sir Giles.

"Have I your Highness's gracious promise of pardon to all except the principals in these great offences?" pursued Lanyere.

"As it may materially serve the ends of justice that such promise should be given, I do not hesitate to comply with your request," replied Charles.

"In that case I shall be able to confound the villains with a witness whom they little expect to be produced against them," replied Lanyere. "Let Lupo Vulp be called," he added.

The summons was responded to as before by Luke Hatton, and the next moment the ill-favoured scrivener emerged from behind the tapestry, and made his way through the assemblage, who recoiled with abhorrence from him, towards the Prince.

"Who art thou?" demanded Charles.

"I am named Lupo Vulp, your Highness, and have for many years been a money-scrivener in the employ of these two gentlemen," replied the individual addressed.

"Thou knowest all their transactions?" said Charles.

"No man better," answered Lupo; "unless it be Clement Lanyere."

"You remember a certain deed of mortgage from Sir Ferdinando Mounchensey to your two employers?" said Lanyere.

"I remember it perfectly," returned the scrivener, "as I should do, seeing I prepared it myself."

During all this time Lupo Vulp had kept his eyes upon the ground, and had never dared to raise them towards Sir Giles, though he felt that the gaze of the latter was fixed upon him.

"Was Sir Ferdinando's signature attached to that deed?" demanded Lanyere.

"Look at me, Lupo, ere thou answerest," cried Sir Giles. "Look at me well—and take heed what thou say'st."

"Be not influenced by him," interposed Charles. "Look only at me, and speak truly, as thou valuest thy safety. If thou hidest aught, or falsifiest aught, the heaviest punishment awaits thee!"

"Hark ye, Lupo," said Sir Giles, in a low tone. "Be warned by me. Utter a word to my detriment, and as surely as thou art suborned to injure me, I will hang thee. I *can* do so, as thou knowest!"

"Fear him not, Lupo," said Lanyere. "Thou hast his Highness's gracious promise of pardon."

"If my life be but spared, most gracious Prince," said the scrivener, falling on his knees, and clasping his hands together in supplication, "I will reveal all I know touching the malpractices of these two persons."

"Speak, then, without fear," said Charles.

"I repeat my question," said Lanyere, "and demand an explicit answer to it. What was the nature of that deed?"

"It was a forgery," replied the scrivener. "Sir Ferdinando Mounchensey had nothing whatever to do with it. His signature was imitated from other deeds in the possession of my employers, and his seal was likewise fabricated."

"What say you to this, Sir?" said Charles, to Sir Giles.

"I deny it, as I do all the rest," he replied. "'Tis a foul conspiracy against me, as will appear in the end."

"This is only one amongst many such frauds committed by them, your Highness," said the scrivener. "Since I have your gracious promise of pardon, I will make a clean breast of it, and reveal all I know. Many and many a fair estate has been wrongfully wrested from its owner in this way—by forged deed or will. I will name all the parties to your Highness."

"Hereafter, I will listen to thee," rejoined Charles, motioning him to rise; "but I shall now confine myself to the case immediately before me. Proceed, Sir," he added, to Lanyere.

"I have come to the saddest and darkest part of all," said the promoter. "Your Highness has seen that a deed was forged to obtain possession of the Mounchensey estates—and the fraudulent design was only too successful. It was in vain Sir Ferdinando denied all knowledge of the instrument—in vain he refused payment of the large sum demanded—his estates were seized by the extortioners—and he was deprived of the power of redemption. He commenced a suit against them in the Star-Chamber, but here again he was baffled by the cunning and knavery of Sir Giles, and having unwittingly incurred the censure of the Court, he was cast into the Fleet Prison, where he perished miserably."

"A lamentable history," exclaimed Charles. "It is grievous to think that justice cannot be done him."

"Justice may be done his son," said Buckingham, "who has been oppressed in like manner with his father. Restitution may be made him of the estates of which he has been plundered."

"It is well," said Sir Giles, glancing at Lanyere. "You will not enjoy them."

"What means he?" inquired Charles.

"The estates were assigned to this treacherous knave, your Highness," said Sir Giles, pointing to Lanyere, "for a certain consideration, which was never performed. But, while denying, as I do most energetically, that any underhand means whatever were used by us to obtain possession of those estates, and repeating my declaration that a most artful conspiracy has been formed against us,

I assert, as will appear on investigation, that if I fail in sustaining my claim to the Mounchensey estates, they cannot go to Sir Jocelyn."

"Wherefore not?" inquired Charles.

"Because Sir Ferdinando left them to his brother Osmond. I have possession of his will."

"It may be a forgery," said Charles.

"Not so, your Highness," observed Lupo Vulp. "This statement is correct."

"I have it with me now," cried Sir Giles, producing a document. "Will it please your Highness to look at it?" he added, handing it to the Prince. "You will see that the estates are wholly left to Osmond Mounchensey. If, therefore, your Highness should seek to deprive me of them, you must bestow them as they are herein bequeathed."

"Undoubtedly, if this instrument be valid," said Charles, looking at Lanyere.

"I do not dispute it, your Highness," said the promoter.

"But there is no proof that Osmond Mounchensey is living, your Highness," observed Lupo Vulp. "He has not been heard of for many years—not, indeed, since the time when his debts were paid by Sir Ferdinando. Though Sir Giles has used every exertion for the purpose, he has never been able to discover any traces of him—and it is reasonable, therefore, to suppose that he is no more."

"That is false," cried Sir Giles. "It is true I have long sought for him in vain—but within these few days I have obtained some tidings of him, which, if followed up, will assuredly lead to his detection. Nay more, Lanyere himself must know that he is alive, since, from the intelligence I have received, he must have been recently in company with him."

"Is this assertion correct?" said Charles, to the promoter.

"It is, your Highness," replied Lanyere; "but I had good reasons for concealing the circumstances."

"Undoubtedly," cried Sir Giles; "because you had ascertained from the traitor Lupo that this will existed, and feared a claim might be advanced to the estates—but they will never be yours, or Sir Jocelyn's. If not mine, they are Osmond Mounchensey's."

"He says right," remarked Charles.

"Then learn to your confusion, villain, that Osmond Mounchensey stands before you!" cried the promoter, addressing Sir Giles. "Behold him in me!"

"You Osmond Mounchensey!" exclaimed Sir Giles; eyeing him with an astonishment which was shared by Sir Francis and by the greater part of the spectators. To judge from their manner, however, Prince Charles, together with Buckingham and De Gondomar, did not seem unprepared for the announcement.

"Ay," rejoined Osmond to Sir Giles. "Look on me if you can. Never should my name have been revealed to you, except at a moment when there should have been no chance of its repetition, on your part, but for my brother's will, of the existence of which I have only been lately aware, and which has obliged me to avow myself. But for this, I would have remained for ever in obscurity, and have perished as I have lived—the despised Clement Lanyere. The name of Mounchensey should not have been shamed in me. But if I am the reproach of that ancient and honourable house—untarnished by any other member of it—I am also its avenger, and will wipe out effectually the stains you have cast upon it. By your machinations, villain, was my brother destroyed—by your machinations has his son been imprisoned, and his life endangered—by your machinations I myself was censured by the terrible Star-Chamber, and its severest punishments inflicted upon me. You knew not whom you tortured; and had you been aware of my real name, even this wrong might not have contented you. But no matter. From the hour when the tormentor, by your order, did his work upon me, I devoted myself to vengeance—slow, sure vengeance. I resolved not to interfere with your career of villany till you were full-blown in crime; and though I have had some difficulty in holding back my hand, I have been patient. The hour at length has arrived, and I hold you firmly in my grasp. I have crushed in pieces the whole of the fabric you have been at such pains to rear. Your estates and all your possessions will be forfeited to the Crown; and, if you escape with life, you will bear the indelible marks of disgrace which you have inflicted upon me!"

Overpowered by what he heard, Sir Giles threw himself at the feet of Charles.

"Do not sue to me, Sir," replied the Prince, regarding him with stern displeasure. "Enough for you to know that I have been in this much-injured gentleman's secret. Let your nephew now be introduced, Sir," he added, to Osmond Mounchensey.

"His nephew!" muttered Sir Giles, as he arose. "Nay, then, all is indeed lost!"

"I have felt that for a long time," groaned Sir Francis.

CHAPTER XXXII.
JUDGMENT.

On the intimation of the Prince's wishes, the tapestry was again raised to admit Sir Jocelyn Mounchensey, who, stepping forward, made a profound reverence to the Prince.

"I greet you well, Sir Jocelyn," said Charles, in the kindest and most gracious tone, as the young knight advanced towards him. "As your disgrace was public, so shall your restoration to the King's favour be likewise public. Your return to Court will be a satisfaction to his Majesty. Any imprudence of which you have been guilty will be entirely overlooked. All graver faults imputed to you have been explained—so that no unfavourable impressions against you remain upon my royal father's mind—or on mine. Let me assure you that you have now no more zealous friends than the Conde de Gondomar and the Marquis of Buckingham."

"For any wrong I may have done Sir Jocelyn I am heartily sorry," said Buckingham, frankly. "And he may rely on my present oiler of friendship."

"And on mine, too," subjoined De Gondomar. "The services I have rendered him must be set against any mischief I have subsequently done."

"You make me more than amends," said Sir Jocelyn, bowing to them, "and I at once accept your proffered friendship."

"You are in the midst of friends and foes, Sir Jocelyn," said Prince Charles, "and have before you a new-found relative; and not far distant from you one, whom—unless I am greatly mistaken—has the strongest hold upon your affections; but before you turn to her, or to any one, listen to the sentence, which in the King's name I shall pronounce upon those two offenders—a sentence which most assuredly will be ratified by his Majesty in person, and by the Lords of the Council of the Star-Chamber, before whom they will be brought.

Hear me, then, ye wrong-doers. Ye shall be despoiled of your unjustly-acquired possessions, which will be escheated to the Crown. Where restitution is possible, it shall be made."

"Restitution by the Crown!—a likely thing!" muttered Sir Giles.

"Moreover, ye shall pay for your misdeeds in person," pursued Charles. "Degraded from the knighthood ye have dishonoured, and with all the ceremonies of debasement, when ye have become Giles Mompesson and Francis Mitchell, knaves, ye shall undergo precisely the same ignominious punishment, with all its dreadful details, which ye caused to be inflicted upon him you supposed to be Clement Lanyere. This being done to you, and no part of the torture being on any plea omitted, ye shall be brought back to the Fleet Prison, and be there incarcerated for the residue of your lives."

Mompesson heard this sentence apparently unmoved, though his flashing eye betrayed, in some degree, his secret emotion. Not so his partner. Flinging himself on his knees before the Prince, he cried in piteous tones—"I confess my manifold offences, and own that my sentence is lenient in comparison with them. But I beseech your Highness to spare me the mutilation and branding. All else I will patiently endure."

"He merits no compassion," said Buckingham, "and yet I would intercede for him."

"And your intercession shall avail to the extent which he himself hath mentioned—but no further," rejoined Charles.

"I solicit nothing—and I confess nothing," said Mompesson, in a tone of defiance. "If I am ever brought to trial I shall know how to defend myself. But I well know that will never be. I can make such revelations concerning those in high places—ay, in the highest places," he added, with a vindictive look at Buckingham, "that they will not dare to molest me."

"The hound must be muzzled," said Buckingham, in a low tone, to the Prince.

"He must," replied Charles. "Let the prisoners be removed. They are committed to the Fleet Prison."

"Prisoners!" exclaimed Mompesson.

"Ay, prisoners," repeated Osmond Mounchensey, "*my* prisoners. I have a Star-Chamber warrant for your arrest. Behold it. Under this warrant his Highness has committed you, and you will be taken hence to the Fleet, where you, Giles Mompesson, shall occupy the cell you destined for my nephew! Now, your sword."

"Take it," rejoined Mompesson, plucking the rapier from its sheath, "take it in your heart. You, at least, shall not live to enjoy your triumph."

But Osmond was too quick for him, and seizing his arm, ere he could deal the meditated blow, with almost superhuman force, he wrested the sword from him, and broke it beneath his feet.

At the same time, other personages appeared on the scene. These were the Serjeant-at-arms and a party of halberdiers. Advancing slowly towards the prisoners, the officer received the warrant from Osmond Mounchensey, while the halberdiers closed round the two extortioners.

"Before the prisoner, Mompesson, is removed," said Charles, "see that he delivers up to you his keys. Let an inventory be taken of all monies within the house, and let the royal seal be placed upon all boxes and caskets. All deeds and other documents must be carefully preserved to be examined hereafter. And let strict search be made— for I have heard there are many hidden depositories of treasure— especially within the prisoner's secret cabinet."

"Take heed that the strictest examination be made," subjoined Buckingham, "in accordance with his Highness's behests—for the knave smiles, as if he thought his precautions were so well taken that the searchers would be baffled."

"Fear nothing, my Lord Marquis," replied the Serjant-at-arms. "Now, prisoner," he added, to Mompesson—"your keys!"

While the officer was thus employed, Luke Hatton stepped forward.

"Those keys will be of little use," he said, to the Prince. "Others have been beforehand with your Highness."

"How, Sir—what others?" demanded Charles, bending his brows.

"The extortioner's lawless band of attendants—generally known as his myrmidons, your Highness," replied Hatton. "Instinctively discerning, as it would seem, that all was over with their master, they had determined to quit his service, and without giving him any notice of their intention. Not content with deserting him in the hour of danger, they have robbed him as well—robbed him of the bulk of his treasure. They have broken into his secret cabinet—and stripped it of all its valuables that could be of use to them, and have not left one of his hidden hoards unvisited."

"Hell's curses upon them!" exclaimed Mompesson, with irrepressible rage. "May they all swing upon the gibbet!"

"The chief among them—a rascally Alsatian, known as Captain Bludder—has been captured," pursued Luke Hatton. "And a large sum, together with a rich casket of jewels, has been found upon him; and it is to be hoped that the officers will succeed in finding the others. Will your Highness interrogate Bludder?"

"Not now," replied Charles. "Let him be taken to the Fleet. But there were other matters of more importance than the treasures—the deeds and legal instruments. These, as being useless to the robbers, were probably left untouched."

"They were so, your Highness," replied Luke Hatton.

"Would they had burned them!" ejaculated Mompesson. "Would all had been destroyed!"

And he gave utterance to such wild exclamations of rage, accompanied by such frenzied gestures, that the halberdiers seized him, and dragged him out of the room. The old usurer was removed at the same time.

"And now," said Charles, rising from his chair, "one thing only remains to be done ere I depart, and it will he pleasanter to me than aught that has preceded it. I must again address myself to you, Sir Jocelyn Mounchensey, ay, and to you, also, fair Mistress Aveline. I pray you to come near me," he continued, with a gracious smile, to the damsel.

And, as she blushingly complied,—for she half divined his purpose,—he said—"As I have already told you, Sir Jocelyn, your restoration to the King's favour is complete, and your re-appearance at Court would be a gratification to his Majesty, but, after the events which have occurred, a brief retirement will, I conceive, be most agreeable to you, and I would counsel a visit to the hall of your ancestors."

"Nothing could be more in accordance with my own wishes, most gracious Prince, if my newly-found relative will accept me as his guest."

"Not as his guest, my good nephew," said Osmond. "You are sole lord of Mounchensey. I have made over the mansion and all the estates to you. They are yours, as by right they should be."

Sir Jocelyn's emotion was too great to allow him to express his gratitude in words.

"A noble gift!" exclaimed Charles. "But you must not go there alone, Sir Jocelyn. You must take a bride with you. This fair lady has well approved her love for you—as you have the depth of your devotion to her. Take her from my hands. Take her to jour heart; and may years of fondest wedded happiness attend you both! When you re-appear at Court, you will be all the more welcome if Lady Mounchensey be with you."

So saying, he placed Aveline's hand in that of her lover; and, with a look of ineffable delight, they knelt to express their gratitude.

The Prince and the courtly train passed out—and, lastly, Sir Jocelyn and the object of his affections. Vainly did he seek for his relative and benefactor. Osmond Mounchensey had disappeared. But, just as the young Knight and his fair companion were quitting the house, Luke Hatton, followed by two porters, bearing a stout chest, approached them, and said—

"Sir Jocelyn, you have seen the last of your uncle. He has charged me to bid you an eternal adieu. You will never hear of him again, unless you hear of his death. May no thoughts of him mar your happiness—or that of her you love. This is what he bade me say to you. This chest contains the title-deeds of your estates—and amongst them is a deed of gift from him to you. They will be conveyed by these porters whithersoever you may direct them. And now, having discharged mine office, I must take my leave."

"Stay, Sir," cried Sir Jocelyn; "I would fain send a message to my uncle."

"I cannot convey it," replied Luke Hatton. "You must rest content with what I have told you. To you, and to all others, Osmond Mounchensey is as the dead."

With this, he hastily retreated.

Three days after this, the loving pair were wedded; and the ceremony—which was performed with strict privacy, in accordance with the wishes of the bride—being concluded, they set out upon their journey into Norfolk. Sir Jocelyn had noticed among the spectators of the marriage rites, a tall personage wrapped in a sable cloak, whom he suspected to be his uncle; but, as the individual was half hidden by a pillar of the ancient fabric, and as he lost sight of him before he could seek him out, he never could be quite sure of the fact.

Sir Jocelyn's arrival at the hall of his ancestors was the occasion of great rejoicings; and, in spite of the temptations held out to him, many years elapsed ere he and Lady Mounchensey revisited the scene of their troubles in London.

CONCLUDING CHAPTER.

Retribution.

As will have been foreseen, the judgment pronounced by Prince Charles upon Mompesson and his partner, was confirmed by the King and the Lords of the Council, when the two offenders were brought be them in the Star-Chamber. They were both degraded from the honour of knighthood; and Mitchell, besides being so heavily fined that all his ill-gotten wealth was wrested from him, had to endure the in of riding through the streets—in a posture the reverse of the ordinary mode of equitation—name with his face towards the horse's tail, two quart pots tied round his neck, to show that he was punished I for his exactions upon ale-house keepers and hostel-keepers, and a placard upon his breast, detailing the nature of his offences. In this way,—hooted and pelted by the rabble, who pursued him as he was led along, and who would have inflicted serious injuries upon him, and perhaps despatched him outright, had it not been for the escort by whom he was protected,—he was taken in turn to all such taverns and houses of entertainment as had suffered most from his scandalous system of oppression.

In the course of his progress, he was brought to the Three Cranes in the Vintry, before which an immense concourse was assembled to witness the spectacle. Though the exhibition made by the culprit, seated as he was on a great ragged beast purposely selected for the occasion, was sufficiently ludicrous and grotesque to excite the merriment of most of the beholders, who greeted his arrival with shouts of derisive laughter; still his woe-begone countenance, and miserable plight—for he was covered with mud from head to foot— moved the compassion of the good-natured Madame Bonaventure, as she gazed at him from one of the upper windows of her hostel, and the feeling was increased as the wretched old man threw a beseeching glance at her. She could stand the sight no longer, and rushed from the window.

In the same room with her there were four persons, who had been partaking of a plentiful repast, as was proved by the numerous dishes and flasks of wine garnishing the table at which they had been seated, and they, too, as well as the hostess, on hearing the noise outside the tavern, had rushed to the windows to see what could cause so much disturbance. As they were all well acquainted with the old usurer and his mal-practices, the spectacle had a special interest to them as well as to the hostess, and they were variously affected by it.

The party, we must state, consisted of Master Richard Taverner, as the quondam apprentice was now styled, and his pretty wife, Gillian, who now looked prettier than usual in her wedding attire— for the ceremony uniting them in indissoluble bonds had only just been performed; old Greenford, the grandsire of the bride; and Master John Wolfe, of the Bible and Crown in Paul's Churchyard, bookseller, erstwhile Dick's indulgent master, and now his partner, Master Taverner having very prudently invested the contents of the silver coffer in the purchase of a share in his employers business, with the laudable determination of bestirring himself zealously in it ever after; and, as another opportunity may not occur for mentioning the circumstance, we will add that he kept to his resolution, and ultimately rose to high offices in the city. Dick's appearance had already considerably improved. His apparel was spruce and neat, but not showy, and well became him; while his deportment, even under the blissful circumstances in which he was placed, had a sobriety and decorum about it really surprising, and which argued well for his future good conduct. He began as he meant to go on; and it was plain that John Wolfe's advice had produced a salutary effect upon him. Old Greenford looked the picture of happiness.

With Master Richard's predilections for the Three Cranes we are well acquainted, and it will not, therefore, appear unnatural that he should choose this, his favourite tavern, for his wedding-dinner. Madame Bonaventure was delighted with the bride, and brought the blushes to her fair cheeks by the warmth of her praises of her beauty; while she could not sufficiently congratulate the bridegroom on his good luck in obtaining such a treasure. The best in the house was set before them—both viands and wine—and ample justice was done by all to the good cheer. Cyprien, as usual, brought in the dishes, and filled the flagons with the rare Bordeaux he had been directed by his mistress to introduce; but Madame Bonaventure personally superintended the repast, carving the meats, selecting the most delicate bits for Gillian's especial consumption, and seasoning them yet more agreeably with her lively sallies.

The dinner had come to a close, and they were just drinking the health of the bonny and blushing bride, when the clamour on the quay proclaimed the old usurer's arrival. As he was the furthest person from her thoughts, and as she had not heard of the day appointed for his punishment, Madame Bonaventure was totally unprepared for the spectacle offered to her when she reached the window; and her retreat from it, as we have related, was almost immediate.

To his shame be it spoken, Master Richard Taverner was greatly entertained by the doleful appear of his old enemy, and could not help exulting over his downfall and distress; but he was quickly checked by his bride, who shared in the hostess's gentler and more compassionate feelings. So much, indeed, was the gentle Gillian touched by the delinquent's supplicating looks, that she yielded to the impulse that prompted her to afford him some solace, and snatching up a flask of wine and a flagon from the table, she rushed out of the room, followed by her husband, who vainly endeavoured to stay her.

In a moment Gillian was out upon the quay; and the mounted guard stationed round the prisoner, divining her purpose, kindly drew aside to let her pass. Filling the goblet, she handed it to the old man, who eagerly drained it, and breathed a blessing on her as he returned it. Some of the bystanders said the blessing would turn to a curse—but it was not so; and so well pleased was Dick with what his good wife had done, that he clasped her to his heart before all the crowd.

This incident was so far of service to the prisoner, that it saved him from further indignity at the moment. The mob ceased to jeer him, or to hurl mud and missiles at him, and listened in silence to the public crier as he read aloud his sentence. This done, the poor wretch and his escort moved away to the Catherine Wheel, in the Steelyard, where a less kindly reception awaited him.

In taking leave, as we must now do, of Master Richard Taverner and his pretty wife, it gives us pleasure to say that they were as happy in their wedded state as loving couples necessarily must be. We may add that they lived long, and were blessed with numerous issue—so noumerous indeed, that, as we have before intimated, Dick had to work hard all the rest of his days.

In bidding adieu, also, to Madame Bonaventure, which we do with regret, we have merely to state that she did not reign much longer over the destinies of the Three Cranes, but resigned in favour of Cyprien, who, as Monsieur Latour, was long and favourably known as the jovial and liberal host of that renowned tavern. Various reasons were assigned for Madame Bonaventure's retirement; but the truth was, that having made money enough, she began to find the banks of the Thames too damp and foggy for her, especially during the winter months; so the next time the skipper entered the river, having previously made her arrangements, she embarked on board his vessel, and returned to the sunny shores of the Garonne.

Mompesson's sentence, though far more severe and opprobrious than that of the elder extortioner, was thought too lenient, and most persons were of opinion that, considering the enormity of his offences, his life ought not to be spared. But they judged unadvisedly. Death by the axe, or even by the rope, would have been infinitely preferred by the criminal himself, to the lingering agonies he was destined to endure. Moreover, there was retributive justice in the sentence, that doomed him to undergo tortures similar to those he had so often inflicted on others.

The pillory was erected at Charing Cross. A numerous escort was required to protect him from the fury of the mob, who would otherwise have torn him in pieces; but, though shielded in some degree from their active vengeance, he could not shut his ears to their yells and execrations. Infuriated thousands were collected in the open space around the pillory, eager to glut their eyes upon the savage spectacle; and the shout they set up on his appearance was so terrific, that even the prisoner, undaunted as he had hitherto shown himself, was shaken by it, and lost his firmness, though he recovered it in some degree as he mounted the huge wooden machine, conspicuous at a distance above the heads of the raging multitude. On the boards on which he had to stand, there was another person besides the tormentor,—and the sight of him evidently occasioned the criminal great disquietude. This person was attired in black, with a broad-leaved hat pulled down over his brows.

"What doth this fellow here?" demanded Mompesson. "You do not need an assistant."

"I know not that," replied the tormentor,—a big, brawny fellow, habited in a leathern jerkin, with his arms bared to the shoulder,— taking up his hammer and selecting a couple of sharp-pointed nails; "but in any case he has an order from the Council of the Star-Chamber to stand here. And now, prisoner," he continued roughly and authoritatively,—"place your head in this hole, and your hands here."

Since resistance would have been vain, Mompesson did as he was bidden. A heavy beam descended over his neck and wrists, and fastened him down immovably; while, amid the exulting shouts of the spectators, his ears were nailed to the wood. During one entire hour the ponderous machine slowly revolved, so as to exhibit him to all the assemblage; and at the end of that time the yet more barbarous part of the sentence, for which the ferocious mob had been impatiently waiting, was carried out. The keen knife and the branding-iron were called into play, and in the bleeding and mutilated object before them, now stamped with indelible infamy, none could have recognised the once haughty and handsome Sir Giles Mompesson.

A third person, we have said, stood upon the pillory. He took no part in aiding the tormentor in his task; but he watched all that was done with atrocious satisfaction. Not a groan—not the quivering of a muscle escaped him. He felt the edge of the knife to make sure it was sharp enough for the purpose, and saw that the iron was sufficiently heated to burn the characters of shame deeply in. When all was accomplished, he seized Mompesson's arm, and, in a voice that seemed scarcely human, cried,—"Now, I have paid thee back in part for the injuries thou hast done me. Thou wilt never mock me more!"

"In part!" groaned Mompesson. "Is not thy vengeance fully satiated? What more wouldst thou have?"

"What more?" echoed the other, with the laugh of a demon,—"for every day of anguish thou gavest my brother in his dungeon in the Fleet I would have a month—a year, I would not have thee perish too soon, and therefore thou shalt be better cared for than he was. But thou shalt never escape—never! and at the last I will be by thy side."

It would almost seem as if that moment were come, for, as the words were uttered, Mompesson fainted from loss of blood and intensity of pain, and in this state he was placed upon a hurdle tied to a horse's heels, and conveyed back to the Fleet.

As threatened, he was doomed to long and solitary imprisonment, and the only person, beside the jailer, admitted to his cell, was his unrelenting foe. A steel mirror was hung up in his dungeon, so that he might see to what extent his features had been disfigured.

In this way three years rolled by—years of uninterrupted happiness to Sir Jocelyn and Lady Mounchensey, as well as to Master Richard Taverner and his dame; but of increasing gloom to the captive in his solitary cell in the Fleet. Of late, he had become so fierce and unmanageable that he had to be chained to the wall. He sprang at his jailer and tried to strangle him, and gnashed his teeth, and shook his fists in impotent rage at Osmond Mounchensey. But again his mood changed, and he would supplicate for mercy, crawling on the floor, and trying to kiss the feet of his enemy, who spurned him from him. Then he fell sick, and refused his food; and, as the sole means of preserving his life, he was removed to an airier chamber. But as it speedily appeared, this was only a device to enable him to escape from prison,—and it proved successful. He was thought to be so ill that the jailer, fancying him incapable of moving, became negligent, and when Osmond Mounchensey next appeared, the prisoner had flown. How he had effected his escape no one could at first explain; but it appeared, on inquiry, that he had been assisted by two of his old myrmidons, Captain Bludder and Staring Hugh, both of whom were prisoners at the time in the Fleet.

Osmond's rage knew no bounds. He vowed never to rest till he had traced out the fugitive, and brought him back.

But he experienced more difficulty in the quest than he anticipated. No one was better acquainted with the obscure quarters and hiding-places of London than he; but in none of these retreats could he discover the object of his search. The potentates of Whitefriars and the Mint would not have dared to harbour such an offender as Mompesson, and would have given him up at once if he had sought refuge in their territories. But Osmond satisfied himself, by a perquisition of every house in those sanctuaries, that he was not there. Nor had any ore been seen like him. The asylum for "masterless men," near Smart's

Quay, and all the other dens for thieves and criminals hiding from justice, in and about the metropolis, were searched, but with the like ill result. Hitherto, Mompesson had contrived entirely to baffle the vigilance of his foe.

At last, Osmond applied to Luke Hatton, thinking it possible his cunning might suggest some plan for the capture of the fugitive. After listening with the greatest attention to all related to him, the apothecary pondered for awhile, and then said—"It is plain he has trusted no one with his retreat, but I think I can find him. Come to me on the third night from this, and you shall hear further. Meantime, you need not relax your own search, though, if it be as I suspect, failure is sure to attend you."

Obliged to be satisfied with this promise, Osmond departed. On the third night, at a late hour, he returned. He did not, however, find Luke Hatton. The apothecary, it appeared, had been absent from home during the last three days, and the old woman who attended upon him was full of uneasiness on his account. Her master, she said, had left a letter on his table, and on investigation it proved to be for Osmond. In it the writer directed him, in the event of his non-return before the time appointed, to repair without delay, well armed, to the vaults beneath Mompesson's old habitation near the Fleet, and to make strict search for him throughout them. He also acquainted him with a secret entrance into the house, contrived in the walls beneath the lofty north-eastern turret. On reading this letter, Osmond at once understood his ally's plan, together with its danger, and felt that, as he had not returned, he had, in all probability, fallen a victim to his rashness. Telling the old woman whither he was going, and that inquiries might be made there for him on the morrow, if he did not re-appear with her master, he set out at once for the place indicated.

We shall, however, precede him.

Ever since Mompesson had been taken to the Fleet, his habitation had been deserted. The place was cursed. So much odium attached to it,—so many fearful tales were told of it,—that no one would dwell there. At the time of its owner's committal, it was stripped of all its contents, and nothing was left but bare walls and uncovered floors. Even these, from neglect and desertion, had become dilapidated, and a drearier and more desolate place could not be imagined. Strict search had been made by the officers of the Star-Chamber for concealed treasure, but little was found, the bulk having been carried off, as before related, by the myrmidons. Nevertheless, it was supposed there were other secret hoards, if a clue to them could only be found. Mompesson had been interrogated on the subject; but he only made answers calculated to excite the cupidity of his hearers without satisfying them, and they fancied he was deceiving them.

On the night in question, to all outward appearance, the house was sombre and deserted as usual, and the city watch who passed it at midnight, and paused before its rusty gates and its nailed-up door, fancied all was secure. The moon was at the full, shining brightly on the sombre stone walls of the mansion,—on its windows, and on the lofty corner turret, whence Mompesson used so often to reconnoitre the captives in the opposite prison; and, as certain of the guard looked up at the turret, they laughed at its present emptiness. Yet they little dreamed who was there at the time, regarding them from the narrow loop-hole. After the pause of a few minutes they moved on, and the gleam of their halberts was presently seen, as they crossed Fleet Bridge, and marched towards Ludgate.

About two hours afterwards the watch re-appeared, and, while again passing the house, the attention of their leader was attracted by an unusual appearance in the masonry near the north-east angle, above which the tall turret was situated. On closer examination, the irregularity in the walls was found to be produced by a small secret door, which was left partially open, as if it had been recently used. The suspicions of the party being aroused by this singular circumstance (none of them having been aware of the existence of such a door), they at once entered the house, resolved to make strict search throughout it. In the first instance, they scaled the turret, with which the secret outlet communicated by a narrow winding staircase; and then, proceeding to the interior of the habitation, pursued their investigations for some time without success. Indeed, they were just about to depart, when a sound resembling a deep groan seemed to arise from the cellars which they had not visited. Hearing this, they immediately rushed down, and made an extraordinary discovery.

To explain this, however, we must go back to the time when they first passed the house. We then mentioned that there was a person in the turret watching their movements. As they disappeared in the direction of Ludgate, this individual quitted his post of observation, and, descending the spiral staircase, threaded a long passage in the darkness, like one familiar with the place, until he arrived at a particular chamber, which he entered; and, without pausing, proceeded to a little cabinet beyond it. The moonlight streaming through a grated window, showed that this cabinet had been completely dismantled; stones had been removed from the walls; and several of the boards composing the floor, had been torn up and never replaced. The intruder did not pass beyond the door, but, after gazing for a few minutes at the scene of ruin, uttered an ejaculation of rage, and retired.

His steps might have been next heard descending the great stone staircase. He paused not a moment within the entrance-hall, but made his way along a side passage on the left, and down another flight of steps, till he reached a subterranean chamber. Here all would have been profound obscurity, had it not been for a lamp set on the ground, which imperfectly illumined the place.

As the man took up the lamp and trimmed it, the light fell strongly upon his features, and revealed all their hideousness. No visage, except that of Osmond Mounchensey, could be more appalling than this person's, and the mutilation was in both cases the same. It is needless to say it was Mompesson. His habiliments were sordid; and his beard and hair, grizzled by suffering rather than age, were wild and disordered. But he was armed both with sword and dagger; and his limbs looked muscular and active as ever.

Casting a glance towards the entrance of the vault as if to make quite sure he was not observed—though he entertained little anxiety on that score—Mompesson stepped towards a particular part of the wall, and touching a spring, a secret door (not to be detected within the masonry except on minute examination) flew open, and disclosed another and smaller vault.

Here, it was at once evident, was concealed the treasure that had escaped the clutches of the myrmidons and the officers of the Star-Chamber. There was a large open chest at the further end, full of corpulent money-bags, any one of which would have gladdened the heart of a miser. On this chest Mompesson's gaze was so greedily fixed that he did not notice the body of a man lying directly in his path, and well-nigh stumbled over it. Uttering a bitter imprecation, he held down the lamp, and beheld the countenance of Luke Hatton, now rigid in death, but with the sardonic grin it had worn throughout life still impressed upon it. There was a deep gash in the breast of the dead man, and blood upon the floor.

"Accursed spy and traitor," cried Mompesson, as he took hold of the body by the heels and dragged it to one corner—"thou wilt never betray me more. What brought thee here I know not, unless it were to meet the death thou hast merited at my hands. Would a like chance might bring Osmond Mounchensey here—and alone—I would desire nothing more."

"Be thy wish gratified then!" cried a voice, which Mompesson could not mistake.

Looking up, he beheld his enemy.

In an instant his hand was upon his sword, and the blade gleamed in the lamp-light. Osmond had likewise plucked forth his rapier, and held a poignard in his left hand. For a few moments they gazed at each other with terrible looks, their breasts animated with an intensity of hatred which only mortal foes, met under such circumstances, can feel. So fiercely bloodthirsty were their looks that their disfigured features seemed to have lost all traces of humanity.

"Yield thee, murtherous villain," cried Osmond at length. "I will drag thee to the hangman."

"Call in thy fellows, and thou shalt see whether I will yield," rejoined Mompesson, with a laugh of defiance.

"I have none at my back," rejoined Osmond; "I will force thee to follow me alone!"

"Thou *art* alone then!" roared Mompesson; "that is all I desired!"

And, without a word more, he commenced the attack. During the brief colloquy just detailed, he had noticed that his enemy was doubly armed, and before beginning the conflict he drew his own dagger, so that there was no greater advantage on one side than the other.

Both were admirable swordsmen, and in strength they were nearly matched; but the combat was conducted with a ferocity that almost set skill at defiance.

After the exchange of a few desperate passes, they closed; and in the terrific struggle that ensued the lamp was extinguished.

The profound darkness prevented them from seeing the frightful wounds they inflicted on each other; but both knew they were severely hurt, though each hoped he was not so much injured as his adversary.

Exhausted, at length, by loss of blood, and ready to drop, they released each other by mutual consent; and, after making a few more feeble and ineffectual thrusts, leaned upon their swords for support.

"Wilt thou yield now, villain?" demanded Osmond, in a hoarse voice. "Or must I finish thee outright?"

"Finish me!" echoed Mompesson, in tones equally hoarse. "Strike another blow against me if thou canst. But I well know thou art sped. When I have recovered breath, I will make short work with thee."

"About it quickly, then," rejoined Osmond: "I am ready for thee. But thy boast was idle. Thou art bleeding to death. Twice has my poignard pierced thy breast."

"Thou wilt never use thy poignard again. Thy left arm is disabled," rejoined Mompesson—"besides, my sword passed through thee almost to the hilt."

"It glanced from my doublet: I scarcely felt the scratch."

"'Twas a scratch deep enough to let thy life-blood out. But since thou hast more to be spilt, have at thee again!"

"Where art thou?" cried Osmond, staggering towards him.

"Here!" rejoined Mompesson, avoiding the thrust made at him, and dealing one in return that stretched his adversary lifeless at his feet.

In the exultation of the moment, he forgot his own desperate condition, and, with a fierce, triumphant laugh, set his foot upon the body of his prostrate foe.

But a mortal faintness seized him. He essayed to quit the vault— but it was too late. His strength was utterly gone. With an irrepressible groan, he fell to the ground, close beside his enemy.

There they lay, the dying and the dead, for more than an hour. At the end of that time, they were discovered by the watch.

Mompesson yet breathed; and as the torch-light fell upon the scene of horror, he slightly raised his head, and pointing to his slaughtered adversary, with a ghastly smile, expired.

THE END.